**The lovely young countess
eyed the retreating
Thomas thoughtfully.**

The insolent make-bait had even taken liberties with
her! True, Thomas had mistaken her ladyship for a
housemaid, nevertheless...

With a sudden, sharp pang, Camilla recalled the near-
ness of him, his admiring, laughing eyes... Was
Camilla, Countess of Wyckfield, widow of the late
Earl, to be denied the freedom to love that the lowliest
parlormaid enjoyed?

Elizabeth Mansfield
The Counterfeit Husband

BERKLEY BOOKS, NEW YORK

THE COUNTERFEIT HUSBAND

A Berkley Book / published by arrangement with
the author

PRINTING HISTORY
Berkley edition / September 1982

ISBN: 0-425-05336-9

A BERKLEY BOOK® TM 757,375

PRINTED IN THE UNITED STATES OF AMERICA

Prologue

October, 1803

Thomas Collinson stood leaning on the rail of the merchant ship *Triton*, watching the waves slap away at the worn piles of the Southampton dock where the ship was moored. The wharf was dingy and rotting, but it was what the crew of a merchantman had come to expect in these days of war. Nelson's naval vessels had first choice of moorage space, and the vessels of the East India Company had their own prime anchorages. So ships like the *Triton* took what was left.

It was already dark; the sails had been furled and the rigging secured an hour earlier. The captain and most of the crew had already gone ashore, but a few stragglers were still making their way down the gangplank toward the waterfront taverns or, if they were lucky, a woman's bed. Most of these tag-tails were the ones who hadn't signed on for the next voyage and had spent the past hour packing their gear. Tom gave an occasional wave of the arm to a departing sailor. He, the ship's mate, had been given the watch, but he felt no resentment as his glance followed his shipmates, their seabags slung over their shoulders as they walked across the wharf and disappeared into the dark shadows beyond the dock where the light from the ship's forward lantern couldn't reach. He didn't mind having the watch. He was in no hurry to get ashore; there was no place on land for which he had any particular fancy.

A man came stealthily up behind him—a sailor, moving quietly toward the railing on tiptoe. He was not as tall as Tom but so powerfully built that the heavy seabag resting on his shoulder seemed a lightweight triviality. His approach was soundless, but some instinct made Tom whirl about. He gave a snorting laugh. "You didn't think you could sneak up behind me with success, did you, you whopstraw, with me waiting to see you off?"

The stocky sailor lowered his seabag to the deck and shrugged. "Tho't I'd give it one last try." He grinned at Tom with unabashed admiration. "I guess no press-man'll take *you* unawares."

Tom's answering grin soon died as the two men stared at each other in silent realization that it might be for the last time. "So you've packed, eh, Daniel? Ready at last?" He forced a smile. "It's goodbye, then."

Daniel pulled off his cap and ran his fingers through his shock of curly red hair. "It's the only thing I regret about leavin', y' know . . . sayin' goodbye to ye, Tommy lad." His soft brown eyes, usually gleaming with good cheer, now looked watery, as if the fellow was holding back tears. He thrust out his hand for a last farewell.

Tom ignored the hand and threw his arms about his friend in a warm embrace. "No need for the dismals, Daniel," he said softly, patting his friend's back with affection. "Where did you say Betsy is? Twyford, isn't it? That's less than a dozen miles north of here. We'll see each other from time to time."

"No, we won't," Daniel muttered, breaking out of the embrace and turning away his face. "Betsy an' me'll be movin' to God-knows-where, an' ye'll get yerself a berth with the John Company, an' we'll lose track—"

"Stow the gab," Tom ordered with an attempt at a laugh. "We can keep in touch if we try. There are letters . . ."

"I ain't much good at writin'."

"Then Betsy can do it for you. I've seen her letters . . . your wife writes a fine hand."

Daniel sighed and put on his cap. "Aye, I suppose so." He lifted his seabag to his shoulder and gave his friend a pathetic mockery of a grin. "Be seein' ye, then, eh? We'll let ye know where we'll be settlin'."

Tom nodded, finding himself suddenly too choked to speak. They walked together slowly toward the gangplank. "Are you sure you won't sign on again? Just one more voyage?" he asked at last.

"What's the use of it? Betsy's heart'd break fer sure. It's different fer you, Tommy. You haven't a wife t' cling to yer knees, sobbin' her eyes out every time ye make fer the door. Besides, one more voyage an' ye'll have yer master's papers. Why, next time I hear of ye, ye'll be mate on a John Company ship."

"Not very likely. East India Company berths are saved for rich men's sons, not for the vicar's daughter's bastard."

"You can try, can't ye? Ol' Aaron swears he heared that a mate on a company ship can pile up a couple o' thousand quid on a single voyage!"

Tom shook his head dubiously. "Two *thousand?* What gammon! Don't put your trust in those dreamers' yarns. Besides, if I get to captain a ship like this tub we're on, it'll be good enough for me."

"Aye, if that's the sort of life ye want."

"It is." Tom threw his friend a worried look. "But what about you? What will you do now, do you think?"

"I dunno. I'll find somethin'. I'll *have* to, y' know—what with Betsy makin' me a father by spring."

"Aye, you lucky bag-pudding," Tom chuckled. "A *father!* Before you know it, there'll be a strapping, red-headed whelp sitting astride your shoulder instead of that seabag. It's a sight I'd give a yellow-boy to see."

Daniel's face clouded over. "Per'aps ye will," he muttered without much conviction. "Per'aps you will."

Tom felt a wave of depression spread over him. Daniel was probably right. They were about to set off on widely diverging paths, and the likelihood of ever meeting again was slim. And even if they did, the close camaraderie of the past months would have long since evaporated into the unreality of nostalgic memory.

Daniel stuck out his hand again, and Tom gripped it tightly. They held on for a long while, and then, by some manner of wordless communication, let go at the same moment. The red-headed man turned abruptly away and marched purposefully down the gangplank. Tom watched him from his place on the railing, feeling bereft. *A sailor's life is always leavetaking*, he told himself glumly as he watched his friend trudge stolidly across the wharf. Just before Daniel was completely swallowed up by the shadows, Tom saw him pause, turn and give one last wave of farewell.

Tom waved back, his throat tingling with unexpected emotion. He grunted in self-disgust, annoyed at this indulgence in sentiment. If there was one requirement for a ship's master, it was hardness—hardness of body and of feeling. If he was ever to become a master, he'd better learn to behave like one. He'd be—

"Tom! *Tom! Press-gang!*" came a shout from the shadows.

Tom felt the blood drain from his face. "Good God! *Daniel!*"

He could hear, above the noisy slap of the water against the side of the ship, the sounds of a violent scuffle in the dark of the dock. His heart began to hammer in his chest, for he knew that the worst had happened. An attack by a press-gang was a merchant seaman's direst fear. He glanced about him desperately for some sort of weapon. Snatching up a belaying pin, he vaulted over the railing onto the gangplank and dashed down.

The sounds from the shadows became louder and more alarming as he tore across the wharf and neared the shadowy part of the dock beyond. "No, no, don't use the cutlass," he heard a voice bark. "He's a good, stalwart specimen. I don't want him spoiled."

Tom raced round a mound of crates and gasped at the sight that met his eyes. Daniel was struggling like a wild stallion against the tugs and blows of half-a-dozen ruffians armed with cutlasses and cudgels. Standing apart, his arms folded over his chest, was a King's officer watching the proceedings with dispassionate interest. Tom would have liked to land him a proper facer, but the six bruisers had to be tackled first. He threw himself headlong into the melee. "All right, Daniel," he shouted, "let's give it to 'em!"

There was no answer from the beleaguered Daniel, but he struggled against his attackers with renewed energy. Tom swung the belaying pin about in violent desperation, striking one press-man on the shoulder hard enough to make him squeal and drop his hold on Daniel's arm. Turning quickly about, he swung the pin at the head of another attacker and heard a very satisfactory crack of the skull as the fellow slumped to the ground.

The shouting was deafening as shadowy figures swirled about him. He swung his makeshift weapon wildly, hoping desperately that he wouldn't accidentally strike his friend. "Daniel, are you . . . there?"

"Aye, lad," came a breathless, discouraged answer from somewhere behind him.

"Don't despair," Tom urged, swinging the belaying pin vigorously about him, keeping two of the ruffians at bay. Just then, from behind, came a sharp blow. The flat side of a cutlass had struck powerfully and painfully against his ear. He swayed dizzily. The pin was wrenched from his weakened grasp, and three men jumped on him at once. He felt himself toppling over backwards, but he kept swinging his fists as he fell. With a string of curses, his assailants slammed his head down upon the cobbles. It struck with an agonizing thud. Streaks of red and yellow lightning seemed to obscure his vision and sear his brain with pain.

By the time he could see again, the fight was over. He lifted his head and looked about him. Two of the press-men were leading Daniel off, his shoulders pathetically stooped and his hands bound behind his back. Three others of the gang, looking very much the worse for wear, were trussing up his own wrists with leather straps. And the sixth lay stretched out on the cobbles, blood trickling from his nose. Above it all, the King's officer stood apart, his hands unsullied by the struggle he'd just witnessed. Catching Tom's eye, the officer smiled in grim satisfaction. Tom well understood the expression. The man on the ground might be dead, and another of his gang might not have the use of his right arm for a long spell, but the two men the officer had caught were trained seamen. He and Daniel were the sort of catch the press-gangs most desired. This had been, for the officer, a very good night's work.

After having been alternately shoved and dragged along the waterfront for what seemed like miles, his head aching painfully and his spirits in despair, Tom was pushed into a longboat manned by eight uniformed sailors. Daniel was nowhere in sight. The King's officer dismissed the ruffians of the press-

gang and climbed into the boat, giving Tom a smug smile as
he seated himself on a thwart facing his prisoner. Tom's fingers
ached to choke that smile from his face.

The sailors began to row toward an imposing frigate (painted
with the yellow and black stripes that Admiral Nelson required
of naval vessels) which rode at anchor some distance from the
dock. It was His Majesty's Ship *Undaunted*, and despite the
darkness Tom could see that it carried at least fifty guns and
floated in the water at over six hundred tons. As the longboat
drew up alongside the vessel, a sailor prodded Tom with an
oar, urging him to climb up the ladder to the upper deck.

Despite the desperation of his condition, Tom couldn't refrain from peering with considerable interest through the darkness at the activity on deck. While the King's officer, who had
followed him up the ladder, held a whispered colloquy with
the vessel's first lieutenant, Tom looked around, marvelling
at the pristine neatness of the ship. But before he had an opportunity to scrutinize what was a vastly different vessel from
the one he'd just abandoned, the lieutenant, a stocky, balding
man in his mid-twenties, with a florid complexion that bespoke
a hot temper, gave an order to the two sailors who were guarding him, and he was roughly dragged across the deck to the
companionway.

At the end of the passage, he was unceremoniously ushered
into what he instantly recognized was the captain's cabin. It
was a low-ceilinged, unpretentious compartment with panelled
walls and a row of wide windows (which usually graced the
stern of a sailing ship) covering the far wall. The captain himself
was nowhere in evidence, for the chair behind the huge desk
(a piece of furniture which gleamed with polish and importance
in its impressive position at the dead center of the room) was
empty. The only sign of the cabin's inhabitant was a coat
trimmed with gold braid which had been thrown over a cabinet
in the corner.

After his eyes became accustomed to the light—provided
by a lamp swinging at eye level from the rafters on a long,
brass chain—he could see that the desk was covered with
navigational charts and a heavily-bound ship's log. But his
eyes were immediately drawn to the group of men who had
been standing at the desk when he'd entered. Two of them
were uniformed sailors, set to guard the prisoner standing
between them. It was Daniel, his face chalky-white in the

lamplight, his hands still secured behind him and blood dripping from a cut on his upper lip. Tom felt his stomach lurch with nausea as their eyes met. Daniel's face was rigid with terror. *And no wonder,* Tom thought miserably. Daniel's life was no longer worth a brass farthing.

The worst circumstance that life could impose on Daniel had occurred: impressment. All through their sailing days, merchant seamen were edified with blood-chilling tales of the sort of life they could expect if they were so unfortunate as to be impressed into naval service. Service in His Majesty's Navy was hell for impressed seamen. They were forced to fill the most unwanted posts, to work at the dirtiest jobs and made to expose themselves to the greatest dangers. The food the King allotted for ordinary seamen was rotten beyond belief, and the pay a pittance. And the chance of coming out of the experience alive—after who-knew-how-many forced voyages—was slim indeed. The Navy, unable to recruit enough seamen to staff its ships because of this notorious mistreatment, had for centuries used the nightmarish device of impressment to fill its berths. And this time, Tom and his best friend had been caught in the net. For *him* there was a ray of hope—the ship-master's apprentice papers in the pocket of his coat; but for Daniel there was no hope at all.

He started across the cabin to stand beside his friend, but he was jerked back to his place by the sailors who were guarding him. The lieutenant and the King's officer conferred again briefly, and then the lieutenant went to a door near the far corner of the wall at Tom's right and tapped gently. At the sound of a voice from within, the lieutenant opened the door and disappeared inside. He emerged a few moments later, followed by a tall, lean man of late middle age with a head of iron-grey hair, a short beard and a pair of narrow, glinting eyes. The man was in his shirt-sleeves, but Tom knew it was the captain even before he reached for the gold-trimmed coat and shrugged himself into it.

The lieutenant, meanwhile, came into the circle of light which surrounded the desk and, bending over, began to shuffle the papers about until he found what appeared to Tom to be a ship's roster.

"Sit down, Mr. Benson, sit down," the captain muttered from the shadows where he stood leaning his elbow on the cabinet and looking from Tom to Daniel and back again.

"Aye, aye, Captain." Mr. Benson, the lieutenant, took the chair behind the desk, picked up a pen from the inkstand and wrote something on the paper. Then he looked up at the two prisoners coldly. "Which one of you is the murderer?" he asked.

"It's the taller one, of course," came the captain's voice from the shadows. "Isn't that so, Moresby?"

The King's officer chuckled. "You're right again, Captain Brock."

At the sound of the captain's name, Daniel's eyes flew to Tom's with a look of desperation. Sir Everard Brock was notorious. His reputation for cruelty was legendary among seamen.

"Start with the other one," the captain ordered.

Mr. Benson nodded. "What's your name, fellow?" he demanded of Daniel.

"Dan'l Hicks, sir."

"You were an ordinary seaman on the *Triton?*"

"Aye, sir, but...I..."

"Yes?"

"I've finished my time."

"Finished? Didn't sign up again, eh? Had enough of the old scow?" Mr. Benson asked with a sardonic grimace.

"Well, I...I suppose ye could say that."

"Good. If they're not expecting you back on board the *Triton*, no one will be looking for you." He dipped the pen carefully in the inkwell.

"But ye see, sir, there *will* be someone—"

"What?" the lieutenant asked, writing.

"Someone lookin' fer me. I have a wife, y' see, an' she—"

"Forget your wife, fellow. Can't worry about wives. Haven't you heard that the Prime Minister, Mr. Addington, declared war on Napoleon this past May? This is wartime," Mr. Benson said pompously, adding Daniel's name to the roster. "Cut his bonds," he ordered the guards.

"Y' don't understand, sir," Daniel pleaded as a sailor stepped behind him and sliced the cords at his wrists with a small, curved-bladed knife. "I—"

The lieutenant paid no attention but merely held out the pen. "Here. Put your X right here."

Daniels's hands were trembling. "But...y' see...I *can't*

sign on. My wife's in the family way, if y' know what I mean. She'll starve t' death if I—"

Mr. Benson's eyes narrowed angrily. "Are you daring to contradict me, Hicks? If I don't have your X on this sheet at once, it'll be ten stripes for you!"

"Twenty," came the captain's voice ominously out of the shadows.

"Twenty!" Mr. Benson echoed.

Daniel cast Tom a look of stricken anguish. Tom, his mind racing about to think of a way out of this rat-trap, could do nothing at the moment but signal with a blink of the eyes that Daniel should acquiesce. Poor Daniel groaned despairingly, stepped forward and took the pen from the lieutenant's hand. He knew well enough how to sign his name, but he wrote an X as a gesture to himself that he still had a spark of rebellious spirit within him.

Mr. Benson threw a look of satisfaction over his shoulder at the captain and turned to Tom. "Now *you*, murderer," he said with a kind of malicious enjoyment, "what's *your* name?"

"Collinson, sir. Thomas Collinson." Tom used the opportunity to move closer to the desk and Daniel's side.

"You don't appear to be overly disturbed about having killed a man," the lieutenant remarked, looking him over interestedly.

"If you're speaking of the press-man I laid low, he damn well deserved it."

Mr. Benson's self-satisfied expression changed to one of discomfort. He was not accustomed to back-talk. This fellow was a cool one, and that type could make him look foolish before the captain. "Watch your tongue, fellow," he growled threateningly, "if you know what's good for you."

Tom shrugged. "May as well be hanged for a sheep as a lamp," he said, brazenly directing his words to the captain.

Captain Brock said nothing, but he moved in closer to the light and peered at Tom intently. The lieutenant, meanwhile, jumped angrily to his feet. "Oh, you won't hang, fellow," he sneered, "but you'll wish by tomorrow that you had. Hanging's too good for the likes of you."

"Don't think to frighten me with this fustian," Tom retorted. "A civil trial might be more damaging to the Navy than to me, and *that's* why I won't hang."

The lieutenant, red-faced with fury, reached out and grasped

Tom by the collar of his coat, but before he was able to do anything further, the captain's voice stopped him. "Hold on there, Mr. Benson. Let the fellow be for a moment." He walked into the circle of light and studied Tom's face before turning to the King's officer. "Speaks the King's English, Moresby, did you notice? You haven't made a mistake again, have you?"

The officer stepped forward, his brow wrinkled with sudden alarm. If a member of the nobility had been mistakenly caught in his net, he could find himself in a great deal of difficulty. He circled Tom slowly, looking carefully at his clothing, his hands and the careless way his hair had been cut. "I don't think so, Captain Brock," he said thoughtfully. "Looks all right to me. He came off the *Triton,* after all, and that's not the sort of berth a gentleman would seek."

"Where did you learn a gentleman's English, fellow?" the captain asked Tom.

"At Cambridge. Where else?" Tom responded flippantly.

The captain drew in his breath and nodded at the lieutenant.

Mr. Benson, who still clutched Tom's collar with one hand, smashed him in the mouth with the other. "The captain asked you a question, sailor. Answer him properly, or you'll feel the taste of wet leather!"

Tom pulled himself free of the lieutenant's grasp and licked the blood from his split lip before he answered. "I read a bit, that's all," he muttered.

"That's *not* all," the captain said in a voice so icy that Tom understood how he could command this ship with its crew of hundreds. "One doesn't learn to speak well only by reading. Well?"

Tom gave the captain a sardonic shrug. "I had a mother who set great store by appearances. She trained me. She thought that if her boy *appeared* to be a gentleman, he might be taken for one."

"How very interesting," the captain murmured, his voice, even while tinged with amusement, still chillingly cold. "And *were* you taken for one?"

Tom smiled wryly. "Not until now."

The captain let out a grudging laugh. "You've a sharp wit, Collinson, but you'll find that wit is no advantage here. Carry on, Mr. Benson." And he walked back out of the light.

The lieutenant sat down and leered up at Tom with satisfaction. "As I was saying, sailor, you're not going to hang.

That would be too easy a punishment for you. You're going to serve on this ship. You're going to labor through two watches every day. *Two!* And once a week, the bo'sun will deliver upon your back at least . . . er . . ."

"Thirty-five," came the voice from the shadows.

"Thirty-five stripes. Do you understand, Collinson? *Thirty-five*. Every week. Why, when we put into port, you'll be so bone-weary and sore you'll be glad that you have to stay behind in the brig instead of going ashore with the rest of the scum you'll be calling your shipmates. What have you to say to *that* with your clever tongue, eh, Collinson?"

Tom moved close to the desk, carefully stepping on Daniel's foot and pressing down on it with just enough weight to indicate that the pressure was not accidental. He hoped Daniel would recognize it as a signal to stay alert. Meanwhile, he faced Mr. Benson with a leer of his own. "What I have to say, sir, is that you can't do it. I'm sorry to disappoint you . . . and you too, Captain Brock. You may be able to bring me to the magistrates on the charge of murder, but you can't make me sign on. I have papers."

"Papers?" The lieutenant looked nonplussed. "What papers?"

"If you'll permit your men to untie my hands, I'll show you."

Mr. Benson looked over his shoulder for guidance. The captain nodded, and the lieutenant motioned to the guard with the knife to slice the straps. Then Tom reached into his coat and pulled out an oilskin packet. He was about to untie the strings when the lieutenant reached out his hand. "Here, give it to me."

Mr. Benson nervously undid the strings as if he feared a snake might emerge and sting his finger. He pulled out the contract which Tom had signed with the captain of the *Triton*, and his eyes slid over the closely-written words. Then, biting his lip, he looked hesitantly over his shoulder. With a sigh of annoyance, the captain came up behind him and picked up the document.

After a quick scan of the papers, the captain looked up at Tom, his lips twisted in a small smile. "So," he said with quiet menace, "you're a mate, are you? Well, well! You *have* brought me a good haul this time, Moresby. It's not often we get recruits who know the difference between main and mizzen."

"But you can't recruit me," Tom argued. "Those papers prove I'm exempted by law—"

"Papers?" the captain asked. "What papers?" He ripped the document in half and then in half again. "Did you see any papers, Mr. Benson?"

The lieutenant smirked. "No, Captain."

"Did anyone here see any papers?" Captain Brock asked, looking around at all the faces pleasantly, all the while tearing the precious sheets into shreds.

"No, Captain," the sailor-guards said in unison.

Captain Brock turned and walked back into the shadows, reappearing again with a washbowl in his hand. He placed the bowl on the deck before Mr. Benson and threw the shreds of paper into it. "Burn it," he said curtly, turned on his heel and strode off to his inner cabin, slamming the wooden door behind him.

Every man around the desk watched soundlessly as Tom's papers burned. They all knew that a man's future was going up in smoke. But Tom felt no emotion but a sharp, alert tension. *There'll never be a better time*, he thought, and he pressed down hard on Daniel's foot while, at the same moment, he snatched up the flaming washbowl and smashed it down on the lieutenant's head. "Use the log book!" he shouted to Daniel, and he ducked down and lunged at the legs of the guard closest to him.

Daniel, with a cry of elation, snatched up the heavy volume and swung it at the head of the guard at his right, while the other one was busily occupied putting out the fire on the desk. Tom, meanwhile, from his place at the top of his first guard, grabbed the legs of the second and pulled him down. Before they'd recovered from their surprise, he scrambled to his feet in time to see the King's officer advancing on him with a drawn cutlass. Again he ducked and dived for the fellow's midsection. They toppled over in a heap, the officer waving his deadly implement wildly in the air. Tom grabbed at his wrist, for the officer was trying urgently to hack him to pieces. Suddenly Daniel loomed above them and, using the log book as a broadsword, knocked the cutlass out of the officer's hand and sent it spinning across the floor. The fellow cried out in pain. Tom seized the moment and administered a smashing right to his jaw, while Daniel used the log book to good effect on the heads of the two tackled sailors who were just getting to their feet again.

Tom leaped up, fists ready, but only Daniel was still erect, his breast heaving and his eyes shining with the glow of victory. Tom chortled in delighted surprise at the sight of six men sprawled about in various degrees of semi-consciousness. "We *did* it!" Daniel crowed, hugging Tom and slapping him on the back.

"Don't congratulate yourselves too soon," came the captain's icy voice from the shadows, and they wheeled about to see him step into the light, pointing at them with the black, ugly barrel of a very long pistol.

"Go ahead and shoot, Captain Brock," Tom said, moving in front of Daniel and motioning behind his back for Daniel to edge toward the cabin's outer door. "I'd rather be dead than serve under you."

"But you'll live," the captain muttered with chilling calm. "You'll live . . . and you'll serve!"

Tom wished he could look up at the lantern to gauge its distance accurately, but he knew that if he moved his eyes from the captain's face he'd give his scheme away. *"Duck,* Daniel!" he shouted and swung his arm at the lantern.

A shot rang out, and he felt the ball whiz by the side of his face as the lantern swung across the desk, a glowing missile aimed right for the captain's head.

They didn't stay to watch it reach its mark but bolted for the door. The companionway was already filling with sailors who'd heard the noises, but they were either too startled by the sudden appearance of the fleeing men or too sympathetic to their plight to grab hold of them. "Head starboard," Tom gasped as they broke onto the deck. They ran across the deck, meeting with no obstruction in the darkness, and came to the railing near the stern. With the sounds of shouts and running footsteps hot behind them, they climbed up on the railing and, with one quick look at one another, leaped overboard into the black water.

Chapter One

Camilla stared out of the library window at the sunny lawns and chaste gardens of Wyckfield Park (a vista which had been acclaimed for generations as the most beautiful in the county) and admitted to herself that she hated the very sight of the place. The entire world might admire the grounds—those lawns which were mowed, edged and cultivated until they resembled lush velvet; the hedges which were clipped, trimmed and manicured until there was not a twig that would dare to pop crookedly out of place; the fall flowers which were lined up below her window in rigid neatness, each row bearing blooms of only one color so that the rows of reds could never presume to mix with the pinks—but *she* found nothing admirable about the view.

The carefully tended, rich and spacious grounds of Wyckfield Park were an anathema to her. To her eyes they seemed a travesty of natural beauty—a place where the Goddess of Nature had been bound, shackled and restricted at every turn.

Nowhere on the estate's vast acreage had any living thing been allowed to develop in its own way. Each hedge and shrub had been made to conform to the Wyckfield's grand plan, every natural instinct compelled to yield. That was why Camilla hated the grounds—they were a monument to repression. *Like my own life,* she thought, crossing her black-clad arms over her chest as if to ward off a cold draught.

"What's the matter, Mama?" came a child's voice behind her.

Camilla put on a smile and turned to face her ten-year-old daughter who was curled up on the sofa with a copy of *Evelina* on her lap. "Matter? Nothing at all. What makes you ask?"

The child looked over the spectacles perched on her nose and fixed her blue eyes on her mother's face with a gaze that was unnervingly mature. "You sighed three times," she accused.

"Did I?" Camilla's smile lost its strained insincerity and widened into a grin. "Have you been sitting there counting my sighs?"

The child grinned back. "It's no great task to count to three, you know."

"True, but I thought you were absorbed in your reading."

"I was, until your heartrending breathing distracted me."

"Heartrending? *Really,* Pippa!" Camilla couldn't prevent a gurgling laugh from welling up into her throat. Her daughter, Philippa, was her joy—the only real joy that life had ever offered her. Small in size but gifted in intellect, the child was the only creature in the household whose development had been miraculously unaffected by the repressive atmosphere. Pippa was perhaps too bookish and precocious, but her nature had a pervasive serenity and self-confidence. She was capable of such outpourings of affection and good cheer that the cold aridity of the Wyckfields seemed unable to penetrate her spirit.

To Camilla, her daughter was a miracle. Pippa's father, now deceased, had been cold as steel, his sister Ethelyn rigid and forbidding and Oswald, Ethelyn's husband, weakly indifferent. Each of them had attempted to control the child's growth, yet Pippa had developed a clear-eyed optimism, an honest, straightforward way of thinking and an amazingly strong spirit. In this house of gloomy religiosity and fanatical repression, the little girl had learned to laugh.

Best of all, in Camilla's view, was the combination of precocity and innocence in Pippa's character. It was a combination so charming that even Ethelyn couldn't bring herself to scold the child with nearly the animosity with which she scolded the rest of the world. No matter how angry Ethelyn would become at one of Pippa's blithe infractions of the rules, Pippa could turn the wrath aside with her sturdy, unafraid, logical explanations. Camilla wished that she herself had been gifted with some small part of the child's courage and ability to adapt to these sterile surroundings.

Camilla sat down beside her daughter on the sofa. She hated to see the little girl clad in the depressing mourning dress, but Ethelyn insisted that they both wear black until the entire year of mourning had passed. Camilla put an arm about the little shoulders and drew Pippa close. "Why are you studying me so speculatively, love?" she asked. "Miss Burney's tale must be disappointing to you if your attention is so easily diverted by my sighs."

"I *love* Miss Burney's story," Pippa declared earnestly, snuggling into the crook of her mother's arm, "but I *don't* love to hear you sighing. You can tell me, you know, Mama, if something's troubling you. I'm quite good at understanding worldly problems."

"Are you indeed?" she squeezed Pippa's shoulders affectionately. "Are you trying to make a romance out of my breathing, my dear? If you're looking for worldly problems, stick to Miss Burney's book."

The bright, spectacled eyes turned up to Camilla's face with a look of disdain. "You needn't try to put me off, Mama. I know you're worrying about something."

"Perhaps I am, but even if I *did* have 'worldly problems,' I shouldn't wish to burden you with them. I've no intention of permitting you to grow old before your time." She planted a light kiss on the girl's brow. "You've plenty of time to cope with worldly problems when you're older."

"If your problem concerns Aunt Ethelyn, I can help, you know," the child insisted.

"Hush, dear. Do you want Uncle Oswald to hear us?"

Pippa and her mother both turned their eyes instinctively to the huge wing chair near the fireplace across the room. Oswald Falcombe, Lady Ethelyn's lethargic husband, was slumped upon it, fast asleep, the handkerchief still spread over his face as it had been for the past two hours. "He's sleeping

quite soundly," Pippa whispered reassuringly. "You can see
it in the way the handkerchief pops up and down with his
breath."

"You seem to have made quite a study of breathing," her
mother said drily.

Pappa giggled. "It's just observation, Mama. Keen observation." Her smile faded, and she sat up straight and looked
at her mother in mild rebuke. "That's how I know that something is bothering you. Observation."

"You, my girl, are a persistent little *witch!* I've already told
you that I don't intend to discuss my problems—if there *are*
any—with you. You are not to worry about me, Pippa! I'm
perfectly capable of handling my problems without the advice
or assistance of a ten-year-old, even if she *is* a prodigy."

"I'm not certain you *are* capable of handling them, Mama,
if they require facing up to Aunt Ethelyn."

Camilla drew herself up in mock affront. "Is that so?"

"Yes, it is. You've been trying for two months to convince
her to let us put off these mourning clothes, and you still haven't
succeeded," the girl pointed out frankly.

"I know."

"After all, it's been almost a year since Papa died—"

"Passed to his reward," Camilla corrected in perfect imi-
tation of Ethelyn's words and manner.

Pippa laughed. "Passed to his *just* reward," she amended
with an almost equal talent for mimicry. "Aunt Ethelyn is a
great stickler for rules, isn't she? Everything must always be
exactly proper . . . proper dress, proper demeanor, proper wording. I wonder why she thinks the longer phrase 'passed to his
just reward' is better than just saying he died?"

"I don't know, love. Perhaps she thinks 'died' is too
blunt . . . or too disrespectful to God."

"You mean 'Our Blessed Lord,'" Pippa quipped, using her
aunt's tone again. *"Is* it disrespectful, Mama, to speak bluntly?
To say 'God' or 'died' straight out?"

"I don't think so, dear. It's just that your aunt is . . . well,
a stickler as you said."

Pippa made a face. "A *real* stickler. That's why we've had
to wear black for so long. I wish she'd change her mind and
let us put off full mourning. I don't think wearing black helps
one to remember Papa any more than one would if one were

wearing *pink*. To tell the truth, I barely remember his face any more."

"That, Philippa Wyckfield," came an ominous voice from the doorway, "is a *sinful* thing to say!" And Lady Ethelyn Falcombe, her large frame draped in a round-gown of heavy black bombazine, her wiry grey hair rolled up in a knot at the back of her head and looking like a twenty-gun frigate ready for battle, sailed into the room.

"Eh? What's that?" muttered Oswald, shaken awake by his wife's booming voice and pulling the handkerchief from his face.

"Come now, Ethelyn," Camilla said placatingly, "what Pippa said was only natural—"

"As if that excuses it! If we all were permitted to give in to our natural instincts, we'd still be *savages*. How *dare* she say she's permitted herself to forget her father!"

"I'm sorry, Aunt Ethelyn," Pippa said, calmly cheerful. "I didn't say I'd forgotten Papa. I said I'd forgotten his *face*." She got up from the sofa and took her aunt's hand affectionately. "It's quite the truth, you know. I've tried to remember his face, but I can't seem to bring it to mind. Can you?"

"Can I what? Remember my beloved brother's face? What an absurd question."

"I mean actually *see* him in your mind whenever you wish to. Can you do it now, this moment? Close your eyes, Aunt Ethelyn, right now, and try to remember him. Tell me if you see him clearly, just as he was."

"But of *course* I..." Ethelyn stared at the child looking innocently up at her. Then she shut her eyes tightly. After a moment she blinked her eyes open and glanced down at her niece who still held her hand and was watching her closely. "Well, I *think* I..." She shut her eyes again. Her heavy cheeks quivered, and her brow wrinkled as her effort intensified. "Isn't that strange?" she murmured. "I see the *portrait* of him that we've hung on the drawing room wall, but..."

"I remember his nose," Oswald put in reflectively. "Had a slight hook in it, from having been tossed from a horse during that hunt—"

"Oswald, don't speak like a fool!" Ethelyn barked, her eyes still shut. "Desmond's nose was perfect."

"Remembering that his nose had a hook doesn't count,

Uncle Oswald," Pippa explained reasonably. "You're remembering a fact, not seeing a face."

"Ummm," he nodded, shutting his eyes to try again.

Camilla sank back against the sofa cushions and looked at the others in wonder. There they were, the three of them, trying to conjure up the face of the deceased Desmond in their minds merely at the behest of the little girl. Her ingenious daughter had managed to turn what could have been an unpleasant scene into a little game. Pippa was truly an amazing child.

Of course, Camilla herself could see Desmond's face all too clearly in her mind. She didn't even need to close her eyes to conjure up a vision of those steely eyes, that thin-lipped mouth, that wiry, grey hair that had been steadily receding from his forehead in recent years. Even after almost a year, the memory of his face could make her blood run cold. In her dreams she still heard the cutting sarcasm of his voice and the sound of his icy scoldings. At unexpected times of the day she still found herself stiffening when she heard a certain sort of footstep on the stairs. And sometimes at night, when she blew out her bedside lamp, she had to remind herself to relax . . . to will herself to recall that he could no longer pay his devastating fortnightly visits to her bed.

"The child's right," Oswald admitted. "I can't bring his face to mind either."

"I think it's shocking!" Ethelyn muttered irritably. "We must ask our Blessed Lord's forgiveness this evening at prayers. Perhaps with His Divine Assistance we may find the strength to overcome this lapse in our mental powers. Meanwhile, Philippa, I will refrain from any further comment on the unfeeling words you spoke when I entered. I suppose you meant no harm."

"Thank you, Aunt Ethelyn," the child said pleasantly.

"Now, my dear, I desire you to run off and occupy yourself elsewhere," Ethelyn ordered. "I have something of importance to discuss with your mother."

Pippa, with a sidelong glance at her mother, bobbed obediently and turned to go. Her mother handed her her book with a reassuring smile.

"What have you there?" Ethelyn demanded as the girl skipped to the door. "I hope, Philippa, that it isn't one of those dreadful novels for which you seem to have such an appetite."

"It's only *Evelina*. And it can't be *very* dreadful, for it was written by Fanny Burney whom you told me you'd met in your youth." With that the girl smiled, waved a cheery goodbye to her uncle, gave her mother an encouraging wink which seemed to say, *Don't let the old dragon bully you,* and whisked herself out of the room.

Lady Ethelyn glared at the door as if trying to decide whether to call the child back for a scold or let her go. After a moment, she wheeled about to face her sister-in-law on whom, she concluded, a scolding would have more effect. "Really, Camilla, how can you permit the child to read *novels?* If I know Miss Burney's interests, the book deals with nothing but flirtations and matchmaking and the like. I can't approve of so frivolous a piece of reading matter even for an adult, but to permit a mere *child* to—!"

Camilla clenched her fists in her lap and tried to keep Ethelyn's booming voice from overwhelming her courage. "I believe it best," she said quietly, "to let Pippa choose her own reading matter, since she is so advanced."

"Choose her own? Are you *mad?* A child, no matter how gifted, needs direction. She should be reading books which are *edifying* rather than entertaining—like Mr. Watt's *Divine and Moral Songs for Children.* Or, if she must read stories, let her peruse the one I gave her last week."

"If you mean the tale by Mrs. Sherwood called *The Fairchild Family,* she's already read it." Camilla's lips turned up in a tiny, almost unnoticeable smile. "She said it was excessively silly."

"Silly? It was recommended by Harriet More herself!" Ethelyn's breast heaved in outrage that anyone could question the judgment of the famous evangelical.

"Nevertheless," Camilla said, her chin coming up bravely, "Pippa said it's fit only to frighten little children, making them believe that at each and every second of their lives they are walking the tightrope between eternal bliss and eternal damnation. She said she's sorry for the little ones in the charity schools who have to read it, but that *she's* too old to be frightened by it."

"Shocking! The child's too clever for her own good!" Ethelyn frowned down at her sister-in-law darkly. "I suppose it's too much to hope that you took her to task for saying such sinful things."

"There was nothing sinful—!"

"You are as aware as I am that we *do* walk a tightrope, every moment of our lives, between bliss and damnation, and the sooner a child knows it the better. You, of all people, should show some concern for Philippa's immortal soul!"

A flash of anger seared through Camilla's chest. "There's not the least reason for me to have concern for her soul!" she retorted, a touch of waspishness in her voice. As if Pippa had anything in her soul but the purest, sweetest innocence!

But there was nothing to be gained by pursuing this subject with Ethelyn. Camilla had never been able to argue against either of the Wyckfields—Ethelyn or Desmond—with any degree of success. Even when she was in the right, they could put her on the defensive and make her feel inadequate. Often in the past, she would find herself at the end of a dispute defeated, choked with frustration and shamefully giving way to a flood of tears. Even now that Desmond was dead, and she was legally mistress of this house, she found herself intimidated by her sister-in-law's sheer forcefulness. She realized that she'd have to face up to Ethelyn one of these days, if she was ever to have any sort of life for herself. But it was silly to have an altercation now on so ludicrous a subject as the danger to her daughter's soul from a bit of innocuous reading. "Did you say earlier, Ethelyn, that you have something to discuss with me?" she asked, turning the subject.

"Yes, I did." Ethelyn seated herself imperiously on the chair facing the sofa and folded her hands in her lap primly. "It's the matter of *your* butler."

"Hicks? Again? What's he done?"

"The man actually uttered a foul blasphemy . . . and in my presence!"

"Oh, Ethelyn, he *couldn't* have," Camilla said, leaning forward worriedly. "I've known him all my life, and I've *never* heard him—"

"But *I* heard him!" Ethelyn retorted coldly. "I gave him an order, and I heard him mutter something under his breath."

Camilla felt her stomach tighten. The matter of Hicks had been a subject of contention between them for years, and Camilla instinctively felt that the matter was about to explode in her face. She got up from the sofa and returned to her place at the window. Staring out on the prim grounds with unseeing eyes, she said hesitantly, "Perhaps you misunderstood . . . or didn't hear him quite accurately . . . ?"

"Camilla, I am sick and tired of listening to your weak-kneed defense of that incompetent, disobedient, *godless* knave! While this is, of course, just as much your home as mine—and the Good Lord knows that you may have an equal say in running it—you cannot expect me to have to endure obscenity and blasphemy from the servants!"

Camilla's fingers clenched. *An equal say in running it, indeed!* she thought, gritting her teeth furiously. Never once in the eleven years since she'd come to this house as a bride had Ethelyn permitted her to make a decision regarding the running of the house. Everything from the planning of the week's menus to the decoration of the sitting room was decided by her sister-in-law. Even the servants knew whose word was law in this house. While Desmond had been alive, he'd been the undisputed master, but the domestic details had been the province of his sister, not his wife. And now that he was dead, nothing had changed. Even though he'd left everything to his only issue—his daughter Philippa—Ethelyn still ruled with an iron hand. Desmond had left both his wife and his sister generous independencies and had stipulated that the estate of Wyckfield Park should be open to them whenever they wished to reside therein, but Ethelyn still behaved as if the property were her own.

Only two members of the household staff considered Camilla to be mistress of the house—Hicks and Miss Ada Townley, her old governess. Camilla had brought them with her when she'd come to Wyckfield Park eleven years ago. During all those years, Ethelyn had attempted to oust the two servants whom Camilla had (as Ethelyn like to put it) "inflicted" on her. But Camilla, even though she'd been too young and frightened to take a stand on anything else, had been adamant about keeping them with her. She'd felt (and she *still* believed) that they were her only friends in the household of cold antagonists who surrounded her.

In defense against the houseful of indifferent or icy adversaries, Camilla, Miss Townley and Hicks seemed to form a small enclave of cheerfulness and affection which embraced little Pippa and protected them all from feelings of loneliness and ostracism. But Camilla soon realized that it was an enclave which Ethelyn was determined to break apart. Ethelyn had often and openly declared that Hicks and Miss Townley encouraged Camilla and even Pippa in keeping secrets, in scornful attitudes toward the rest of the household, in engaging in frivolous pursuits, and in latitudinarian—nay, *godless*—behavior. Ethelyn had long ago convinced herself that she and she alone was responsible for the welfare of the immortal soul of every member of the household, even the staff. Anything which interfered with that Godly Mission was sinful in the extreme.

Camilla knew that Ethelyn's resentment ran deeper than her repeated protestations that she was concerned only for the welfare of their souls. The little circle of four had managed, by sticking together, to keep from being completely dominated by the strong-willed, dictatorial woman. The truth was that Ethelyn had convinced herself that if she could rid the household of Hicks, she'd be able to control the others.

Camilla could feel, in the determined fury of Ethelyn's voice, that her sister-in-law had made up her mind to force a confrontation. Hicks's blunt, country honesty made it hard for him to hide his feelings, and his outspoken manner had always roused Ethelyn's ire. But Camilla had managed, until now, to keep matters from coming to a head. With her legs trembling under the black skirts, she turned to face her irate sister-in-law and try again. "I'll speak to him, Ethelyn," she offered with a sigh.

"You've spoken to him any number of times already, and it hasn't made one particle of difference in his manner."

"But I shall be . . . *most* severe," Camilla promised.

Ethelyn hooted. "It's not *in* you to be severe! You've never shown the servants that you have an ounce of strictness in you. It is your nature to be lenient and indulgent, and *this* is the result. I've warned you, Camilla, that softness of character eats away at the discipline of a human being as well as a household. If it weren't for my God-given strength, this house would be a shambles."

"If I've been lenient and indulgent," Camilla declared, lifting her chin in self-defense, "it's only because you've never given me the opportunity to—"

"Oh, how many times do I have to listen to *that* argument? It won't wash, Camilla. If you feel superseded in the running of this house, you have only yourself to blame. I've said to Oswald time and again—haven't I, my dear?—that if you'd shown any sign of the rigor and forcefulness needed to run an establishment of this sort, I would have gladly surrendered the responsibility into your hands. Just ask Oswald if those weren't my very words."

"I think, ladies," Oswald murmured, pulling his bulk from the wing chair awkwardly, "that I had better toddle off and let you pursue your discussion uninterruptedly."

Camilla frowned in disgust. It was just like Oswald to wish to evade the scene. She supposed that, many years ago, when he'd been with the Admiralty, he might have been a tolerable sort, but he'd long ago lost any vestige of purposefulness of character. Now he was careful only to avoid confrontation or any involvement in the stressful situation developing around him. He seemed to wish for nothing but peace and his daily allowance of sweets.

His wife fixed a firm eye on him. "Sit down and be still, Oswald! I want you to be a witness to this. I mean to settle this matter once and for all, and I want no recriminations later."

"I don't see what there is to settle," Camilla said with quiet constraint. "I know that Hicks's manner is annoying to you, but there doesn't seem to be any way to change him at his advanced age, so we may as well make the best of it."

"I *intend* to make the best of it, Camilla, by insisting that we get *rid* of him."

"Oh, Ethelyn, you can't mean that. Surely you see that I couldn't discharge a man who has been in my family's employ all his life."

"No, I *don't* see. You may pension him off or do anything else you wish, but you will direct him to *leave this house!*"

"Ethelyn, I can't do that. It would be the cruelest sort of blow to the old fellow. You mustn't ask it of me."

"I am not asking. I'm demanding. My brother made it clear in his will that this is where I'm to live, did he not? And since I cannot live in the same house with that *depraved* butler, there is nothing for it but to let him go."

Camilla's heart sank in her chest. There it was . . . an ultimatum. And although the impasse had been erected by her sister-in-law, she herself had made it mountainous by eleven years of evasion. Now she would either have to make a complete surrender or attempt to surmount it by having it out with Ethelyn once and for all.

She raised her eyes and met Ethelyn's cold, inflexible stare. Her spirit quailed, but she warned herself that the security of a beloved servant, the respect of her daughter and the hope of her own future contentment were at stake. She drew in a deep breath, clenched her fingers into tight fists and said firmly, "See here, Ethelyn, I—"

At that moment the door burst open. "Miss *Camilla!*" Miss Townley said breathlessly from the doorway, "the fat's in the fire this time. Hicks is packin' to *leave!*"

•

Chapter Two

Dinner that night was a strangely silent meal, in spite of the fact that everything in the household was at sixes and sevens. Ethelyn was not speaking to Camilla at all; Oswald had decided to keep his eyes on his plate and to use his tongue only for tasting; and Pippa, not having been told the details but aware that a crisis had struck, watched everyone carefully from the corners of her eyes but said nothing. Even the servants walked about as if on eggs, terrified that the least mischance would set off an explosion.

Camilla had managed to persuade Hicks (who had been pushed beyond his limit by what he said was "Lady Ethelyn's wrongful abuse") to retire to his room for the rest of the day until she could find time to think . . . and to decide what was best to be done. Ethelyn, feeling that postponement to be "a most dastardly placating of a reprehensible servant," had fallen into a rage and had ranted at Camilla for almost the entire afternoon. When she'd finally realized that Camilla would make no decision until she could sleep on the matter, Ethelyn had stalked off, declaring furiously that Camilla would get "not one more word from me until the despicable fellow has been sent packing!"

Even Miss Townley had given Camilla a scold. The elderly governess, taking advantage of her life-long intimacy with her mistress, told her roundly that she'd "better show Lady Ethelyn some backbone—and mighty soon!—if you ever intend to call your soul your own," and had marched off in a huff.

After dinner, Camilla accompanied her daughter to her room and, with Miss Townley's assistance, dressed the child in her nightclothes. "Aren't you going to tell me what's amiss?" Pippa asked when her mother tucked her into bed.

"No, I'm not," Camilla answered firmly.

"Then I'll coax Miss Townley to—"

"No, you won't, my girl," Miss Townley said briskly, folding away Pippa's mourning dress. "If your mother doesn't think you should know, then neither do I."

Pippa looked from one to the other. "I shall worry all the more if I'm kept in ignorance."

Camilla sat down at the edge of the bed and stroked her daughter's silky hair. "There's no need to worry, love. I promise you that all will be well by morning."

"I'd surely like to know," Miss Townley said disgustedly after they left Pippa's room, "what magic it is you'll use to get out of this fix by mornin'."

Camilla smiled with more reassurance than she felt. "Never mind, Ada. You can put off your Friday-faced frown. I shall think of something." And she walked airily away down the hall.

With Ada Townley thus dismissed, she had only her Abigail to send to bed to be alone at last. When this had been done, she locked her door, took off her shoes and climbed into bed. She would really need an inspiration to solve this vexing problem which she'd avoided for so long. Her avoidance and lack of firmness had enlarged the problem until it had become a true crisis, and she would need a veritable stroke of genius to solve it now. Here, in the comfortable silence of her bedroom, she hoped to find it. She sat back against the pillows, pulled an eiderdown quilt over her legs and tried to concentrate.

The problem was truly a knotty one, with ramifications beyond the obvious one—the antagonism between her sister-in-law and Hicks. First there was Hicks himself. All day he'd repeatedly declared he would not remain in this house, but Camilla was certain he'd be hurt beyond repair if she permitted him to leave. Even a generous pension would not salve the blow to his pride if she let him go. It would be, in his eyes, an admission that Camilla *agreed* with Lady Ethelyn's disdainful assessment of his worth.

Another ramification of the problem was its reflection on her own character. If Hicks left his house, both her daughter and Ada Townley would be justified in believing that she was completely lacking in backbone. And they would be quite right. Whenever there had been a confrontation with Ethelyn, Camilla had backed down. If she yielded again—especially over something as important as Hicks's future—they would despise her.

Yet she had to think of Ethelyn too. This *was* the only home that Ethelyn had ever known. Ethelyn had often remarked that it was unthinkable for her to live anywhere else but on the land that her family had owned for generations. Was it fair or just for Camilla to make her uncomfortable in a home to which she really had more right than Camilla?

She sighed again as she'd been sighing all day—helplessly. If only she could make her sister-in-law understand her attachment to the stubborn old butler. But Ethelyn would never understand. Ethelyn had never been poor, and she didn't know anything of what Camilla's life had been like twelve years before. Twelve years ago . . . when her father had died. Camilla needed only to shut her eyes, and the scenes of that dreadful year would come crowding back to her mind . . .

They weren't memories so much as a series of sounds— voices, noises, cries. Her father's voice on his deathbed, muttering brokenly, "I'm sorry, dearest . . . forgive me." The solicitor's voice explaining why the home she'd always lived in was now no longer hers. She hadn't understood anything about the entail and the debts, but she'd understood, when Miss Townley had held her in her arms and crooned brokenly, "Oh, my little lamb, my poor little lamb," that at the age of seventeen she was orphaned, homeless and almost penniless.

Then Hicks's voice, gentle and optimistic, explaining that the shabby, ugly little cottage he'd found for them was only temporary . . . that as soon as she turned eighteen, she and Miss Townley could start a school for young ladies and that they would then make out very well. But she'd known that the school was only a dream.

And there'd been the sound of Miss Townley's clatter in the smoky cottage kitchen as she banged the pots in anguish over her meager talents in cookery, frustrated beyond words at being unable to turn oatmeal and turnips into a palatable meal. Worst of all had been the scratching of the rats behind the walls of her cottage bedroom as she lay sleepless during the dark, endless hours of the night.

And finally there'd been Desmond's voice. Desmond, the Earl of Wyckfield, one of her father's creditors, who'd come to collect an unpaid debt and remained to woo the terrified girl who was twenty years his junior. Oh, it had been a very mellow voice, well-modulated and velvet with promises. She would have everything, he'd said. All her dreams would be fulfilled. She'd be a Countess, with a magnificent home, a stable full of horses, her very own carriage, the Wyckfield Necklace made of emeralds and diamonds, and a cloak lined with sable . . .

Camilla gave her head an abrupt shake and opened her eyes, hoping to dissipate the sounds of those echoing voices from the past. But no mere movement, no matter how sharp or sudden, could dissipate the gloom that twelve years of painful regret had pressed upon her spirit. It had all been her own fault. It had been she who'd persuaded herself to marry Desmond in the first place. Miss Townley had warned her that his air of cold reserve might run deeper than mere outward manner. But Camilla had been too eager for the security of wealth; those months of poverty had been too terrifying.

She told herself that she would grow to love him, and she'd married Desmond in a self-deluding glow of optimism. It didn't take long to discover that the ice in his manner was an integral part of his nature. It took a bit longer to learn that wealth and security make inadequate substitutes for inner contentment, but she'd learned it well. She'd soon realized that she would never find contentment in this house. But when that realization had finally burst upon her, escape had become impossible—she was bearing his child.

The thought of the child immediately cheered her. Little Pippa had been a life-saving gift—a sign of God's grace. It was as if she'd been forgiven for having married for the wrong reasons. From the child she'd learned that happiness was still possible. Every evening, at the family prayers which Ethelyn's domination turned into a cold and almost meaningless ritual,

Camilla sat apart and gave thanks for the miracle of her daughter's existence.

More for her daughter's sake than for any other reason, Camilla had to find a solution. Pippa could not be permitted to believe that her mother was a spineless jellyfish. Yet a bitter, recriminative collision with Ethelyn would be horrible. Even if she remained firm and refused to let Hicks go, Ethelyn would never back down, and life in this house would be even more unpleasant.

Camilla winced in self-disgust. Her thinking was as shilly-shallying as her character. Here she was, a grown woman of twenty-nine, and no more capable of handling her problems than a child. Why, a child like Pippa could probably handle it without a blink!

She shut her eyes, wondering what Pippa would do in her place . . . and suddenly the answer came like a candle flame shining through the mist. Of *course!* How simple and how *perfect!* She threw off the coverlet, jumped out of bed and gleefully danced about the room in her stockinged feet, smiling broadly. She, Camilla Wyckfield, was not such a ninnyhammer after all.

Early the next morning, Camilla leaped out of bed and, without ringing for her Abigail, hurried into her clothes. Halfway through buttoning the back of her mourning dress, she stayed her hands. *If I'm about to play the rebel,* she thought with amusement, *I may as well go all the way.* Quickly she stripped off the black dress and replaced it with a poplin gown of soft lilac. Thus attired, she sped quickly downstairs and hurried into the morning room. But she was not the first to arrive. Miss Townley was already there, setting a pot of tea in the center of the table. "What *is* this, Ada?" Camilla asked, pausing in the doorway. "Where's Hicks?"

Miss Townley didn't look up. "He asked me to set breakfast in his place," she said, her voice cold with disapproval. "He's packed his things and is all ready to leave."

"Good," Camilla said promptly. "Will you ask him to—"

"Good?" Miss Townley's head came up angrily. "Are you backin' down, then, after—? *Good Lord!*" She gaped at her mistress openmouthed. "Where's your mournin'—"

"Hush, Ada, hush. Leave the breakfast things, and ask Hicks

to come here to see me, will you, please?"

"Then you *do* have a plan!" The governess smiled at Camilla proudly. "I *knew* you'd think of some—"

"You knew no such thing, you humbug. Just a second ago you were ready to eat me whole."

Miss Townley ignored the chastisement and rubbed her hands eagerly. "You're goin' to have it out with her!" she chortled. "I can't wait to see—"

"Hush, I tell you! Please, Ada, don't jump to conclusions. Just do as I ask, and get Hicks for me. And don't say anything to anyone."

"Not even about the gown?" the governess asked as she scurried to the door.

"Not even about that."

Miss Townley nodded, gave Camilla an approving wink and left. Camilla seated herself at the table facing the door and, with hands that shook only slightly, filled her cup with tea. Bracing herself with a quick gulp of the steaming brew, she sat back and waited. She was quite ready.

The first to arrive was Pippa, who took immediate note of her mother's change of attire. "Oh, *my!*" she breathed in amazement, stopping in her tracks and gaping in admiration. "Does Aunt Ethelyn *know?*"

Camilla grinned. "Isn't it customary to say 'good morning' when you first come in?"

Pippa skipped around the table and flung her arms about her mother's neck. "Never mind the good mornings. You look *beautiful!* May I go up and change, too?"

"Perhaps later. Sit down, love, and have your breakfast."

Pippa threw herself upon a chair and reached for a biscuit. "I suppose there's a deeper meaning in this, isn't there, Mama?" Her eyes twinkled expectantly. "This has something to do with yesterday's crisis, hasn't it?"

"It's not a bit ladylike to speak with your mouth full, you know," her mother chided as a tactic of evasion.

"Very well, don't answer," Pippa said calmly, helping herself to tea. "I shan't leave your side until I learn for myself just what's going—"

"Good morning, good morning," came Oswald's voice from the doorway. "We have two early birds at the table, I s—" He was about to pull out a chair when he noticed Camilla's garb. "My *word!* You've put off mourning!"

"Yes, I have," she said, buttering a slice of toast.

"Does Ethelyn . . . that is, I mean to say . . . is everything—"

"If you are asking whether I've been given Ethelyn's *permission*, Oswald, the answer is no."

Pippa gave a little giggle, but Oswald stiffened. "I . . . er . . . think I'll put off breakfasting a little while," he mumbled, backing to the door. "Perhaps later, when—"

"Oh, do sit down, Oswald," Camilla said impatiently. "This has nothing to do with you. There's no reason for you to run off without your breakfast."

Trapped, Oswald clumsily sank into a chair, but it was clear to all of them that he would take no pleasure from this morning's meal. He was reaching half-heartedly for the covered platter containing the coddled eggs when Hicks tapped at the door and came in. He was dressed in his Sunday coat instead of his butler's garb, and he carried a shabby beaver in one hand and a stuffed portmanteau in the other. "I've come to say goodbye, Miss Camilla," he said stiffly.

"And a good riddance!" Ethelyn said, sailing into the room behind him. "Then this will be the last time I'll have to take you to task for calling her ladyship 'Miss Camilla.'" She breezed past the infuriated butler and took her place. "I'm delighted, Camilla, that you've come to your senses. Good heavens, *what* are you *wearing?*"

"Never mind that," Camilla said. "I've something important to say to Hicks before he leaves."

"Mama, you're not going to let Hicks *leave*, are you?" Pippa asked, jumping up and running to the butler's side in alarm.

"Don't worry, poppet," whispered Miss Townley, who was watching the proceedings from the open doorway. "Your mother has a plan."

"Don't care if she has," the butler muttered. "There's nothing she can devise to make me remain."

"Well, Camilla, say what it is you have to say, and let the fellow take his leave," Ethelyn ordered impatiently, "for I have a thing or two to say to *you*, and I don't want to wait all day to say it!"

Camilla folded her hands tightly in her lap and sat up very straight. "If you wish to say something about my putting off mourning, Ethelyn, you may as well save your breath. The length of my period of mourning is my own affair."

"I think, my dear," Oswald said uncomfortably, "that I'll just pop out for a . . . a stroll. Glorious morning, you know. Glorious. So if you'll excuse me—"

"Be quiet, Oswald," Ethelyn ordered, motioning him to remain in his chair. "Really, Camilla, you've no need to take that tone. If you wish to incur the disapproval of all our friends and neighbors by appearing in colors before the year has passed, I'm sure I wouldn't take it upon myself to chastise you."

"Thank you. Then I may speak to Hicks without further interruption." Camilla stood up and walked round the table to the butler. "I know you no longer wish to remain here in this house, Hicks, and I won't insist that you do, but—"

"Thank the Good Lord for *that*, at least," Ethelyn muttered.

"I've had quite enough breakfast, my dear," Oswald mumbled, "so if you don't mind—"

"Be *quiet*, I said!" his wife barked.

Camilla gave them both a look of reproval and turned back to Hicks. "As I was saying, I won't insist that you remain, but you wouldn't object to remaining in my employ, would you?"

The butler looked at her, puzzled. "Well, no, Miss Camilla, but I don't understand how—"

"I'd like you to execute a commission in London for me."

"Camilla, what is this all about?" Ethelyn asked, her brow wrinkled in annoyance. "Why do you want *him* to do it? We have any number of servants who would be much more capable—"

"Hicks is the perfect choice for *this* commission, I assure you."

"But what is it you want him to *do?*"

"I want him to find me a house. And since the house will be in his charge, he's the best one to find it."

"A *house?* What are you talking about?"

"I'd better take myself off to—" Oswald said in desperation.

"Oswald, will you be *still?* How can you wish to scurry off when Camilla has obviously lost her mind? Really, Camilla, it's the outside of enough to buy a house for the fellow in London! You can certainly find him a retirement abode in some less expensive—"

"But the house in London is not for *him* to live in . . . not alone, that is."

"Why . . . what on earth do you mean?" Ethelyn demanded, half rising from her chair.

"I've decided," Camilla said, turning to face them all and speaking with a tense firmness, "that Pippa and I shall be taking up residence in London."

There was a moment of complete silence, during which no one in the room seemed able to draw a breath. Then Oswald spoke up. "I really *must* ask to leave the room."

"Oh, *Mama!*" Pippa cried, jumping up and down jubilantly. "What a perfectly *splendid* notion!"

"Miss Camilla," Miss Townley exlaimed, "you're a *genius.*"

Hicks pumped her hand. "You've made me a happy man, Miss Camilla. A very happy man."

"Camilla!" The room fell silent as Ethelyn rose grandly to her feet. "You are speaking utter nonsense. You will do nothing of the sort."

Everyone watched intently while Ethelyn and Camilla faced each other. But for Camilla, the war was over. She'd made a decision she knew in her bones was right, and Ethelyn was powerless to stop her. Her trembling ceased. With a look of compassion, she crossed the room and put a light hand on her sister-in-law's arm. "I *will* do it, Ethelyn," she said quietly. "Don't look so thunderstruck. In a very short time you'll get used to the idea. And one day, much sooner than you think, you'll agree that I've made the very best decision for us all."

Chapter Three

By the time the last customer had stumbled out of the taproom of the Crown and Cloves, Twyford, and into the rain, it was well past midnight. But Betsy Hicks, the barmaid, still had the washing-up to do. The innkeeper's wife had, as usual, followed her husband up to bed, leaving every remaining chore to Betsy. Wearily, she washed and dried the glasses, wiped down the tables and swept the floor. Then, every bone aching, she got down on her knees, smothered the remainder of the fire with a bucketful of ashes and, patting her slightly swelling belly as if making a promise to the budding life within that only one more chore remained, swept the ashes back into the bucket and deposited it outside the back door.

The rain was coming down heavily now. Although her room over the stable was only a step away, she pulled off her apron and held it over her head as she dashed across the cobbled courtyard and into the stable door. Every step up the rickety ladder to her room seemed an enormous effort, and she was breathing heavily by the time she reached the top. She longed for sleep. Tonight she'd make only a hasty washing before throwing herself into bed. Usually she liked to daydream of Daniel when she snuggled under the blankets, but tonight she would probably be asleep before she could even bring his face to mind. It was cruel of Mrs. Crumley to keep her working so late, especially since she was four months pregnant. She limped down the short passageway with the painful shuffle of an aged crone. *If only Daniel would get home*, she prayed, *before these endless hours of work make an old woman of me*.

She'd barely opened the door and stepped over the threshold, wondering if she'd left herself a match with which to light the candle, when she was seized about the shoulders from behind, and a hand clamped down firmly on her mouth. Terrified, she struggled wildly. "Shhh, girl," a man's voice whispered in her ear, "it's only me. Don't make a noise when I let ye go."

"Daniel!" Betsy, trembling from head to toe, couldn't decide whether to kiss him or strike him. "How *could* ye—"

But he pulled her into his arms and kissed her with all the hunger that more than three months of separation had built up in him, and she forgot her fright and anger and let herself surrender to the urgency of his embrace. "Oh, Dan'l, love," she murmured breathlessly between kisses, "I thought ye'd never . . . I'm so *happy!*" It was not until she heard a match being struck by someone behind her that she realized there was someone else in the room. "Daniel," she asked with a troubled start, "who—"

The match flared up, revealing a shadowy figure on the other side of the room. "Don't make any noise, love," Daniel warned in a hissing whisper. "It's my friend, Tom, that I wrote ye of. We been sittin' here in the dark for three hours, waitin' fer you t' finish yer chores."

"Sorry we had to break in on you this way, Mrs. Hicks," Tom said quietly, lighting a candle on Betsy's bedside table.

Betsy put a hand to her heaving breast and sank down on the bed, looking from one man to the other. "Somethin's gone wrong, ain't it? That's why ye didn't come to the inn to fetch me. Somethin's terrible wrong. I've felt it in my bones all day."

Daniel sat down beside her, took her hand and stroked it gently. "Don't take on when I tell ye. I . . . can't stay with ye. We're on the run."

"On the *run?*" In the dim light of the candle she searched his face, taking agonized note of his puffed right eye, and ugly bruise on his left cheek and a bit of dried blood on his lip. "Oh, my God! What is it ye've *done?*"

Quickly, without going into minor details, he related to her the events of the evening before—the encounter with the press-gang and the struggle in the cabin of the *Undaunted*. "We're in fer it now, y' see," he concluded glumly. "They'll be lookin' fer us up and down the coast."

"But, why?" Betsy asked, fingering her husband's bruised face tenderly. "Ye've given them the slip, haven't ye? They'll forget all about ye as soon as they nab some other poor sot in yer place."

He shook his head. "I don't think so. That Captain Brock'll remember us, fer sure. And the officer—what was his name, Tom?"

"Moresby."

"Aye, Moresby. He'll not forget us, neither. We've got to get away, love." His voice choked. "We only waited so's I could say goodbye to ye."

"No!" the girl cried, flinging her arms round his neck. "Ye'll not go a step without me! I swore to myself ever since ye left that I'll never say goodbye to ye again."

Daniel buried his face in her neck. "Nay, love, don't be foolish," he murmured brokenly. "We don't know where we'll end. We can't—"

She put a hand to his mouth to stop his words and shook her head. They clung to each other for a long moment. Then she pushed him away and got to her feet. "Y're wet and cold and prob'ly hungry. We can't think straight in such a state." She wiped her eyes, sniffed bravely and tried to pull herself together. Straightening her shoulders, she looked at Tom shyly. "Excuse me, sir," she said, holding a hand out to him. "I been very rude. I'm most pleased t' meet ye after all Daniel's wrote me about ye."

Tom took her hand and smiled down at her. "Daniel told me about you, too, especially how pretty you are. I was sure the fellow was lying, but I see now that he didn't exaggerate a bit."

A pathetic little smile made an appearance at the corners of her mouth. "Oh, pooh, I must look a sight." She blushed and pushed aside a fallen lock of hair. "But I want t' thank ye,

Mr. Collinson, for bein' such a good friend to my Daniel."

"I haven't been a very good friend in *this* matter," Tom muttered ruefully. "I'm afraid I've gotten him into deeper trouble than he'd have had without my interference."

"Belay that, Tom," Daniel ordered. "If it warn't fer you, I'd be prisoned on the *Undaunted* like a slavey, with no hope of any life at all, and no way t' get word to Betsy."

"And it was only t' help him that y're in this fix at all," Betsy added. "We'll always be grateful to ye."

"There's no earthly reason for that," Tom sighed, "for all the good my 'help' has done. But standing here talking won't pay the piper. We'd better be on our way."

"He's right, Betsy, love." Daniel got up from the bed reluctantly. "Laggin' in the valley won't get us over the hill."

"No, I won't have it," Betsy declared firmly. "Ye can't leave me behind, nor the baby neither. Besides, you'll never get away dressed in seamen's clothes and lookin' all battered, like ye do."

"But, Mrs. Hicks," Tom said gently, "there's nothing else to be done. We may even endanger *you* if we're caught in your company."

"My name is Betsy, if you please, and we're not *goin'* to be caught if we think of a good-enough plan. Y're both too cold and miserable to see things straight. I'll slip down t' the kitchen an' fetch some bread an' cold meat—"

"Nay, lass," Daniel cut in, although the prospect of food was painfully tempting, "someone might see ye."

"No one will see me, I promise," She wrapped a shawl around her and moved toward the door. "After ye've filled yer bellies, ye'll be able to think better on what t' do next."

Betsy proved to be right. A tray of food and a few mugs full of home brew made the whole world seem brighter. And after they'd discarded their damp clothes, wrapped themselves in dry blankets and permitted Betsy to tend their bruises, it became difficult to see how they could get along without her. Finally, she pointed out that they would look less suspicious travelling about with a woman, and they agreed that, wherever they should decide to go, she would be with them.

With that decided, they turned their attention to the problem of their destination. It had to be a place far from any seaport where press-gangs were likely to be active, yet somewhere which would offer opportunities to find work. Betsy, her weariness forgotten in the anticipation of the start of a new life in the company of her husband, was full of suggestions. But each one was ruled out by the men for being either too optimistic or too impractical.

She paced the tiny room animatedly, while the two men sat huddled near the fire staring discouragedly into the flames. Although their spirits were too depressed to permit their minds to function, *her* brain seethed with fertile imaginings. She would not permit herself to succumb to discouragement. "I have it!" she clarioned excitedly for the sixth time. "The perfect plan at last!"

"Now, love, don't carry on," Daniel admonished with gentle hopelessness. "Ye've said that about *all* yer ideas."

"But this one will work, I *know* it! I been thinkin' on it all these months, tryin' to puzzle out where we might go when ye returned from the sea. I put the idea out o' my head, figurin' ye wouldn't take kindly to it. But now it seems t' me to be just exac'ly what we need."

"Why? If I wouldn't take kindly to it afore—"

"Well, matters 'er different now. It'd be a perfect place to hide."

Daniel tried to stop her effusions, but Tom put a hand on his arm. "Let her talk, Daniel. She's the only one of us who's shown a spark of imagination. Perhaps she has something, this time."

"I do, Dan'l, truly. The best suggestion yet. Yer uncle Hicks."

"My uncle? What're ye talkin' about?"

"He's in Dorset, somewheres near Shillingstone, ain't he? That must be a goodish distance from the sea, and as good a place as any I can think of to—"

"But he's a butler, ain't he? On a grand estate. Workin' fer a duke or an earl. Wyckfield Park it's called, if I remember rightly. You ain't imaginin' he could take us in an' hide us, are ye?"

"No, but per'aps he could find us places there. To work, I mean. I could serve as a housemaid, couldn't I? At least 'til the baby comes. And you both could be gardeners or stable hands or footmen or somethin'."

"Nay, girl, ye're talkin' like a witlin'. What do we know about gardenin' or horses or household service?"

"What do ye know about *anythin'* save seafarin'?" she

countered bluntly. "That sort of work's as easy t' learn as any-thin' else."

Daniel was silenced but unconvinced. Dubiously, he looked at Tom. Tom shook his head. "She may be right, Daniel. Certainly no impressment officer would go seeking you in the house of a nobleman. It isn't the sort of work for *me*, but you and Betsy might do very well—"

Betsy planted herself before him, her eyes flashing and her arm akimbo. "We already decided we'll stick t'gether, so let's hear no more you-and-Betsys! An' if the work would do fer Daniel an' me, why wouldn't it do fer you?"

Tom made a face. "I'll be dashed if I want to be a footman for a puffed-up nobleman to step upon."

"Are ye tryin' to say ye're too good fer household service? Per'aps it'd be better t' be trussed up like a sack o' mutton and dumped on the deck o' that navy ship ye spoke of, eh?" she demanded tartly.

Daniel grinned at his wife's spirit. "She has ye there, old man. An' she may be right. No King's officer would recognize us all spruced up in footmen's livery."

Tom looked from one to the other questioningly. "Are you seriously saying you want to go to Dorset and ask this uncle of yours for work as *servants?*"

"That's exac'ly what I'm sayin'," Betsy declared. "Nothin's wrong with bein' servants. The quarters are clean, the pay's reg'lar, and the food's always good an' plentiful."

"That's true enough," Daniel agreed. "You'll probably like it better 'n ye think, Tom, fer there's sure t' be a goodish number of pretty young maids about to kiss under the stairs—"

"Oh, hush, Dan'l! What a thing to say! Tom ain't the sort to maul the girls under the stairs," his wife objected. "He's far too gentlemanly."

Tom grinned at her. "No man's too gentlemanly for that, my dear. In fact, the promise of some pretty girls to cuddle is the only part of your plan which I find pleasing, if the truth were told."

"There, y' see?" Daniel chortled, pinching his wife's cheek. "I know this fellow better 'n you do, my girl. I seen 'im fondle and forsake more 'n one lass in our time together."

"Shame on ye, Dan'l, trying to make me b'lieve yer best friend is a rake! I don't want t' hear no more o' this. Besides, it ain't gettin' us no closer to solvin' our problem. Are we goin' to Dorset or ain't we?"

"But Betsy, love," Daniel said, his grin dying, "it ain't very likely, is it, that my uncle Hicks could find posts fer all three of us?"

"How can we tell 'til we try?" Betsy responded reasonably. "Stake nothin', draw nothin', as they say."

Daniel shrugged. "Well . . . it's the best scheme we've come up with so far. What do y' say, Tom? Shall we chance it?"

Tom stared into the fire. It *was* the best suggestion to come forth, yet it only served to deepen his despond. He suddenly perceived that his dreams of mastering a vessel were now completely beyond the possibility of fulfillment . . . and for the first time since they'd encountered the press-gang, that truth swept over him with the finality of death. No more would he feel the rocking of the deck beneath his feet, the salt wind cracking his lips, the wheel fighting for supremacy under his hands. No more would he wake up in the morning, climb up on deck and stare out at the grey mist rising from the immensity of grey sea. Now he'd probably wake up to the smell of horse dung in the stable, or, if he were housed in the servants' quarters, he'd probably look out on a backyard court piled with kitchen refuse waiting to be burned. At sea the work had seemed to him to be purposeful and important; the way he'd order the sails trimmed or how he'd chart a course would determine how quickly and safely the ship would reach its destination. He'd had rules to obey, but they'd made sense. Now his work would be trivial, and the rules would be made—and arbitrarily changed—at the whim of a spoiled nobleman with nothing more to do than give orders. At sea he'd had a chance to become a master. Now he'd be subjected to orders from an army of superior beings, and the hope of ever becoming his own man would be an empty dream.

A hand on his shoulder made him look up. Daniel was standing above him, looking down at him with eyes that revealed his complete understanding of his friend's feelings. "I'm . . . right sorry," he mumbled miserably. "Things shouldn't 've turned out like this fer ye . . ."

Filled with shame at his attack of self-pity, Tom forcibly shook off his dejection. "No, Daniel, don't mind me," he said, getting to his feet and smiling reassuringly. "Being sorry for myself won't buy any barley, as your sensible little wife would be quick to tell me. She seems to have more brains than the two of us together. Well, Betsy, it seems we're going to Dorset. What are your plans, then? Give us our orders, my dear. You're the captain of this voyage."

Betsy threw her arms around him in a grateful hug. Then, clapping her hands happily, she looked at them both with eyes shining in excited anticipation. "If I'm to be captain," she said, laughing, "my first order is to warn you, Tom, to stop usin' all that mariner's talk. Next, I say we should all go to sleep, fer there's nothin' more we can do tonight. We'll be able to think better after we've rested. Dan'l, you and Tom take the bed. I'll fix myself a pallet on the hearth—"

"Not on your life," Tom interrupted, grinning. "I'll obey your orders on almost anything, Betsy, but not on this. You and Daniel take the bed. I'll do very well on the hay in the loft outside. Goodnight to you both." And with a wink at his friend, he wrapped his blanket about him and fled.

Betsy proved more than equal to the task of organizing their departure. First thing next morning, she had them pool their resources. Betsy had managed to save—after months of slaving in the taproom—only a meager pile of coins, and Tom, having left the *Triton* so abruptly, had only a few shillings in the pocket of his coat. But Daniel had sewn into his coatlining the twenty pounds which the paymaster had given him before his departure from the *Triton*. Betsy decided that most of the money had to be spent on clothing. "We ain't likely to get posts as respectable servants if we look like shabby beggars," she informed them.

To avoid arousing suspicion while they prepared themselves for the trip to Dorset, the men kept hidden in the stable while Betsy took steps to procure the items of clothing they would need. First she informed her employers at the Crown and Cloves that she was leaving to live with distant relatives until her child was born. Then, quite openly, she ordered a warm and amply cut gown for herself from a seamstress in Twyford. An extra few shillings convinced the woman to set aside her other work and stitch up the dress as soon as possible. Meanwhile, Betsy unobtrusively made her way by cart, wagon and shank's mare to the town of Winchester to buy clothing for the men. She waited until dark to make her way back, and her husband was in a state of considerable agitation by the time she slipped back into the room. "Where've ye been, woman?" he almost shouted when he saw her safe. "Ye had me fearin' you'd been trampled by a horse or worse!"

"Hush, ye great looby, do ye want them t' hear ye in the taproom? I had to wait 'til dark so no one'd see me carryin' these parcels. I'm fine, as ye can see. And just wait 'til ye glimpse what I've bought fer ye."

The packages were eagerly unwrapped, and the merriment was hard to contain as they watched Daniel struggle into a pair of almost-new buff-colored breeches which were much too tight for him. But they all roared aloud when Tom stood before them fully dressed. The coat Betsy had purchased for him had been cut for a much shorter man. The waist was too high, and his wrists hung from the sleeves like those of a fifteen-year-old youth who'd grown too quickly. And the high-crowned, curly-brimmed top hat she'd purchased, while certainly fit for a gentleman, fit him not at all. It was so large that it slipped down over his ears. The entire effect of his altered appearance in those ill-fitting clothes set them all in stitches. But Betsy sat up all night, letting out the seams of Daniel's "smalls" and lengthening the sleeves of Tom's new coat. And the next day, after exchanging Tom's top hat for the low-crowned, soft-brimmed headpiece she'd bought for Daniel, she was quite pleased with their appearances.

It took one more day for Betsy's dress to be ready, but they looked a very presentable trio when they finally set out, on foot, before the sun had risen the next morning. Daniel was surprisingly gentlemanly in his top hat (which Betsy had made to fit by stuffing paper into the inner hatband), Tom was quite "sporting" in his more informal headgear, and Betsy was neatly demure in her plum-colored kerseymere gown and black bonnet. All their extra linens were packed into one small parcel wrapped in brown paper and tied with a cord, which Tom and Daniel took turns carrying.

By midmorning they reached Winchester, where they boarded the stage bound for Bath. Although they were going only to Deptford—a distance the coach would cover in less than seven hours—they found the ride completely nerve-wracking, for the coach had started out from Southampton, and it seemed to them that every passenger who'd boarded before them was staring at them with suspicion. They disembarked at Deptford, however, without any untoward incident having occurred. In joyful relief, they squandered a large portion of their meager funds on a substantial dinner and lodgings at a respectable inn. And the next morning, after a whispered conference over the breakfast table, they decided to throw what remained of their finances into hiring a private carriage to take them the rest of the way to Wyckfield Park.

The carriage ride was a merry one, for the privacy was heady luxury. There was no one aboard to stare into their faces or eye their makeshift clothing with suspicion. Their spirits rose to dizzy heights as they laughed and joked and made optimistic predictions about their futures. "My uncle'll be delighted t' see us, don't ye think, Betsy, love?" Daniel asked. "He always like me as a boy. Tossed me up in the air and pinched my cheek..."

"I'm certain he'll be glad t' see you, my dear," his wife smiled confidently. "By tonight, we'll be comfortably moved into neat bedrooms, an' we'll be havin' our supper in a nice, warm kitchen with the rest o' the staff, all smilin' and friendly."

No cloud could be envisioned to dim their bright prospects. Betsy was convinced they were embarked on a promising new path. She painted a glowing picture of how she imagined their new mistress would be: a sweet, generous lady who'd be delighted that her new maid was with child, and who'd kindly provide a midwife to see her through the birthing safely. Daniel dreamed of the small apartment they would be given all for themselves, and of the kitchen gardens and the ample grounds where the child would be permitted to run and play quite freely.

Betsy and Daniel together made predictions even for *Tom's* future. Tom, because of his gentlemanly speech, would soon be promoted to the favored post of gentleman's gentleman. Tom laughed at the absurdity and acted out a comical pantomime in which he attempted to tie an impatient gentleman's neckcloth with staggering ineptitude. By keeping everyone laughing, he was able to mask, even to some extent from himself, the despair with which his altered prospects had overwhelmed his spirit.

The ride was briefer than they'd expected. By midmorning they'd arrived at the impressive gates of Wyckfield Park. They quickly sobered at the sight. Ordering the coachman to set them down just outside the gates, they climbed from the carriage and trudged along the drive leading to the great house. Silently, with unspoken fears beginning to hammer away at their previous optimism, they made their way round to the kitchen door.

Before knocking, the men removed their hats, and Betsy nervously looked them over. She straightened Daniel's neckcloth, picked a piece of lint from Tom's shoulder and nodded. Daniel stepped forward and, with a deep breath, knocked firmly at the door.

It was opened by a plump, fuzzy-haired woman in a very large, stiffly starched white apron and neat cap. "Yes?" she asked, eyebrows raised.

Betsy dropped a quick curtsey. "Beg pardon, ma'am," she said politely, "but we was wonderin' if we could see Mr. Hicks."

The woman, taking note of their dusty shoes and strained expressions, looked at them with a twinge of sympathy. "Mr. Hicks? I'm sorry to have to disappoint you, but he ain't here no more. He's gone off to London, he has, not a se'ennight since. An' he ain't expected back."

Chapter Four

For three days following Camilla's announcement of her intention to leave Wyckfield Park for London, a painful war had ensued. Ethelyn had subjected her sister-in-law to a most trying ordeal, attacking Camilla repeatedly with every weapon of persuasion or coercion available to her. There had been hours of argument, during which Ethelyn described London as a place of vice and iniquity, declaring it to be completely unsuitable for a woman of Camilla's sensitivity and sheltered background, "and positively *unfit* for a child like Philippa!"

When the arguments had proved ineffective, Ethelyn had resorted to shouts, demands, threats, and even a shocking and most uncharacteristic flood of tears. Finally she'd taken to her bed, accusing Camilla of driving her to death's door. But Camilla, through it all, had remained adamant. Once she'd breathed the whiff of freedom . . . once she'd realized that escape from the repressive confines of her sister-in-law's domination was possible . . . once she had permitted herself to believe that a new life was within her grasp, she couldn't turn away from the joyful prospect.

Patiently, and with a quiet steadfastness that was as surprising to Ethelyn as it was irritating, Camilla tried to bring her sister-in-law to a calm acceptance of the inevitable separation. She explained that her decision to move to London was not a sign of depravity. They would choose a house in a quiet neighborhood. They would not indulge in hectic socializing but would keep very much to themselves. But they *would* avail themselves of the many cultural and artistic activities that London offered—the museums, the libraries, the opera, the shops and the parks. Pippa needed more intellectual stimulation than she could find in the country. "And I myself," she added gently, "need to get away from these surroundings which remind me so much of . . . of death and mourning."

Ethelyn remained unconvinced, but she was powerless to force her sister-in-law to accede to her will. Camilla was, after all, twenty-nine years old and possessed of more-than-adequate means. What Ethelyn would have found consoling would have been to remove Philippa from her mother's guardianship. She'd even consulted the family solicitor about the possibility. But there were no legal grounds on which they could build a case. Ethelyn, being female, had no stronger claim to the guardianship than the child's mother. If only she'd thought about it before her brother had died, she could have persuaded him to place the guardianship in Oswald's hands. Now, of course, it was too late . . .

Ethelyn had never set foot in London in her life and therefore despised the place with the unshakable conviction of prejudiced ignorance. She'd heard enough lurid tales and gossip to convince her that it was as iniquitous as Sodom, and she warned Camilla that she would never, as long as she lived, set foot in her sister-in-law's London establishment. "So you needn't expect any visits from *me!*" she warned. "Although I shall be willing to welcome you here. I shall expect you for all the important religious observances, of course, and for the warm-weather months as well." She fixed an eye on Camilla coldly. "And when you've realized that I am right about the unsuitability of those surroundings for your daughter, you will, of course, send her promptly home to me."

Camilla, who had chosen London as the locus of their new home for precisely the reason that Ethelyn never would visit there, merely lowered her eyes and kept silent. She'd won the war; there would be little harm in letting Ethelyn believe she'd won a small part of this last battle.

When they realized they'd been victorious, Camilla, Pippa and Miss Townley gathered behind the closed door of Camilla's bedroom and hugged each other in unrestrained elation. The future was suddenly wide open with exciting possibilities. "What wonderful adventures we'll have!" Pippa exclaimed, whirling about the room deleriously. "It will be like living a *novel!*"

Her mother tried to restrain the child's imagination from running riot. "It certainly will *not,*" she said, trying to frown. "We shall live in quiet modesty, just as we always have." But her imagination was scarcely less riotous than her daughter's, and she concluded her reprimand by lifting the child in her arms and spinning her about until, laughing and breathless, they both fell dizzily upon the bed.

While waiting to hear from Hicks that a house had been found and made ready for them, the three hurled themselves into a frenzy of packing. Besides their clothing and personal effects, there were some paintings, household articles, pieces of furniture and a great number of books which Camilla had purchased over the years that, if Ethelyn should not object, she wished to take with her. The next few days were spent going over lists of these items with her sour-faced sister-in-law and setting aside those things which Ethelyn agreed could be removed. Later, Miss Townley and Camilla packed the articles carefully with their own hands, and often with Pippa's assistance. It was the only activity which seemed to ease their impatience to be gone.

For Pippa, the waiting was almost unbearable. With typical childish avidity, she chaffed at the delay as day followed day without a word from the butler. "Why doesn't he write?" she asked nightly, when her mother tucked her into bed. "Why does it take so long to find a house?"

After several days, Camilla decided it was best to make it clear to the child that buying a house was not a task that could be easily concluded in a short time. "It's only been a week, dearest," she said soothingly. "We'll hear from Hicks before long."

"Yes, but *when?* A day? A week? A fortnight?"

"I don't know. Perhaps even longer."

Pippa winced. *"Longer?* Oh, no! I don't think I could *bear* it!"

"But why not, my love? You've lived here all your life in perfect contentment. Why does the prospect of spending a few more weeks under this roof seem suddenly unbearable to you?"

"I don't know," Pippa answered thoughtfully. "Perhaps it's because I never expected any sort of change before." She gave her mother a sudden, mischievous grin. "Now that I have the prospect of adventures, I just can't wait for them to begin to happen!"

"Oh, my *dearest,"* Camilla admitted, enveloping the girl in a warm embrace, "neither can I!"

It was midmorning of the very next day that Mrs. Nyles, the fuzzy-haired cook, stood in the kitchen doorway staring interestedly at a trio of travelers who seemed inordinately disappointed at the news that Mr. Hicks had gone. The three, who'd introduced themselves as Betsy and Daniel Hicks and their friend Collinson, were gaping at her as if she'd announced the end of the world. "Ye've come a long way, I wager, and all for naught," the cook murmured sympathetically, tucking a crimped lock of hair under her cap. "Come in an' have a spot o' tea with me. It'll cheer ye som'at to rest yerselves a bit."

Betsy, the elected captain of this ill-fated expedition, tried to push aside her feeling of despair as she nodded gratefully. Mrs. Nyles seemed a woman of hearty good nature, and she and her companions needed to sit themselves down and think. They'd foolishly squandered all their money and were now stranded in the middle of Dorset with no resources and no plan. Why had they never even *considered* what to do if the first plan failed?

Mrs. Nyles ushered them into a huge, square kitchen, brightly lit by the October sunshine streaming in through a row of windows in the south wall. The wall adjoining the windows contained two large ovens and an immense fireplace, and in the corner opposite was an open stairway which they surmised led up to the main part of the house. The cook led them to a long table in the center of the room and, as soon as they were seated, turned to two young kitchen maids who were lolling near the fire and ordered them into action. As the maids set plates and cups before the visitors, Mrs. Nyles took a seat beside Betsy and looked her over interestedly. "Did ye wish t' see Mr. Hicks fer some partic'lar reason?" she asked, turning away only to slice a loaf of bread which one of the maids had set before her.

"Oh, yes," Betsy admitted, eyeing the large loaf, the wedge of cheddar cheese, the platter of cold, sliced ham and the basket full of warm raisin buns which the maids set on the table, "he's my husband's uncle, y' see."

"His uncle, eh? My, my." Mrs. Nyles leaned toward Daniel and looked at him closely for a family resemblance. "Now you mention it, I mind as how he sometimes spoke of a nevvy he had as was a sailor. Is that you?"

Daniel cast Tom an uneasy glance, but Betsy covered quickly. "No, no," she said hastily. "Ye're thinkin' of his . . . er . . . brother."

"Right," Daniel said, nodding earnestly. "My brother. He's at sea."

"Ah, yes. Well, Mr. Hicks'll be sorry he missed ye, I'm sure."

"Not nearly as sorry as we are," Tom muttered.

Mrs. Nyles looked at him curiously. There was nothing she liked better than an opportunity for idle gossip. "Did ye have somethin' special ye wanted to see him about?" she asked, pouring out the tea.

Tom hesitated, but Betsy nodded frankly. "We was hopin' he could find us places here at Wyckfield Park," she admitted, hoping desperately that the friendly seeming cook could be of help. "I've had some years as a . . . a housemaid, y' see, and these two strong fellows could be of all sorts of use—"

"Ye weren't expectin' *Mr. Hicks* to find you places here, were ye?" The cook snorted in scornful amusement. "Ye're way out, if that's what ye come for."

The two kitchen maids, lingering about behind her and eyeing the two men covetously, giggled loudly.

Mrs. Nyles turned round. "What're ye doin' hangin' about here?" She swung her arm at them, catching one a good cuff at the hip. "Get about yer duties, both of ye!" The maids scurried off under Mrs. Nyles's glare. When they'd vanished, she sighed and shook her head. "Impudent snips! They'd rather stand about gossipin' than do anythin' else. If there's anythin' I can't abide, it's a lazy tittle-tattle."

"But, Mrs. Nyles, I don't understand why you all laughed," Betsy said, confused. "Mr Hicks *is* the butler here, ain't he?"

"He *was* the butler. But her ladyship—Lady Ethelyn Falcombe, y' know—wouldn't never take on nobody of *his* recommendin'." She turned in her chair and leaned toward Betsy in eager confidentiality. "She never could abide him, y' know. If it wasn't fer the young Lady Wyckfield, Lady Ethelyn would've let him go years past."

"Are you saying that he's been given the *sack?*" Tom asked.

"In a manner o' speakin' he has."

"It's a fine kettle o' fish we're in," Daniel groaned, dropping his chin on his hand gloomily.

Tom studied the cook with a puzzled frown. "What do you mean, 'in a manner of speakin'? Has Mr. Hicks been sacked or hasn't he?"

"He still works fer the younger Lady Wyckfield. He's gone to find her a house in town. She's movin' away, y' see."

"And he won't be comin' back here?" Betsy queried.

"Not him. Swore he'd never set foot in this house again, he did. It was a reg'lar to-do he had with her ladyship afore he left, I can tell ye."

"Then we are in the soup an' no mistake," Betsy said, stirring her tea dispiritedly.

"Perhaps not." Tom eyed the cook speculatively. "Are you saying that Mr. Hicks is setting up a household for Lady Wyckfield in London? Won't he have to hire a number of servants to staff it?"

Mrs. Nyles eyebrows rose delightedly. "O' *course!*" she exclaimed, clapping a hand to her forehead. "What a *codshead* I am! He'll need t' find parlormaids, an' a groom, an' footmen, an' a cook, an' all manner of help."

"That's right," Daniel chortled in relief. "He'll have a real *need* fer us."

"But Dan'l," Betsy murmured, frowning worriedly, "London . . . ?"

Daniel blinked. He'd completely forgotten the necessity for hiding. Would they be safe among the crowded masses of the city where, it was said, all roads cross? He looked over at Tom questioningly.

Tom shrugged. "I'd be willing to chance it, if you are," he murmured in an undervoice. "Now all we have to do is find the wherewithal to get there."

Daniel sagged in his chair. Life was one problem after the other. "That's the facer, ain't it?"

Mrs. Nyles looked from one to the other. "What's worryin' ye now?" she asked in her direct, curious way.

"We used all our blunt to get here," Betsy explained. "How are we to get to London without a shillin' in our pockets?"

"Is *that* all that troubles ye?" She got to her feet and, smiling broadly, went to the fire for the kettle. "Ye can catch a ride with my Henry. He's the coachman, y' see, an' he's settin' off this very afternoon to deliver some boxes fer Lady Wyckfield to the new house. She got word this mornin' that Mr. Hicks has found a place on—where did she say?—Upper Seymour Street, if I remember rightly." She poured the boiling water into the teapot, feeling quite pleased with herself. "There, y' see?" She beamed at them, clapping Daniel on the shoulder with enthusiasm. "Ye haven't a care in the world. Now ye can drink yer tea without wearin' them long faces."

With the seemingly insoluble problem so easily dispensed with, the three travelers set upon the food before them with hearty appetites. Mrs. Nyles smiled encouragement and pressed them to refill their plates as often as they wished. It was not often she could welcome congenial visitors to her table, and she revelled in the opportunity to reveal tidbits of household gossip to strangers who hadn't heard the tales before. With an innate sense of the dramatic, she began to regale them with a detailed account of Lady Ethelyn's eleven-year battle with Mr. Hicks. She started with their initial encounter (a scene which Mrs. Nyles had been privileged to witness with her own eyes) when they'd taken an instant dislike to each other, and, providing her amused and fascinated listeners with almost verbatim accounts of the numerous altercations which followed, was just approaching her rendition of the final confrontation when her voice suddenly faded. With mouth open, she gaped up at the stairway in the corner of the kitchen. Her three guests, surprised at her change of expression, turned in the direction of her stare.

Coming down the stairs, her eyes fixed on a long sheet of paper in her hand, was a youngish woman whose appearance set Tom's pulse racing. She was slim as the stem of a seaweed, with a slightly pointed chin and a pale complexion. A mane of silky, light-auburn hair was carelessly tied in a knot at the top of her head, but many strands spilled over her forehead in what Tom felt was enchanting disarray. Her face was smudged with dust, as was the voluminous apron which covered her dress. With her attention focussed on the paper she held, he couldn't see her eyes, but the hand which held lightly onto the bannister to guide her down was as graceful as a gull. "Mrs. Nyles," she was saying in a soft, musical voice, "I wonder if you'd mind going over this list of equipment with me. Hicks writes that the kitchen in the London house is sadly lacking in—*oh!*"

Her eyes, as she looked up in startled embarrassment, were, Tom thought, beautifully dark in that pale face. *"Lord!"* he gasped, getting to his feet and moving trance-like toward the stairs, "someone should have told me household service could be like this!"

"What?" the woman on the stairs asked, blinking down at him in confusion.

A strangled gurgle came from deep within Mrs. Nyles's throat.

"The name is Tom," he said, taking her hand and helping her down the last two steps, "and I was saying that if I'd known there were housemaids like you on the premises, I should have entered service years ago." He grinned down at her, amused and delighted by her complete astonishment. He put one hand on the bannister and the other on the wall, thus quite effectively preventing her from being able to move away from him.

"Told you that he'd like it," Daniel chortled, delighted at seeing his friend involved in a flirtation.

"Hush, Dan'l," Betsy murmured, an instinct warning her that something was wrong. "The poor lass looks frightened."

"Frightened?" Tom asked, glancing at Betsy over his shoulder. "Don't be foolish. I mean her no harm." Looking back at his prisoner, he took her chin in his hand. "You aren't afraid of me, are you, girl? Surely every fellow for miles about must be after you—and more forcefully than *this*. Why, I haven't even tried to *kiss* you yet."

The astonished woman gasped. "Mrs. Nyles!" she sputtered furiously. "Who *is* this person?"

Mrs. Nyles choked, unable to speak. "I . . . I . . ." she managed in a choking voice, her face reddening alarmingly.

"Go ahead and kiss 'er," Daniel urged, laughing. "There ain't a female in the world wouldn't prefer the deed to the word."

"You're quite right," Tom agreed, slipping an arm about his quarry and pulling her to him.

"Don't you *dare!*" the woman exclaimed in a voice of unmistakable authority. "I realize you've mistaken my identity, but even a *maid* ought to be safe in the kitchen of this house!"

Tom's grin faded. "Mistaken your identity?" he asked, his eyes narrowing.

"Oh, *heavens,*" Mrs. Nyles cried, finding her voice at last. "I'm so . . . I d-didn't *dream* . . . oh, yer *ladyship,* I—"

"Your *ladyship?*" Betsy gasped.

Daniel choked and Tom whitened. Dropping his hold, he backed away from her aghast.

"Yes, I'm Lady Wyckfield," Camilla said furiously. "And *who,* may I ask, are you?"

The three strangers, utterly confounded, stood rooted in their places. Mrs. Nyles rose from her chair and approached her mistress fearfully. "I don't know *how* t' apologize, your ladyship," she mumbled. "They're r-relations of Mr. Hicks, y' see, an'—"

"Relations of Hicks's? I don't believe it!" her ladyship said, looking at them sternly.

"It's true, ma'am," Daniel said, stepping forward with head lowered abjectly. "He's my uncle."

"*Is* he indeed! Well, he won't be very pleased with you when I report to him how you comported yourselves in my kitchen!"

"No, ma'am, he won't," Betsy said miserably. "We're dreadful ashamed. We never meant no harm, though. It was the apron, y' see."

"I see quite well. Is it your habit, young man, to accost everyone who wears an apron in that *libertinish* style?"

Tom, recovered from his initial shock at learning her identity, began to find the entire scene very amusing. "Not *every* one, my lady," he said, his lips twitching. "Only the very prettiest ones, I assure you."

"*Tom!*" Betsy protested in a hissing whisper.

Camilla flushed in irritation. "Oh, you find this incident amusing, do you?" she snapped. "You'd do better, fellow, to recognize the depravity of your character and attempt to mend your ways." *Good heavens,* she thought, surprised, *I sound just like Ethelyn.*

"Depravity, ma'am?" Tom regarded her with an irrepressible glint of humor. "If a pinch on the chin is depraved to you, you must be leading a saintly life. However, I'll try to mend my ways if you'll tell me how to go about it."

She frowned at him, not knowing what to make of his unchastened manner. "For one thing," she declared repressively, "you can try to show some sincere *regret*—"

"Am I *not* showing it? I assure you, ma'am, that I'm positively awash in regret."

"One would scarcely notice it," she said suspiciously. "But if you are *truly* sorry for that lecherous behavior, it's at least a beginning."

"Oh, it's not my *behavior* I'm sorry for, ma'am. It's my *lack* of it."

Something in his eyes told her that she would make no headway bandying words with him, but somehow she went on with it. "Lack of it? I don't understand."

He grinned broadly. "What I'm sorry for is that I didn't kiss you when I had the chance—before I found out who you were."

"Tom!" Betsy cried, appalled.

Tom kept his eyes on the lady's face. "Now, you see, my chance is gone forever."

"What I *see*, young man, is that you're quite incorrigible!" She gathered up her skirts and turned to mount the stairs. "I suggest, Mrs. Nyles, that you rid yourself of your 'guests' as soon as possible. When they've gone, please come up to the sitting room to go over this list with me. In the meantime, I hope you will make it clear to these . . . persons . . . that they will not be made welcome in this kitchen ever again!" With that, she marched up the stairs without a backward look and disappeared from view.

There was a moment of stunned silence in the kitchen. Then Mrs. Nyles stalked up to Tom and swatted him smartly on his backside. "You jackanapes! A fine stew ye've got me into!"

"Y' should've told us," Betsy piped up in his defense. "How was he to know?"

"Was *that* Lady Ethelyn?" Daniel asked. "Will she take it out on *you*, Mrs. Nyles, like she did on my uncle Hicks?"

Mrs. Nyles hooted scornfully. "Oh, no, don't worry yer head about *that*. It was only Lady Wyckfield. Camilla, y' know. She's the soft one."

"Camilla," Tom mumbled, staring up at the stairway. "Lovely name. Suits her."

Mrs. Nyles struck him another blow. "Never mind her name, ye great looby! That tongue o' yours'll get ye in fat trouble one o' these days."

She turned away and began busily to clear the table. Betsy, meanwhile, paced about before the fireplace. "Good God!" she exclaimed suddenly. "If that was the *other* lady . . . then *she's* the one goin' to be mistress of the London house!"

"My Lord!" Daniel stared at her in dawning alarm. "Ye mean—?"

Tom groaned and dropped into a chair, struck all at once with shame. "She means that, because of me, Mr. Hicks will never be able to hire us now."

Wordlessly, his friends sank down beside him. This latest blow was too great to permit them even to utter words of consolation to him. The last of the spirit that had sustained them all day deserted them, and they were aware only of the dire hopelessness of their situation.

Mrs. Nyles, crossing from the table to the larder with the left-overs, paused and squinted at them. "Why are ye sittin' about like three stones fer a passerby t' trip over?" she demanded. As far as she was concerned, the incident with her ladyship had been a momentary embarrassment and had passed without causing any permanent harm. She gave it no further thought. "My Henry'll be leavin' without ye if ye don't take yerselves over to the stables."

"No use goin' to London now," Betsy said, unable to keep her unshed tears from showing in her voice.

"No use?" Mrs. Nyles, stowing away the food, wrinkled her brow in confusion. "Why ever not?"

"Didn't ye hear what Tom just said?" Daniel asked morosely. "My uncle won't be able t' take us on now."

"Ye mean because of what just passed?" Mrs. Nyles strode back to them and, taking a stance in the middle of the room, glared at them with arms akimbo. "You three fall more easy into low tide than anyone ought! Don't make so much over nothin'. Just ferget all about that meetin' with her ladyship and go about yer business."

"Ferget it?" Betsy asked. "Ye can't mean it."

"O' course I mean it! Don't even think on it no more."

"But Mr. Hicks would never—"

"I wouldn't even *mention* it to Mr. Hicks, if I was you."

"Not mention it?" Betsy eyed the mettlesome cook dubiously. "But if he should engage us, and then the lady sees us, what then?"

"She won't even remember you, most likely. By tomorrow,

she won't remember yer faces, and by the next day she'll have fergot the whole affair."

"Do ye really think so?" Daniel asked, his eyes brightening hopefully.

"I'm fair certain. Do y' think the lady has nothin' better on her mind than the likes o' *you?* Get along to the stables, now, afore ye miss my Henry altogether."

She shooed them cheerfully toward the door, fluttering her apron after them as if they were a brood of chickens.

"We don't know how t' thank ye, Mrs. Nyles, fer all yer kindnesses," Betsy said at the door. "We shan't ever forget ye."

Daniel leaned down and kissed the cooks's cheek. "No, we shan't. We don't forget as easy as some."

"If it's her ladyship ye mean," Mrs. Nyles retorted with spirit, thwacking him on the arm with a combination of affection and reprimand, "she don't ferget the things she oughtn't. Ye should feel glad that y' ain't important enough fer her to remember. An' you, too, ye lummox," she added to Tom, swatting him on the backside for good measure.

Tom made a mock outcry of pain and rubbed his rear tenderly. Then, just before taking off after his friends down the path to the stables, he gave her a saucy grin. "It may be that her ladyship'll forget us, and it may be she won't," he tossed back, laughing, "but if I'd have kissed her, she'd have remembered me right enough!"

428-9000 AAA

Plane tickets

	Arrive	11:40	1 Pm
Cart	8:00	11:42	Stop
	9:30		11:19
	nonstop		

8:13

34 8

Chapter Five

Mr. Hicks was feeling nervous. It was a most unusual feeling for him; he was not the nervous sort at all. But today, for the first time in all the years he'd worked for Miss Camilla, he was conscious of strong pangs of insecurity and guilt. He and Miss Camilla had always been straight with each other, but now he was about to play her false.

He frowned resentfully at the three troublemakers lined up stiffly before him awaiting his inspection. *Damn* his nephew for placing this awkward situation in his lap! "Let's have a look at your fingernails," he barked irritably.

The three of them stuck out their hands, and Hicks gave them all a thorough inspection. "Very good. Now, stand up straight and let me make certain you look presentable."

If he hadn't been told the lurid tale that lay hidden behind the innocent faces they presented to the world, he'd have had to admit that their appearances were perfectly satisfactory. Collinson, his nephew's friend, was tall and quite prepossessing now that his lightish hair had been properly cut. Daniel, although perhaps a bit too stocky to make an ideal footman, was nevertheless strong and capable. And Betsy was an endearing little puss. Miss Camilla would undoubtedly take a shine to her, especially since she was so modest about the child she was carrying. Betsy had used good sense in decking herself out, for the dark, plum-colored dress she wore lay quite neatly over her swelling belly, and, although it didn't completely hide her condition, it didn't call undue attention to it either. Hicks would have been proud to recommend all three to Miss Camilla, if only he didn't have to hide from her the dark facts of their recent history.

If it weren't for his fond memory of his dead brother, Daniel's father, he'd never do it. As sympathetic as he was to their plight (for no one who'd ever heard an account of a victim of a press-gang could blame them for what they'd done—not if he had a heart in his chest), he never, in ordinary circumstances, would get himself into a situation in which he'd have to lie to Miss Camilla. But these circumstances were different. Daniel was his only remaining relation—his own flesh and blood. Without his help, poor Daniel and his friend might even end up on the gibbet!

If only he didn't have to lie. But the two men had no letters of commendation and no one at all to vouch for them. So he, who had never before said or done a dishonest thing to his mistress, had concocted a fabric of lies and deceits to legitimize their backgrounds. And while one part of him was glad to assist them to start a new life, the other part writhed in remorse and guilt.

But there was nothing to be gained in dwelling on the matter. He'd made up his mind to recommend them, and he would go through with it, nervous or not. More than half-a-dozen candidates for posts on the household staff of Miss Camilla's new abode were probably already awaiting him in the corridor outside Miss Camilla's rooms in the Fenton Hotel. There was very little time left to make certain all would go well. "Let's get on with it," he muttered, looking them over with a last, critical appraisal. "Let's go over our stories once more, before we leave for the Fenton. Remember, I'll present you to her ladyship, and then she'll ask you a few questions. Shall we try it out? I'll be her ladyship. Let's say I turn to you first, Thomas. Step forward."

"A giant step or a baby step?" Tom asked, teasing.

"No levity, if you don't mind, Thomas," Hicks said reprovingly. "Remember that a footman attempts to be invisible and inaudible unless otherwise required."

"Invisible and inaudible, yes, sir," Thomas said agreeably.

"I am not 'sir,' I told you. I'm *Mr. Hicks* to the staff!" He rolled his grizzled eyebrows heavenward to beg for stamina. "May the Lord grant me the patience to deal with these loobies. Now, Thomas, I'm her ladyship, and I turn to you and say, 'What's your name, my good man?'"

"Thomas Collinson, your ladyship."

"And where did you work before?"

"I was underfootman to Dr. Newton Plumb of Derbyshire."

"And why haven't you a letter of commendation?"

"Because the fellow died before I could get one."

Hicks groaned and stamped his foot in annoyance. "Because the 'gentleman' *passed on* without warning and didn't make arrangements for your future, you idiot!"

"Sorry," Tom said with an abashed grin. "I didn't think I had to use those exact words."

"Well, you *do*, so let's hear 'em. Why haven't you a letter?"

Tom straightened, took on a stiff, footmanlike impassivity and repeated obediently, "Because the gentleman passed on without warning, your ladyship, and didn't make any arrangements for my future."

"Very well. And now you, fellow. Your name, please?"

"Daniel Hicks, ma'am."

"And your last employer?"

"I was gardener to the same gentleman as Thomas, here."

"Right. And therefore you couldn't get a letter either. As for you, Betsy Hicks, do *you* have a letter from your last employer?"

"Yes, ma'am, here it is."

"Good." He dropped the aloof manner and shook a warning finger at Betsy. "Now, girl, remember that since the letter says nothing about your last establishment being an inn, you needn't *volunteer* the information that you were a barmaid. But if Miss Camilla should ask, tell the truth. There's no use in lying more than absolutely necessary."

"Yes, sir."

"Yes, *Mr. Hicks!* How many times must I remind you? I'm not your master. And the same goes for Miss Townley. But be sure you always call Miss Camilla 'your ladyship' or 'my lady' or 'ma'am.'"

"Then how is it, Uncle, that ye call 'er Miss Camilla?" Daniel asked.

"Because I've known her since she was a babe. And, to speak the truth, I shouldn't call her that either. I only kept it up to spite Lady Ethelyn. It's a terrible habit with me now. But Daniel, how many times must I remind you not to call me Uncle? It must be *Mr. Hicks* at all times, so you fall into the habit of it."

"Aye, aye, Uncle," Daniel agreed readily.

Tom chortled, but Hicks groaned in irritation. *"Yes, Mr. Hicks!"* he corrected angrily, glaring at Tom for laughing. "Those aye-ayes'll give you both away one of these days. Silly tomdoodles, both of you!"

"Don't be nervous, Uncle," Betsy murmured comfortingly, coming up to him and planting a kiss on his cheek. "We won't joke in front of her ladyship, I promise." She gave Tom a reproving, meaningful look. "Isn't that right, Tom?"

"Aye, that's right, my dear. I'll be so inaudible and invisible that her ladyship'll think I'm only a piece of furniture."

"Me, too, Uncle," Daniel promised.

Hicks sighed deeply. Somehow he knew that the afternoon was going to be a terrible ordeal. He felt it in his bones.

Camilla had taken rooms in the Fenton on St. James Street so that she could oversee the final steps required to ready the house for their occupancy. The suite had two bedrooms (one for Pippa and Miss Townley and the other for herself) and a large sitting room. It was there that Hicks (who himself was already ensconced in the new house) was bringing the various candidates whom he'd chosen to make up the household staff. Camilla had permitted Pippa to run off to explore the neighborhood in the company of Miss Townley, while she herself was occupied with this household business.

It was a great bore to have to stay inside and interview servants when she could be strolling along the busy thoroughfares of London's most fashionable neighborhood, but Hicks seemed to feel that her approval of his choices was absolutely necessary. As a result, she'd moved a table from behind the sofa to a sunny spot before a pair of windows and taken a seat behind it. In the business-like manner recommended by Miss Townley, she'd spoken briefly to each candidate Hicks had brought in, nodded her approval and then carefully entered into a large household-ledger book that person's name, the salary Hicks had promised, the name of the former employer and the title of the exact position for which the person had been engaged. It was all a rather mindless ritual, but it seemed to please Hicks greatly.

Camilla knew quite well that this was a futile exercise. Hicks had made his own records of the information she was recording, and Camilla was certain that all his decisions would be beyond reproach. The only thing that had been left to her discretion was the assigning of the rooms where the servants were to sleep, and even that could easily have been done by Hicks without her help. But both Hicks and Miss Townley had felt that the ritual was required in order to impress the staff. Since Camilla had made up her mind to be a firm and respected mistress of her new establishment, she'd agreed to do what was expected of her.

She had already interviewed and approved Hicks's choice of a cook, two parlormaids, a groom, two scullery maids, a gardner and a coachman, all of whom seemed perfectly suitable, and she would have become quite bored with the proceedings except that Hicks seemed increasingly nervous as the afternoon wore on. She wondered what was troubling him, and her curiosity sharpened her perceptions. When he brought in all three final candidates together, rather than one at a time, the change of routine made her suddenly alert. "Yes, Hicks, whom have we here?" she asked with more interest than she'd felt all afternoon.

"The two footmen and the upstairs maid, my lady. This one here and the woman are a couple, and the other fellow is their friend. That's why I've brought them in together. Here's a letter from the lady's former employer."

Camilla scanned the letter quickly. "Betsy *Hicks?*" she asked with a smile. "Are these people related to you, Hicks?"

He reddened. "Daniel, here, is my nephew, your ladyship."

"Is *that* why you've seemed so uncomfortable?" Camilla smiled in relief. "Did you think I would disapprove of your hiring your relations? You needn't worry on that score, Hicks. I don't mind at all. In fact, if your nephew is half as valuable to me as you've been, I shall be more than satisfied."

"Thank you, Miss Camilla," Hicks said, feeling more guilty than ever.

"Is your name Daniel? Why is there no letter here about you, Daniel?"

Daniel colored. "Well . . . y' see I was . . . er . . . gardener for . . . er . . . Dr. Newton Plumb of Derbyshire . . . an' he passed away sudden-like, y'see . . ."

Hicks felt like giving the slow-top a kick in his rear. "Dr. Plumb passed on before giving a thought to the future of any of his domestics," he offered in quick collaboration, throwing his nephew a look of annoyance.

"Oh, I see. But if Daniel is a gardener, Hicks, is there any special reason why you've made him a footman?"

"A couple of reasons, ma'am. One is that if he works indoors, he'll be close enough to his missus to be able to give her a hand with the heavy work when her time comes near. She's having a baby, you may have noticed. And second, he's worked close with this other fellow, back there, so I've kept them together."

"Very well, Hicks, you know best in these matters. I shall give your Daniel and his Betsy the corner room on the third floor. It's the most adequate room for a couple, I think, and shall afford them some privacy. And, Betsy, I believe it is large enough to be able to accommodate a cradle when you need it."

"Oh, *thank* you, my lady," Betsy murmured, bobbing gratefully.

"In the meantime, Hicks, you must be sure Betsy isn't given work which is too heavy for her, even if her husband *is* near by."

"Yes, my lady. I had that in mind when I made her upstairs maid. So long as he does the fireplaces for her, she'll easily manage the rest."

"Good." Camilla made the appropriate entries in her ledger and then looked up at the third member of the group who was hanging back in the shadows. "And what is the name of the other footman, Hicks?"

"Collinson, ma'am. Thomas Collinson," the butler answered.

"And he has no letter either?"

Hicks motioned with his head for Tom to step forward and

speak his piece, but Tom hung back. Hicks clenched his fists in fury. "Since he was employed by the same Dr. Plumb, he's faced with the same problem," he responded, almost twitching with irritation at having to lie again, and without the assistance of the fellow who, more than the others, stood to gain from the subterfuge.

"Were you footman for this Dr. Plumb, Thomas?" Camilla asked squinting into the shadows.

"Yes, my lady," he answered in almost a whisper.

"You needn't be afraid to speak up, fellow. Step forward, please. You seem to be unduly shy for a footman."

Tom took a step forward. "Not shy, ma'am. I'm just—" A glare from Hicks reminded him of his instructions to keep his answers as brief as possible, so he clamped his mouth shut. *A footman should attempt to be invisible and inaudible,* he reminded himself.

"You're just what, Thomas?" Camilla encouraged, looking at him curiously.

"Just self-effacing, as a footman should be," he responded, unable to treat the situation with proper seriousness. He couldn't seem to take any of what had happened to him in the past week seriously. He seemed to be living in some limbo-like state between the reality of his shipboard life and a nebulous future which he couldn't fathom. This footman business was somehow unreal—an enormous joke that life was playing on him, a temporary aberration that would right itself somehow . . . and some day soon. He couldn't *really* spend his life doing household service. Carrying wood for the fireplace, polishing silver, dressing up in livery to answer a door—those things were not serious work. They were parts of a children's game, like playing house. A man had to do the *real* work of the world—soldiering, or building roads, or sailing a vessel across an ocean.

Something of his inner feelings must have shown in the tone of his voice, because he became aware of Daniel's worried glance and a flashing glare from the eyes of the elderly butler whose neck was growing red. Embarrassed, he tried to back surreptitiously into the shadows again.

But Lady Wyckfield (who was looking even more lovely than he remembered, sitting there in front of the windows with the sunlight etching magical highlights in her hair) was staring at him with an arrested look. Something in the ironic tone of his answer had triggered her memory. For a moment everything seemed to hang suspended—each person in the room watching unmoving, her ladyship's hand hanging in the air over her ledger halted on its way to her cheek. Then she blinked and gasped. "Good *God!* It's the *libertine* who accosted me in the *kitchen!*"

Betsy clapped her hands to her mouth in dismay. Daniel gulped. But Hicks could only gape at his mistress in utter confusion. "What's that you're saying, Miss Camilla?"

"Of *course!*" Camilla exclaimed, rising to her feet. "These are the three who came seeking you in Dorset. They invaded the kitchen at Wyckfield Park, and *that one* had the temerity to assault me on the stairs!"

Poor Hicks could scarcely believe his ears. It was bad enough that they were hiding from the authorities for having escaped from impressment, but this latest crime was too much! "Is this true?" he croaked, staring at the trio as if he'd just discovered they were lepers. "How could you have *done* such a thing?"

"It was all a . . . a misunderstandin', ye might say," Daniel mumbled miserably. "I'm truly sorry, Uncle. We thought she was a housemaid."

"Her ladyship a *housemaid?* Are you all *loony?*"

"Well, in fairness, Hicks," Camilla put in, already filled with sympathy for the pregnant girl who was looking quite stricken, "I *was* wearing an apron—"

But Hicks was beside himself. Already having been functioning on the far edge of nervous balance, he was completely unsettled by this last blow. Hardly aware that he was interrupting his mistress in the middle of a sentence, he shouted, "That's not the least excuse! Any *fool* should be able to see that Miss Camilla is a lady no matter what she wears!" He waved his arms in the air, trying with gestures of frustration to express to each of the three his unmitigated revulsion. "And to think you let me recommend you to her ladyship, knowing all the while that this had taken place and not even telling me a *word*—"

"But, y' see, Uncle," Betsy said, the tears forming in the corners of her eyes, "the c-cook said that her l-ladyship'd never remember—"

"Never *remember?* Never remember being accosted on her

own *stairs?*" Hicks, almost apoplectic, turned away in speechless chagrin.

Betsy came up behind him, the tears spilling down her cheeks. "Please, Uncle," she whispered tremulously, "don't take on so. We're terrible sorry . . ."

"Aye," Daniel sighed hopelessly, "we never meant to—"

"Whay good are your sorrys?" the old man burst out. "I can never face Miss Camilla again with my head up."

"Can't you now!" Tom snorted in sudden and violent disgust. "We've made you lose face, have we? What a terrible pass we've pushed you to. Perhaps we should all fall on our swords, like the Romans, or disembowel ourselves in shame, like the Orientals." He strode across the room and placed himself squarely in front of Camilla. "Put an end to this muddle, ma'am. Tell the old fellow you're not put out with him, and let him proceed with hiring his relations. *I* was the only one to blame in all this. I'll go at once and permit the rest of you to get on with your business."

He turned and started for the door, but Daniel blocked the way. "Shut up, can't ye?" he muttered in an angry whisper. "Y' ain't the mate here, y' know."

"I'm sorry, Daniel, but I've no patience with all this. I don't think I'm cut out for household service. You and Betsy'll do better without me."

"Well, we ain't goin' to do without ye. We've stood up together, an' we'll fall together. Come on, Betsy, we'd best take ourselves off."

"I tell you, there's no need to give up a good place," Tom insisted. "I'll find something—"

"I said no," Daniel retorted. "We been through this afore, an' ye know my feelin's. Come on, Betsy."

But Betsy, whose past experiences working for selfish and thoughtless mistresses had given her an insight into how decent this position might have been, burst into tears.

"There, now, see what you've done?" Tom muttered to Daniel angrily. "You've more to think of than just your own feelings. You've a wife to worry about. Look, man, I can find something on my own—"

"N-No, Tom," Betsy said bravely, wiping her eyes. "Dan'l's right. It's all of us, or none." She took her husband's arm and, before permitting him to lead her to the door, turned back to Camilla. "Ye'll not blame Mr. Hicks, will ye, yer ladyship?" she asked, her lips trembling. "He didn't know nothin' of what happened at Wyckfield Park."

Camilla, who'd been observing the dramatic scene with considerable fascination, gave the tearful young woman a sympathetic smile. "I understand that, Betsy. I don't blame Hicks in the least. In fact, Hicks, if you still want these people on your staff, I shall make no objection. The *contretemps* at Wyckfield *was* a misunderstanding, after all."

Hicks lifted his head and gawked at her. "Miss Camilla! You can't mean . . . after all this, you're *still* willing—"

"It's entirely up to you, Hicks. You are my steward in these matters."

"Thank you, your ladyship, for saying so, especially after seeing my humiliation. If it's up to me, then I say we should let 'em go. First they treated you with disrespect in Wyckfield, and then they kept the knowledge from me. I'm not sure they can be trusted."

"Betsy and Daniel are the most trustworthy pair you'll ever find!" Tom barked impatiently. "I don't see why they are included in this discussion at all. This entire matter is my fault and mine alone."

"That does seem to be true," Camilla said to the butler.

"But it was all *three of them* that didn't tell me what happened," Hicks said stubbornly.

"You're right about that," Camilla agreed thoughtfully, "but I imagine they've learned a lesson from all this."

"Oh, yes'm, we have," Betsy said earnestly.

"Are you saying, Miss Camilla, that you're willing to take all *three?*" Hicks asked in disbelief.

"Yes, if you are."

Hicks looked at Tom dubiously. The part of the story which Camilla did not know hung heavily on his conscience, and in that story as well as this one, Tom's part was most heinous. "I don't think I can recommend the third one, Miss Camilla. Not in good conscience."

"Then yer conscience has misled ye, Uncle," Daniel said firmly. "We thank ye fer yer kindness, my lady, but if ye can't take the three of us, we have t' ask fer permission to withdraw."

"Don't be a fool, Daniel," Tom muttered urgently.

Betsy put a restraining hand on Tom's arm. "It's a settled matter, Tom. Don't keep fightin' over it."

Camilla shook her head in grudging admiration over their loyalty to each other. "They seem to be an unbreakable set, Hicks. What do you think we should do?"

"I don't know, your ladyship," he said, troubled. "Let them all go, I suppose."

"But I hate to permit Betsy to go wandering about the streets looking for a place in her condition . . ."

Hicks sighed. "You're willing to take a chance on them all?"

"I don't see what else we can do, do you?"

Hicks shook his head dubiously. "Very well, my lady. We'll take them on. And I give you my word that I'll do everything in my power to see that you're not ill-served by your kindness."

Camilla nodded, sat down and entered the appropriate items in her ledger-book, while Betsy and Daniel exchanged looks of relieved delight. But Hicks fixed a lugubrious eye on Tom. "I'm warning you, Thomas, that you'll get no further forgiveness if you use your free-and-easy ways as you've done today," he said sternly.

"That's quite true, young man," Camilla said, looking up at the tall, incorrigible fellow with a twinge of misgiving and attempting, by the coldness of her manner, to correct any impression of softness which her previous behavior had probably given. "From now on I shall expect you to behave with impeccable propriety, do you understand?"

"Yes, my lady," Tom assured her. "I shall be the most invisible and inaudible person on your staff, I promise you."

Somehow Camilla had an unshakable conviction that he would turn out to be quite the opposite. "I hope so," she said firmly, rising and dismissing them all with a wave of her hand, "because at the *first* infraction—the very slightest breach of discipline—*out you go!*"

Chapter Six

Dear Ethelyn, I have received your letter of 13 November and hasten to assure you that there has been no calamity. I am sorry that I neglected to write as often as you expected, but in the scramble to make things livable in the new house I was rather preoccupied. We have not fallen into any difficulties of the types you so dramatically suggest in your letter—there have been no robberies, no accidents and no descent into godlessness and sin. In truth, we do very well in all matters. The house is now fully staffed with efficient and respectable help, it is adequately spacious (although I will admit that it is tiny in comparison to Wyckfield), and our neighborhood is as quiet and proper as if it were located in a country town. We have even begun to make a few acquaintances. Pippa, in particular, is delighted to have found a friend her own age, about whom I am sure she will write to you herself. So I hope, my dear, that you will henceforth feel no need to trouble yourself and the Good Lord with concern for our health and happiness.

Pippa and I think of you and speak of you often. With the most fond good wishes for your own and Oswald's well-being, I remain your most devoted, etc., Camilla.

Matters in the house on Upper Seymour Street were indeed going very well. It was a joy to Camilla to be able to rise each morning at any hour she wished, to take breakfast in bed if the inaction suited her mood, or to jump up and dress in the new (and shockingly fashionable) clothes she'd purchased. It was a delight to stroll along the streets with Pippa and Miss Townley (with one of the footmen following along a few paces behind to add an air of propriety to the outings and, incidentally, to carry whatever parcels they managed to acquire during the stroll) and look at the shop windows, the elegant townhouses and the faces of hundreds of interesting passers-by instead of the clipped hedges and rigid flowerbeds of Wyckfield Park. She felt a delicious, heady freedom. There was no one to account to, no one to give her orders, no one whose will was in combat with her own. The feeling was almost too wonderful to be true; sometimes she felt guilty to be so happy.

But every scolding letter from Ethelyn, every stricture, every reprimand, every bit of unsolicited advice which came regularly by post from Wyckfield made that guilt a little less severe. Her sister-in-law's letters merely served to remind her of what she'd escaped. The pleasure, the ease, the freedom of each passing day only confirmed her conviction that she'd done the right thing. She'd escaped from virtual confinement . . . and nothing or no one would ever prevail upon her to return to it.

Even Pippa seemed to be blossoming in the exhilarating atmosphere of what Ethelyn called "the city of sin." The child walked about with eyes wide in perpetual amazement. She drank in every detail of the new sights that greeted her every day. Every new experience filled her with the enthusiasm and excitement that come only to the very young. "Look, Mama," she would cry on a walk down Bond Street, "the lady on the other side of the street has a *finch* pinned to her hat. You don't suppose it's a real one that's been stuffed, do you? A milliner wouldn't—?"

And Camilla would reassure her that the finch had no more been a real bird than the doll in the window of a nearby shop had been a real baby.

Then Pippa's attention would turn to the carriages rattling

by on the busy thoroughfare. "Have you ever seen so many different carriages?" she'd exclaim. "Barouches, and phaetons . . . and there's a cabriolet with the top raised! And that one, there—the one with the horses tandem—do you know what that's called?"

"No, I don't. Do you?"

"Yes. It's called a tim-whiskey. Thomas told me. And look over there, Mama—there's a post-chaise. Do you see the guard standing on the boot? That strange object he's carrying is a real blunderbuss. Thomas says it's a blunder every time someone tries to fire one."

"Thomas is a veritable fount of information, isn't he?" Camilla would murmur drily, unable to keep from throwing a backward glance over her shoulder to frown at him. He was performing his duties in a satisfactory way, as far as she could tell, but for someone who was supposed to be invisible and inaudible, he was certainly making himself noticed.

From the very first day the staff had moved into their new quarters, Thomas had been noticeable. She had called a staff meeting so that she and Hicks could acquaint them all with their duties, explain the rules for daily living and distribute their clothing and uniforms. She'd sat behind her desk and watched as Hicks had explained how they were to dress. Every member of the staff had been given several different costumes; some were for heavy work while others were to be worn when they had to appear at the front of the house. The footmen had three distinct sets of livery. The gold-braided, formal livery, Hicks had explained, was to be worn only when her ladyship held formal dinner parties. "Thank goodness," Thomas had muttered. "I'd hate to have to dress like a popinjay every day of the week." Hicks had delivered a brief scold, but a moment later, when he said that the footmen would not be required to powder their hair except when dressing in the formal livery, Thomas had objected vociferously. "Powder my *hair?*" he'd exclaimed. "Not on your life!" This type of behavior had become the fellow's style ever since.

She'd promised herself to become as good a manager of the household as Ethelyn was of Wyckfield, but she hadn't been able to control Thomas's excesses. Of course, he'd done nothing really reprehensible, and Pippa and Miss Townley seemed to admire what Miss Townley described as his "robust honesty," but he always made Camilla feel uncomfortable. She couldn't understand why she was always conscious of his presence . . . and discomfitted by it.

The trouble was, she supposed, that the fellow was not really like a servant at all. Everything about him, from his long-legged, self-assured stride to his polished speech, seemed more masterful than servant-like. There was nothing about Thomas that was humble or diffident. He behaved as if he were born to give orders rather than to take them. Sometimes she wondered if he weren't a gentlemen of noble birth who was indulging in some sort of irritating masquerade, like certain members of the Corinthian set whom she'd heard of—well-born gentlemen who dressed up like coachmen and drove stage-coaches for excitement.

She'd tried to query Betsy about Thomas's past, but everything she'd learned from the ingenuous girl gave support to the theory that Thomas was exactly what he claimed to be. There was nothing for it but to accept what appeared to be the facts.

But if any one factor could be singled out to be the primary cause of her discomfort in regard to Thomas, it was this very tendency of hers to think about him . . . to take notice of him, and to weave these "romances" about his background. She would have liked to dismiss him from her mind altogether. If only she had the character either to control his behavior with the proper detachment or to banish him from the premises.

Yes, there were problems in this new life, and Thomas was one of them. But there were several others which troubled her too, even though they were minor ones. The other servants still needed training, the household was not yet organized in a purposeful, daily routine, and Camilla suffered occasionally from bouts of loneliness. But for the most part, she was very pleased with her new surroundings. The atmosphere in the house on Upper Seymour Street was one of quiet contentment. Perhaps that contentment had about it an air of precariousness . . . perhaps things were too new and unstable to enable the inhabitants to feel completely relaxed . . . but that would come with time. And meanwhile, the very air was aglow with hopefulness.

Dear Ethelyn, your letter of 23 November was needlessly severe. I am not careless in matters concerning my daughter, and I would certainly not permit her to enter into an intimate friendship with a child whose family I did not know. As a matter

*of fact, little Sybil Sturtevant is a perfectly well-bred girl whose
mother is Lady Sturtevant, wife of Edgar Sturtevant who is a
viscount and a member of Parliament. Even though Lady S.
and I met during a morning walk through Hyde Park, it was
quite obvious at once that she was eminently respectable (she
has five children, and four of them were surrounding her that
very morning, so she could hardly have been engaged in any
activity of a reprehensibe nature) and we took to each other
at once. As for Pippa and Sybil, they make a wonderful pair,
for Pippa is completely bookish and Sybil is completely active.
Each one seems to exert a most beneficial influence on the
other. I do not think that the fact that Sybil taught Pippa to
play cards is a matter to arouse in you such violent antipathy.
They play the most innocuous games, and it seems to me to be
a perfectly permissible activity with which to pass a rainy
afternoon. I think, Ethelyn, that you will feel much more rec-
onciled to the situation if you disabuse yourself of your conviction that London is a hotbed of iniquity. I assure you, my
dear, that it is not. With the fondest of good wishes for you
and Oswald, I remain your devoted, etc., Camilla.*

As a matter of fact, Camilla was not as certain that Sybil
Sturtevant was as good an influence on Pippa as she'd claimed
in her letter. Pippa was enchanted with her new friend, but
Sybil had four brothers and had managed to reach the age of
ten by learning the art of survival. She had made herself as
agile and as strong as they. There was no little boy her age she
couldn't outrun, outbox or outwit. She had a scorn of pretty
dresses, the stride of a tomboy and a vocabulary of boxing
terms that Camilla found a bit shocking. But Pippa was delighted with her. After the quiet, restricted years at Wyckfield,
it was a revelation to Pippa to meet someone whose behavior
was so completely uninhibited. Sybil sat on floors, climbed
trees, dashed in and out of doors, tossed balls, engaged in
fisticuffs, occasionally swore and hated to read. She taught
Pippa how to shoot marbles, how to run like a boy and how
to play cards. In return, Pippa told her stories. Sybil, who had
never spent time with books, was unfamiliar with the most
commonplace of fairy stories and was completely enthralled
as Pippa regaled her by the hour with detailed accounts of *St.
George and the Dragon, Caporushes,* or *The True History of
Sir Thomas Thumb.* It was a friendship made in heaven, and

the two little girls couldn't bear to be parted from one another.

For those times when the girls were not together, Pippa found herself another friend. It was the footman, Thomas, who (if he could be found without a pressing chore to do) would give her a good game of Hearts, make up riddles or tell her the most surprising tales of strange, exotic places like Barbados, Portugal, or India. On a particularly rainy, cold day in late November, when it became clear that Lady Sturtevant and Sybil would not be paying a call, Pippa roamed the house looking for her second-favorite companion. She found him in the warming room, a little room off the large dining room where the food which had cooled on its way up from the kitchen was reheated before being served. The room had a large fireplace, two warming ovens, a number of cupboards in which the large silver serving pieces were stored, and a long worktable at the center. It was at this table that Thomas, busily polishing an appalling number of trays, teapots and candlesticks, was found. "Are you very busy, Thomas," Pippa asked from the doorway.

Thomas looked up and grinned at her. "Busy? What a question, Miss Pippa. Of course I'm not busy. All I need do is say 'Rumplestilskin,' and a little gnome will come and finish all this polishing in a twinkling."

Pippa giggled. "Wouldn't it be wonderful if you could? Then you'd be free to play cards with me."

"It wouldn't be wonderful at all," Thomas said severely. "I already owe you six hundred and forty-nine pounds for games I've lost to you."

"Six hundred and seventy. You're forgetting the twenty-one pounds I won yesterday."

"Six hundred and seventy, then. Do you realize, my lass, that if I spent not a penny of my wages, it would take me thirty-three-and a half years to pay you what I owe?"

"Oh, pooh! The debt is only pretend, as you very well know. Besides, you may be the one to win the next rubber or two, and our situations might well be completely reversed."

"That's true," Thomas agreed, rubbing at the rounded belly of an ornate teapot with energy. "I'm almost sorry, then, that our gambling is only pretend."

Pippa walked thoughtfully to the fire. "Thirty-three-and-a-half years?" She took off her spectacles and shut her eyes. "That means your wages for the year are twenty pounds."

Thomas stopped his work to stare at her admiringly. "That's very *good*, Miss Pippa!"

"Good? It seems to me to be a very paltry amount."

"I don't mean my wages. I mean the way you did that sum in your head."

"Oh, that." She put on her spectacles again and smiled at him. "That's nothing worth speaking of. I've always been very good at sums, you know."

"I *didn't* know. But I should have guessed. That's probably why you do so well at cards. But as for my wages being paltry, I'll have you know that I make three pounds per annum more than Lady Sturtevant's first footman, and I'm only an under."

"No, you're not. Mama says she doesn't approve of firsts and unders. But how can it be that my father left me twenty-*thousand* pounds per annum while your wages are only twenty?"

Tom smiled ruefully. "It's the way of the world, Miss Pippa. But you shouldn't worry yourself about it. You should be pleased that you're such a rich little girl."

"Am I?"

"Indeed you are. I'm fair tempted to run off with you and wed you for your fortune."

Pippa studied him seriously. "No, I don't think you're the sort to make a mercenary match," she decided after brief reflection.

"Am I not? What makes you so certain? How, at your age, have you become so expert in these matters? Has someone tried to run off with you already?"

"What a jokester you are, Thomas," she giggled. "I learned from books, of course. There are many stories in which wicked men try to wed innocent damsels for their wealth. But those men aren't like you. They have narrow, glittering eyes, you see."

"Oh." He narrowed his eyes and leered at her. "Like this?"

She gurgled in amusement. "Not at *all* like that. You just aren't the sort."

He gave a lugubrious sigh. "Too bad. My one chance to become rich . . . gone through having the wrong sort of eyes!"

"But you have the right sort of eyes for gaming," the girl said with inspiration. "If you play cards with me, you may *win* yourself a fortune."

He made a face. "Only a pretend fortune. And I have all these very real trays to do."

"Can't you put off polishing some of them until tomorrow?" she pleaded.

"I'm sorry, Miss Pippa, but tomorrow's taken with other chores. Mr. Hicks has given us a daily schedule. I have it here." He put down his polishing cloth and took from his pocket a closely written sheet. "Let's see now . . . Thursday . . . Thursday . . . ah, here it is. Afternoon, after clearing away the luncheon, there's the stair rods and the brasses."

Poor Pippa's face fell. "Do you mean there's something on that list for *every* afternoon?"

"I'm afraid so. Monday the lamps, Tuesday the glassware, Wednesday the silver and so forth . . ."

"It's quite unfair! Why should *you* be required to do all the work? What about Mary, or Gladys, or Daniel?"

"They've all got their own lists, you know. Daniel, at this moment, is waxing all the oak. Now, don't look so crestfallen. You wouldn't wish me to neglect my duties and get the sack, would you?"

"Oh, you won't get the sack. In my opinion, you're the very best of all the servants."

"Thank you, Miss Pippa. Now if we could only convince Mr. Hicks and your mother of that very obvious truth, we'd have nothing to worry about. We could probably hide in here and play cards all day long."

"But I don't think I can manage it," Pippa admitted, turning with flagging steps to the door. "I don't think either one of them thinks as well of you as I do."

"I'm aware of that. But how did *you* know it?" Tom asked, looking at her curiously.

"I overheard them discussing you. They think you're too bold."

Tom grunted and returned to his polishing. "Hmm. Boldness . . . that's a lamentable flaw in a footman, you know."

The child paused at the door and looked back at him. "Yes, I suppose so. Though it sounds rather heroic to me." She sighed. "I hope there will be *some* time in the week when you can play with me, Thomas."

"Don't worry, lass, we'll manage something. Meanwhile, if you've nothing better to do, you can stay here and listen to me spin a yarn. I can talk and polish at the same time, after all."

The child's face brightened. "Oh, that will be *famous!* I love stories as well as cards, you know."

"Good, then. Here, let me lift you up on the table. It'll be more comfortable than standing about in the doorway."

He cleared away an area on the table to his right and lifted her up. She dangled her legs happily from her elevated perch. "Where are all the chairs?" she asked curiously. "Have they all been taken away somewhere?"

"Oh, there are no chairs in the warming room, ever. This is a workroom, you see. Chairs don't do in a workroom, because their presence might encourage a servant to sit down while working, and that is strictly forbidden. But never mind. You're comfortable up there on the table, aren't you?"

"Oh, yes, it's quite lovely up here," she assured him, picking up a polishing cloth and absently rubbing away at a tray. "What yarn will you spin today?"

"Have I told you the one about the stowaway? No? Well, it begins many years ago, on a schooner called the *Surprise,* when one of the crew who was laying up rigging heard a cough that seemed to come from under the taffrail, where the jollyboat was tied . . ."

The story was well along when Camilla appeared at the warming-room door. "Oh, *there* you are, Pippa," she said in surprise. "I've been searching for you all over the house." She took due note of the tray and polishing cloth in her daughter's lap and the cozy intimacy of the scene before her. It was a scene which struck her as completely inappropriate, and she stiffened in irritation. "Come down from there at once!" she said sharply. *"Ladies* do not perch themselves on *tables."*

"But Sybil would perch on a—"

"Never mind about Sybil. Perhaps Ethelyn is right, and you *are* seeing too much of that child."

"It was my idea to put Miss Philippa up there, ma'am," Tom ventured. "There isn't a single chair in here, you see—"

"Never mind. Just take her down," Camilla said coldly. "And in future, Thomas, I'd be greatly obliged if you'd do your *own* polishing without my daughter's help!"

"He didn't enlist my help," Pippa said quickly. "You're not being fair, Mama. I was only holding the tray in my lap. I don't think Thomas even noticed it."

Thomas, furious, clenched his fists. "Miss Pippa knows I don't approve of her polishing," he said sarcastically. "I only permit her to carry logs for me."

Pippa giggled, but her mother flushed. "Well, never mind. Just help her down. I want her to come along with me at once."

"But may I not stay for a few minutes more?" Pippa asked as Thomas helped her jump down from her perch. "Just to find out what the Captain did to the stowaway?"

"No, you may not." Her mother took Pippa's hand and stalked to the door. "I don't think that fellow will ever learn to have a civil tongue in his head," she muttered. "Irritating rudesby!"

Pippa, just before she was pulled from the room, looked back at the chastized Thomas. *You're just too bold*, she mouthed with a teasing glint.

Thomas grinned and winked. *Much too bold*, he mouthed back.

Dear Ethelyn, I have your letter of 2 December before me, and I regret to have to refuse your kind invitation to return to Wyckfield for Christmas. Pippa has been invited to spend Christmas day at the home of her new friend (who, as I told you, has four siblings of assorted ages) and is quite looking forward to spending the holiday in the company of so many lively children. I, too, have been invited, of course, and I must admit that I share Pippa's eagerness to experience this new sort of holiday celebration. I hasten to assure you that there is nothing godless in the way our new London friends live. Lady Sturtevant, the hostess in question, is a person of whom you would surely approve.

I am sorry that the holiday will find us apart, but in'any case, Ethelyn, I do not believe it would be wise to attempt such a long trip so soon after we've settled in, especially when the weather at this season is so uncertain. Please accept our very best wishes for your good health—and Oswald's, too, of course—and remember that I remain your most devoted, etc., Camilla.

Camilla reread the letter, chewing the tip of her pen worriedly. It was a poor letter in every respect. In the first place, it was awkwardly phrased. Her wording did nothing to hide the bald fact that both she and Pippa preferred to spend the holiday with their new acquaintances rather than return to Wyckfield. And, secondly, she'd added two other excuses— that the trip was too long and the weather uncertain—and anyone with an ounce of sense knew that three lame excuses were not nearly as effective as one good one. Ethelyn would be livid when she read this missive.

But Camilla had already written three earlier drafts. This was the best she could do. Perhaps there was no good way to phrase a refusal. But an acceptance was out of the question.

It was not that the London life was so completely joyful. On the contrary, there were many problems she had to face. She was still very insecure at playing the role of mistress of a household in which she had to make decisions for more than a dozen people. Her daughter was changing before her eyes, and Camilla was not sure the changes were all for the better. And, although she was making friends, she still felt lonely most of the time. No, things were not perfect. Life was teaching her that happiness, even in the best of circumstances, was not easy to achieve. But she did feel hopeful; she did feel alive; she did feel *free*. Those were feelings she'd never had at Wyck-field Park.

She'd had a bad dream just the other night which had made her even more firm about refusing her sister-in-law's invitations. She'd dreamed that she'd returned to Wyckfield and was walking along a hedgerow in the garden, noting again, with distaste, the orderly decorousness of the hedge's shape. Not a twig nor leaf stuck out to mar the even perfection of the trim. Suddenly, however, the leaves withered and dropped off, and the bare twigs began to grow out in frightening, gnarled off-shoots—woodsy, misshapen fingers which began to reach for and clutch at her hair, her arms, her dress. She tried to break free of their grasp, but although the branches appeared to be brittle, they did not break. Before she knew it, she was being held fast. The branches continued to grow and thicken and wind themselves about her. The light was soon blotted out; the hedge became an impenetrable cage, and she knew that she could never, even if she lived a hundred years, claw her way out . . .

With a decisive abruptness, she folded the third draft of the letter and sealed it. No matter how deplorable her sister-in-law would find it, the letter was going to be posted just the way it was, and the devil take the hindmost. She couldn't let it matter to her that her sister-in-law would be offended. She couldn't let herself be weakened by repeated urgings to return to Wyckfield. She couldn't let herself become disheartened, no matter how difficult life in London should become. She had to remember that London was freedom and Wyckfield a cage. No matter what happened, she was never, never going back to Wyckfield again.

Chapter Seven

There was no way in which the country-bred Camilla could have anticipated the excitement of spending the holidays in town. She was not prepared for the number of dinners, outings, balls, luncheons, fetes and routs which, under the aegis of Lady Sturtevant, she was encouraged to attend. By the time the new year had come, and the whirl of activities had finally subsided, Camilla and her daughter had gone through every item in their wardrobes, had been fully occupied every day for a fortnight, and were completely exhausted. It was Pippa who expressed aloud what Camilla felt: "Londoners are wonderful; they have time for everything but sleeping and reading."

They were both glad to be able to return to their previous, more placid routine, but Camilla soon learned that once the door to social life has been opened, it is difficult to close it again. A complete return to the quieter life was no longer possible. Lady Sturtevant, now a close friend, dropped by several times a week with at least two of her children in tow.

And two gentlemen whom Camilla had met during the social whirl of the holidays became frequent callers. One was Lady Sturtevant's bachelor brother, Sir James Cambard, a cheerful, rotund, middle-aged man with a lethargic though generous disposition; and the other was a callow youth of twenty-two, Lord Earlywine, who had been a guest at one of the balls and had tumbled top-over-tail in love with the beautiful widow after merely holding Camilla's hand for one country dance.

It seemed to the servants that the knocker was never still. Unexpected guests were always being invited to stay to luncheon or to tea, thus throwing Mr. Hicks's carefully planned work schedule out of kilter. For all the staff, this meant a great deal of rushing about to catch up with the work, but none of them seemed to mind the extra effort so much as Thomas. Every time one or the other of the gentlemen paid a call, Tom had to grit his teeth to keep his disgust from showing in his face. They were a pair of fools, he thought, each one self-important and encroaching, and his mistress, who was far too good for them, saw them much too often.

Her ladyship usually greeted her callers in the library in the company of Miss Townley, but sometimes, if she were working at her desk in the sitting room, she would permit them to wait upon her there, and alone. It was at those times that Thomas would find an excuse to busy himself outside the door so that he would be at hand if needed. Even if it were Daniel's turn to assist Mr. Hicks in serving the wine or tea to the guest, Thomas would be somewhere in the vicinity. Mr. Hicks often glowered at him, but Thomas always made sure to be occupied with something useful and managed to escape a reprimand.

Thomas was the one on duty, however, the afternoon Lord Earlywine paid his third call in as many days. It was Thomas's task to assist Mr. Hicks to set up the tea things if her ladyship should request that tea be served. Her ladyship had evidently done so today, for Mr. Hicks came down to the kitchen and asked the cook to ready a tray. Thomas, carrying the tray on one shoulder, followed Mr. Hicks up the stairs. "Don't tell me it's Earlywine again," he muttered in disgust.

"It's none of your business, Thomas," Hicks said brusquely. "Just be sure you place the sugar tongs in *front* of the sugar bowl, not behind the scones as you did the last time. I was afraid her ladyship'd have to use her fingers."

"Aye, aye, sir," Tom said absently, standing aside as Mr. Hicks tapped at the sitting-room door.

"Yes, Mr. Hicks," the butler growled as her ladyship's voice invited them to come in.

The butler entered first. "The tea, your ladyship," he said in his formal, company tone.

"Yes, put it on the table near the window, will you, Hicks?" she murmured and turned back to her guest with a fixed smile.

Thomas followed Mr. Hicks into the room and quickly assisted the butler to set up the table. While this was going on, Lord Earlywine, leaning his elbow on the mantlepiece as if he owned the place, prosed on and on about a horserace in which he'd been involved. Thomas, glancing at the lady's face, could see that she was bored and irritated. She even reminded her guest gently, twice, that he'd told her the story before. But the idiotic fellow merely smiled and said, "Yes? And did I tell you that . . ." and went on with his story in greater detail than before.

Lady Wyckfield, seated at the writing desk where she'd been working before her caller arrived, was turned about in her seat so that she could face him. It was an attitude that bespoke a feeling of impatience to have the visit brought to an end. When the tea table had been set, she rose from her place (reluctantly, it seemed to Thomas) and went to the table to pour. "Will you take sugar?" she asked her guest as Hicks handed her the empty cup.

Thomas, stationed behind the table at rigid attention, had nothing to do until it was time to gather up the tea things and remove them. From the corner of his eye, he watched his mistress go through the motions of entertaining her guest, but it was plain to the footman that she would have liked to get rid of Earlywine, and the sooner the better. Thomas racked his brain for some way to help her, but it was not until Lord Earlywine made his way to the tea table to help himself to a second buttered scone that Thomas got an idea. When his lordship drew close, Thomas leaned forward and whispered something into his ear. Then they both looked toward the window. Lord Earlywine nodded and put down his cup. "I think I'd better dash, ma'am," he said with a quick bow. "I hope, next time, that you'll agree to take a ride in my new phaeton. I promise to have a lap-robe, some hot bricks and all sorts of things for your comfort."

"Thank you, my lord. We shall see," Lady Wyckfield said with a polite smile, holding out her hand.

Hicks motioned for Thomas to collect the cups while he led Lord Earlywine to the door. When the butler and the guest departed, her ladyship sighed in obvious relief and went back to her writing table. Picking up her pen, she looked up at the busy footman curiously. "What did you say to his lordship, Thomas, to make him leave so abruptly?"

"Say, ma'm?" Thomas echoed innocently. "Nothing of any importance."

"That is no answer to my question. What did you say to him?"

"Only that his horses were standing, which everyone knows they shouldn't be doing on a cold day like this."

"But Lord Earlywine has a groom. He'd know enough to walk them, wouldn't he?"

"Yes, ma'am."

"Then why wasn't he?"

"Oh, he *was*." Thomas's eyes twinkled. "But not at that moment."

Camilla stiffened. "Are you saying that you *misled* Lord Earlywine into believing that his horses were being neglected?"

Thomas shrugged modestly. "I suppose you could say that."

"But . . . how *dared* you do such a thing? What did you expect to gain by it?" Camilla demanded, rising.

"Well, you wanted to be rid of him, didn't you?"

"I? I wanted—?" Camilla reddened in fury. "Really, Thomas, your presumption is beyond belief! What gave you the right—"

"Are you trying to say you *didn't* want to be rid of him?" Tom asked, bewildered.

Camilla's color deepened. "That has nothing to *do* with it! It's not your *place* to—"

"Oh, my *place*." He picked up the last cup and put it on the tray. "To be honest, your ladyship, I can't keep straight just what my place is. I thought it was my place to be of help to you."

"Well, it's *not* your place to help me unless I ask you!"

"That's the most confusing statement I've yet heard from you, ma'am. I don't wait for you to *ask* me to help you from the carriage or to polish the crystal. I don't have to be asked to perform ninety percent of the tasks I do. Shall I wait to do them, in the future, until I hear from you?"

"You are being purposely dense. You know perfectly well that I needn't give you specific orders when it comes to your routine tasks. Don't stand there and pretend that you don't know the difference between polishing the crystal and sending one of my guests flying out the door on a wild goose chase!"

"I'm sorry, ma'am, if the young man's precipitous departure disturbed you," he muttered with a tinge of sarcasm as he lifted the loaded tray to his shoulder.

"Now you are being *impudent!*" she snapped. "It was not his departure but your *presumption* which disturbs me. And incidentally, in all the time you worked for that physician in Derbyshire, did he never tell you that it is improper to be lifting trays and fiddling about when your employer is speaking to you?"

"No, he never did. I'm sorry, ma'am. Shall I put the tray down?"

"Yes. And when you pick it up again, please carry it before you in both hands, with some semblance of dignity, instead of on your shoulder like a . . . a . . ."

"A seabag?" he supplied.

"Yes, exactly. I sometimes think, Thomas, that you are a complete fraud. You don't speak or act at all like a footman."

He tried to look crestfallen. "I know. Too bold."

"Bold is too mild a word. *Brazen* would be better."

Hicks came in just in time to hear the last few words. "Is anything wrong, Miss Camilla? Has this rogue been up to some deviltry?"

Thomas looked at her with something very like a challenge in his eyes. "Have I, your ladyship?"

She glared at him, but she was more angry with herself. Why could she not handle herself like a proper mistress with this fellow? From the first he'd had a free-and-easy attitude toward her that was completely inappropriate to their positions, yet instead of stifling him permanently and at once, she'd bandied words with him, often to her own disadvantage. By now he'd probably lost all sense of the reverence and awe which a servant should feel toward an employer. What she should do—right on the spot!—would be to dismiss him. He certainly deserved it. The fellow was rude, presumptious, ill-mannered, forward and disrespectful. And he'd undoubtedly become worse if she let this situation pass unpunished.

This was just the sort of situation which Ethelyn could have handled without a bit of hesitation. If she were here, she would sneer at Camilla's "softness." And she would be quite right, for Camilla was already feeling squeamish about sending him out into the streets.

Her gaze flickered before the challenge in Thomas's eyes. The fellow was truly brazen, she knew . . . but had his infraction been great enough to warrant sending him packing? It had been a rather minor indelicacy, hadn't it? And she had to admit to herself that she was glad he'd done it. If he hadn't, the annoying Lord Earlywine might have remained for another hour or more!

"If Thomas has been overstepping again," Hicks was saying, "it'd please me mightily to cut him down to size."

Camilla dropped her eyes from those of her unrepentant footman and shook her head. "It was nothing worth discussing," she said, turning to her writing. "Just have him take up the tea things and go."

She would have liked to take another look at the footman's expression, but she wouldn't permit herself to do so. The brazen fellow was undoubtedly grinning in triumph, but at least he would not have the satisfaction of throwing that smirk in her face. She kept her eyes resolutely lowered on the paper before her and waited for the two servants to leave the room. She heard one man's footsteps recede and the door close, but the other seemed to be lingering behind. A cough sounded behind her, indicating that whichever one it was who remained was waiting for her attention. But she *knew* which one it was. "Yes?" she asked coldly, not looking up.

"Ma'am?" he asked in a voice unwontedly shy.

There was nothing for her to do but turn. He was standing a few paces away, carrying the loaded tray before him with both hands just as she'd instructed. And there was not a sign on his face of a smirk or grin. "Yes?" she asked again.

"I just wanted to . . . to say thank you."

She felt herself flushing. How was it that this fellow—a mere servant whose personality should be unknown to her and completely beneath her notice—could always manage to disconcert her? "Oh, go along, Thomas, go along!" she said in self-disgust and turned back to her letter. "Just try to remember that you promised to make yourself invisible and inaudible."

"Yes, ma'am," he mumbled with what seemed to be utmost sincerity, "I'll try. I'll certainly try."

Chapter Eight

The altercation with Thomas was still on Camilla's mind the next morning when, with a sigh, she entered the empty breakfast room. Pippa had already breakfasted and had gone off with Sybil Sturtevant for an outing in the park; and Miss Townley, despite the fact that Lady Sturtevant, two other Sturtevant offspring, their governess and a nursemaid were of the party, had insisted on going along to supervise her charge. (Miss Townley liked Lady Sturtevant well enough, but the lady's breezy, casual, unconcerned way of rearing children was not, in Miss Townley's view, good enough for Pippa.)

Camilla felt very much alone. She was not pleased with herself this morning (being struck with pangs of humiliation whenever she remembered her cowardly, weak-kneed performance of the day before), and the absence of company at the breakfast table only deepened her discontent. To make matters worse, a letter had been placed alongside her butter knife which she instantly recognized had come from Wyckfield and which her instincts told her would *not* bring news to elevate her spirits.

The letter, written in Ethelyn's firm, decisive, heavy-on-the-downstroke hand, was not very different in substance from the other missives she'd received from her troublesome sister-in-law, but it was much more frightening in tone. Ethelyn insisted that a visit to Wyckfield was past due; this time she was not *requesting* Camilla's return—she was *demanding* it. She wrote that she found it "most peculiar" that Camilla had thus far been unable to arrange matters well enough to be able to spare her sister-in-law "at least a se'ennight's time" in Dorset. She and Philippa had now been gone from Wyckfield for three months, Ethelyn reminded her. Had she already forgotten her promise to return for frequent visits? *Was it fair,* Ethelyn had written, with underlines for emphasis, *to keep our dearest Philippa away from all intercourse with her father's family?*

There was a frightening little addition to all of this. *I have been thinking of something else, Camilla,* Ethelyn had appended in a postscript, *that will make it desirable for you to plan your visit for the week after next. That is the time that our vicar's brother will be visiting. I have met him on several occasions, since he is pastor to a flock located a few miles south of Deptford, and I have often heard him preach. He is filled with fiery conviction and has the same disdain for the comfortable latitudinarianism of some of the clergy which I hold. It seems that this gifted and respected clergyman has often taken notice of you when visiting his brother and has recently expressed an interest in offering for you. While I realize that it is just over a year since Desmond's passing and that it will be difficult for you to think so soon of a successor to my brother, I cannot imagine a more suitable candidate for the position of husband to you and stepfather to Philippa.*

Do not put on your missish airs in this matter, my dear. It is not often that such an opportunity comes along. Mr. Josiah Harbage, the gentleman in question, is not yet fifty, in excellent health and has a character both firm and godly. For Philippa's sake if not your own, you should consider this suggestion with all seriousness. At the very least, you must come for a visit at the time I suggest and permit me to introduce you. The possibilities of such a meeting are most promising. You may find yourself taking up residence in a parish just half an hour's ride from Wyckfield Park and embarked on a new, purposeful, spiritual rejuvenation. How delighted I should be never again to to have to think of you residing in that place of sin and iniquity where you have, for the moment, so inexplicably chosen to bury yourself.

The hand holding the letter was trembling. Camilla could only be glad that she was alone at the table. She wouldn't have wanted Pippa to witness her agitation. Unable to eat a bite, she jumped up and strode across the hall to the sitting room. There she paced about, biting her lip, re-reading the letter, crushing it into a ball, smoothing it out and reading it again. With each re-reading, her agitation grew. It was in this state that Lady Sturtevant found her two hours later, when she brought Pippa home. The two girls had run up to Pippa's room, Miss Townley had gone to her room to lie down, and Lady Sturtevant, completely at home in Camilla's house, had told Hicks not to bother to announce her. In her usual breezy fashion, the feathers of her gaudy blue bonnet waving over her crimped red curls, she strode into the sitting room for a quick visit. The sight of Camilla's pale face and troubled eyes brought her to a standstill. "Good heavens, my dear, what's occurred to drain the color from your face?" she asked in instant sympathy.

"Oh, Georgie, I'm *so* glad to see you!" Camilla exclaimed with a tremulous smile. "I seem to have been working myself into a stew over nothing. Let's not even talk about it. Here, let me take your bonnet and pelisse."

"Never mind my bonnet and pelisse," Lady Sturtevant said firmly, seating herself on the sofa and pulling her friend down beside her. "Now, take a deep breath and tell me everything. What's happened to upset you so?"

Georgina Sturtevant was nothing if not motherly. Tall and large-bosomed, she looked capable of taking the world's troubles to her breast. At first meeting the well-known wife of the taciturn Whig, Lord Sturtevant, one might receive an impression of vulgarity, for she not only wore the brightest colors and the most outrageous hats, but she had a deep, full-throated laugh, a voice that carried across the most crowded of rooms and a way of gesturing with her hands that called immediate attention to the gesturer. On further acquaintance, however, it became clear that Georgina Sturtevant was a woman of remarkable common sense, a complete absence of pretension and an open-hearted generosity of spirit. Camilla, quiet and self-effacing herself, was entirely won over by Georgie's spirited good nature. There was no one in the world in whom she would more readily confide. Wordlessly, she held out the crumpled letter to her friend.

Georgina's eyes flew over the sheet. "Is *this* what troubles you ... this overbearing, presumptious *rodomontade?*" She waved her hands in the air as if she were tossing all Camilla's worries to the wind. "Just tear this up, throw it out and forget it. It's nothing but bluster."

Camilla blinked. "But ... you don't understand. It's from my *sister-in-law.*"

"I know who it's from. And I know that you're still in the habit of jumping when she snaps her fingers. You're independent of her now, Camilla, and you must try to remember it."

"But, you see, in some respects Ethelyn is quite right in what she says."

"Right? *Right?* In wishing you to wed a tub-thumping, hell-threatening, middle-aged country preacher?"

"No, not that. Of course not that. She's only right in the part about my keeping Pippa from her father's family. It *is* wrong of me, I suppose ..."

Georgina cocked her head to one side to study her friend's face, causing her heavily feathered bonnet to fall slightly askew. "Well, if you truly believe it's wrong of you, go ahead and *spend* a week in Dorset."

Camilla bit her lip and dropped her eyes. "Yes, I thought you might say that. It would be the most direct ... the most sensible action." She clenched her hands together but couldn't prevent a little shiver from spreading through her body. "Oh, Georgie, I ..." She looked up at her friend fearfully. "I just *can't!*"

"But why ever not? It would be just for a week," the sensible Georgina asked, her brow knit in an effort to grasp the unspoken undercurrents.

Camilla got to her feet and resumed her pacing. "You'll think me a dreadful fool, I'm afraid ..."

"That isn't very likely." Georgina's smile was reassuring. "Try me."

Camilla paused in her perambulations. "I'm quite ashamed to admit this to you, but I have this ... this *feeling* about it. Ridiculous as it is, I can't shake it off."

"Feeling?"

"Yes. That if I once go back to Wyckfield, I shall never be able to leave."

"Good *God,* Camilla, do you think your sister-in-law would keep you *prisoner* or some such thing?"

Camilla shook her head, smiling a little at her friend's common-sensical literalness. "No, of course not. How could she? I *told* you it was foolish. But my feeling is very real, and I can't rid myself of it."

Georgina reached out her hand and drew Camilla back to the sofa. "My poor girl," she murmured in sudden understanding, "did you hate the place as much as that?"

Camilla lowered her head. "I was not . . . very happy there."

"Then I see no reason for you to go back," her friend said decisively.

"But what about Pippa?"

"Does Pippa feel the same way about Wyckfield as you do?"

"Oh, no, not Pippa. You know Pippa—she's happy anywhere. And it is her home . . . or it will be, when she's of age."

"Then it's all quite simple," Georgina declared, swinging her arms wide in proud acknowledgement of her brilliance in having solved everything. "Send Pippa to Wyckfield without you."

"Without me? Why, I *couldn't—*"

"But, Camilla, it's only for a week."

"But she'd be so *alone.*"

"I'll let Sybil go with her, if you'd like. Miss Townley, who, I assume, will go with them, can be relied upon to see that your sister-in-law doesn't keep them beyond the allotted time."

Camilla gaped at her friend in awe. "Georgie! What a perfectly wonderful idea! The girls would have a marvelous time in the country together, and Ethelyn won't be able to say that I'm keeping Pippa from her." She threw her arms about her friend's neck. "You're a positive genius! And generous to a fault to let Sybil go off for a week. I don't know how to thank you."

Georgina returned the embrace, laughing. "Save your effusions for some other time, silly. It was a perfectly obvious solution which you would have thought of yourself if you'd been less agitated. And as for letting Sybil go, I'm delighted to be rid of her. You've no idea how that tomboy can upset a household. Let your sister-in-law cope with *her* for a few days, and you'll see how quickly the children are sent home."

The vision of the rigid Ethelyn dealing with the mercurial Sybil kept them both laughing for a moment. Then, rising to leave, Georgina adjusted her bonnet and added with sudden seriousness, "I could solve your other problem, too, if you'd let me."

"My other problem?"

"About your sister-in-law's pressure on you to remarry."

"Oh, yes. I'd forgotten that for a moment." She got up to call for Hicks. "Ethelyn will be furious when she learns I won't be there to meet her Mr. Harbage." She smiled as she helped Georgina to straighten her pelisse. "And how, my wise and practical friend, do you think you might solve *that* problem?"

"Again the solution is simple. Just become betrothed to someone *else*—someone of your own choosing. Preferably a Londoner, so that I will always have you close by. As soon as you're betrothed, you know, your sister-in-law will have no reason for matchmaking."

"Oh, that's your 'simple' solution, is it?" Camilla grinned. "I suppose you have a candidate in mind?"

But Hicks came in at that moment. "Will you call Sybil for me, Hicks?" Georgina requested. "It's time we were getting home."

Hicks bowed out, and the two ladies followed him down the hall. Daniel, stationed at the bottom of the stairs, was sent up to fetch the girls, while Hicks sent for Thomas to alert the Sturtevant coachman.

The ladies waited in the entryway. "I don't have a candidate, my dear," Georgina said, picking up the threads of their interrupted conversation, "but I wish I did."

"Candidate?"

"For your hand, of course. I don't fancy myself as a matchmaker, but I wouldn't take it amiss if you showed an interest in my brother."

Camilla lowered her eyes in embarrassment. "I hope, Georgie, that you aren't entertaining serious hopes in that regard."

Georgina sighed. "No, I'm not so foolish. My brother is a dear, but I'm well aware that he's too old, too lazy and too complacent in his bachelorhood to make a satisfactory suitor for you."

Camilla put a hand on her friend's arm. "Your brother *is* a dear. And he does seem happy in his bachelorhood. That's why we get on so well. He understands that I have no wish to remarry, so he feels perfectly safe in my company."

"That may be, Camilla, but there are dozens of other men you might consider. I hate to hear you say you've no interest in remarriage. Just because your previous experience was unhappy is no reason to believe—"

Their conversation was again interrupted, this time by Thomas's return after fetching the Sturtevant carriage. At the same moment, Daniel's step was heard on the stairs. The two women looked up to see him descending rapidly, his face red with chagrin. "I beg yer pardon, yer ladyship, but Miss Sybil refuses to come down," he informed them.

"What?" Lady Sturtevant exclaimed angrily. *"Refuses?* Honestly, that child will drive me to madness! I suppose I'll have to go up and carry her down bodily."

Hicks came toward her from the door. "Is there anything *I* can do, your ladyship?"

Georgina put a hand to her forehead in an exaggerated gesture of helplessness. "I don't see what—"

"Permit me, your ladyship," Thomas offered. "I think I can persuade her to come down." And without waiting for an answer, he bounded up the stairs, taking them two at a time.

Lady Sturtevant stared after him in considerable astonishment. "Your footman seems very . . . er . . . energetic," she murmured to Camilla in some amusement.

"Yes," Camilla responded wryly as she watched Daniel and Hicks move away in perfect, mannerly dignity, "I've noticed, myself, that the fellow's behavior is a trifle . . . unorthodox. I don't know quite what to do about him. I've been thinking of giving him his notice."

"Oh, I wouldn't do that if I were you. I like the servants to be enterprising."

"I shall remember that, my dear," Camilla said with a laugh, "if I'm forced to let him go. In that event, I shall send him straight to you."

Georgina pulled on her gloves. "Why not? In my household of eccentrics, one more or less won't even be noticed. But if I may return to a more important matter, my love, I wish you will think about my suggestion to find yourself a betrothed. I would dearly love to see you happily wed."

"Don't press me on that subject, Georgie, please. I've made up my mind to remain as I am. But there's no need to look so glum about it. Your suggestion has given me a very good idea about what to do about Ethelyn's matchmaking. It's quite a splendid solution that I've thought of all by myself . . . and it will work without my having to become betrothed to accomplish it."

"Really? Then *tell* me—"

But there was no time for Camilla to explain, even if she'd wanted to. A murmur at the top of the stairs made them all look up. Sybil Sturtevant, her bonnet neatly tied on her head and her spencer buttoned, was marching down the stairs in slow, deliberate, completely unaccustomed dignity. Thomas and Pippa followed, both of them watching with interest as Sybil made her majestic descent. "I'm ready, Mama," the girl announced when she'd reached bottom, and, without breaking her even pace, she smiled at Camilla and went out the door to the carriage.

Georgina, her mouth open and her eyebrows raised, watched her daughter's exit with disbelief. "I don't think I've ever *seen* that child move in such a ladylike style!" she whispered to Camilla. "Your footman must have some sort of *gift!* Whenever you want to be rid of him, I'll take him in a snap."

When the visitors had gone and the servants had taken themselves back to their quarters, Camilla accosted her daughter. "What did Thomas *do* to make Sybil behave so well?"

Pippa giggled. "He made a wager with her. He wagered that she couldn't make it all the way down to the carriage without once breaking into a hop, skip or jump."

"Oh, so *that* was his ruse! What did he wager?"

"Nothing much," Pippa said, starting back up the stairs. "Only the four hundred and twenty pounds she owed him."

"Four hundred and twenty *pounds?*" Camilla stared after her daughter, aghast. "What are you *talking* about? Pippa Wyckfield, I see nothing in this matter to *laugh* about! Come back here at once! *Pippa!*"

Chapter Nine

Even after she'd learned from her daughter (who parted with the information only after a prolonged indulgence in irritating and rowdyish hilarity) that the four-hundred-and-twenty-pound wager was only pretend-money, Camilla had the feeling that Thomas ought to be scolded. There was something vaguely disquieting in what he'd done and in the fact that the girls and the footman were on so friendly a footing. It didn't seem right, somehow—but she couldn't put her finger on anything really *wrong* with it. According to Pippa, the footman was clever, humorous, friendly and kind. He was the only adult who was willing to spend time with them, telling them fascinating stories and playing cards with them when all the others—Miss Townley, Sybil's governess, Sybil's brothers, *everyone*—turned away in boredom. There was nothing in Pippa's account of the behavior of the footman toward the two girls to provoke a reprimand, but Camilla was uncomfortable nonetheless. The fellow didn't behave like a footman—that was the long and the short of it.

But she put the matter out of her mind and hurried back to

her writing desk. She had to compose an answer to Ethelyn's letter, and, for once, she was able to frame her response with complete confidence. She knew just what she would say. Her conversation with Georgina had given her the inspiration, and she couldn't wait to put that inspired idea into execution.

At first, her pen flew over the page as she told her sister-in-law that "Philippa and her dear little friend" would be arriving at the suggested time for a brief visit to Wyckfield Park. But the writing slowed down considerably as she struggled to phrase the rest of her message. *I, however, will not be accompanying the girls on this visit,* she wrote, pausing frequently to ponder the effects of her words. *I am very much tied to London at this time. You see, Ethelyn, I've been thinking, just as you have, of the matter of remarriage. You will be pleased to learn that I am seriously considering taking your advice about finding a husband for myself and a father for Pippa.* ("It won't hurt to remind her that she made the suggestion herself," Camilla muttered with a small smile.) *As chance would have it, I have recently become acquainted with a gentleman who has many qualities which would make him suitable.* (What qualities?" she asked herself, chewing the tip of her pen thoughtfully.) *In fact, I'm certain you would agree with me that he is in several ways more suitable than the vicar's brother, of whom you wrote so glowingly. For one thing, the gentleman I speak of is not so far into middle age as Mr. Harbage. The gentleman in question—*

(She scratched out the last phrase. She couldn't keep referring to her imaginary suitor as "the gentleman in question." She had better give him a name. This detail troubled her; she hadn't wanted to dip so deeply into deceit. Giving him a name imparted to the imaginary man a certain discomfiting reality. But there was no help for it. "Thus the liar becomes mired in her dishonesties," she sighed aloud as she pulled out a blank sheet of paper on which to scribble out some experimental names. *Mr. Jonathan Invention,* she began with a nervous giggle and then added, playfully: *Mr. Robert Fiction, Mr. John Ficsham, Mr. John Invensham, Mr. Robert Fabricaysham, Mr. Frederick Falsham, Mr. Peter Fablesham, Mr. Fable Petersham* ... "Petersham," she mused aloud. That was not an unbelievable name. It had a rather honest sound, in fact, when one rolled it comfortably off the tongue. Mr. Petersham, her soon-to-be-betrothed. With a grin, she tore up the scratch sheet and proceeded with her letter.)

Mr. Petersham, the gentleman in question, is not above thirty-five, which you must agree is an age more suited to father a ten-year-old child than a man of fifty. As for his other qualities... (She nibbled the tip of her pen again, trying to think of the sort of qualities she would like in a husband.) *...As for his other qualities, he has a cheerful disposition, a keen sense of humor and a lack of pretension. These, in addition to some of the qualities you admire in your Mr. Harbage, like good health, firmness and godliness, make my Mr. Petersham an even more promising candidate than the vicar's brother.*

It is, of course, much too soon to make a final decision on this matter, and I know you will agree that the matter should not become a subject for public discussion but be kept strictly between the two of us. However, it seems to me that I should not absent myself from London at this delicate juncture in a budding relationship.

Feeling gleefully and mischievously wicked, Camilla reread what she'd written, added her usual wishes for her sister-in-law's good health and signed her name. Then she folded the sheet, sealed it and handed it over to Hicks for posting. The deed was done.

Camilla didn't think about her act of dishonesty during the next few days. She was busily occupied in preparing Pippa for her trip to Dorset, for one thing. And for the another, she was somewhat eagerly making arrangements for the first formal dinner party to be held in her new home. It was to be a small gathering—only Lord and Lady Sturtevant and Sir James Cambard had been invited. (Sir James had arranged for the four of them to attend a performance of *Cosi Fan Tutte* at the King's Theater in the Haymarket, and Camilla had invited them all to dine with her at Upper Seymour Street beforehand.) But although the number of guests would be small, it was to be the first time the Worcester Royal china and the new gold plate would be used, the first time the staff would be required to serve dinner guests, and the first time the cook would be asked to put to use her talent in preparing creams and pastries. With the packing of Pippa's clothing and the readying of the formal dining room for guests, the household was humming with activity, in the midst of which Camilla forgot all about the imaginary Mr. Petersham... not dreaming how ominously his ghostly presence was looming over her future.

A prompt and scathing response from Ethelyn brought the entire matter forcibly back to her mind. With her sister-in-law's acrimonious letter held in a trembling hand, Camilla realized how short-sighted she'd been to have indulged herself in the hope that her invention of a London suitor would put to rest Ethelyn's urge to control her life. It was obvious, from the acerbic tone of the letter, that Ethelyn had no confidence whatever in Camilla's ability to choose a husband for herself. *How dared you take it on yourself to surmise,* Ethelyn demanded, the heavy down-strokes of her pen making the words almost shout in anger, *that your Mr. Petersham can in any way compare with the lofty, zealous, inspired Mr. Josiah Harbage? Who is this Mr. Petersham? From your inadequate characterization I have the impression that he is nondescript at best. What do you know of his family? If he were related to the Petershams of Lincolnshire he would have a title, wouldn't he? What is his income? Have you given a single thought to any of the practicalities of such a match? I very much fear, Camilla, that you are much too fanciful and bubble-headed to be trusted to make a decision of such importance as the choosing of a suitable mate. I therefore insist that you come to Wyckfield and meet Mr. Harbage before you become hopelessly involved in a situation which will lead to disaster.*

Camilla burned with fury. Fanciful and bubble-headed indeed! How dare her sister-in-law so contemptuously presume that she was incapable of choosing a husband for herself! Dashing away a few hot tears of anger, she stalked to her writing desk and penned an impassioned reply. *Even if I were as bubble-headed as you think me,* she scribbed in impulsive wrath, *my own decision in the choice of a marriage partner would be better than anyone else's. I have learned enough of the conditions of matrimony to understand what I require for my own happiness. I know that I need kindness more than firmness, laughter more than solemnity, and freedom more than repression. These are the qualities that I find in my Mr. Petersham, and besides these, the questions of his income and his family fade into insignificance.*

I have no wish to seem unappreciative of your concern for my happiness, but I cannot permit you to assume a parental

*role over me. I am of age and of sound mind. It is my considered
opinion that I would not find happiness as the wife of a clergyman of the sort Mr. Harbage seems to be. Therefore I shall
not subject myself nor Mr. Harbage to the embarrassment or
discomfiture of a meeting. I hope you will respect my wishes
in this matter and not refer to this subject again.*

*Since I know how much Pippa means to you, and how deep
her affection for you and for Wyckfield remains, I shall not—
as I was tempted to do—cancel our plans for her visit. I trust,
however, that you will not discuss this matter with her while
she is with you. My possible remarriage is a subject of the
most delicate intimacy, and I shall confide my plans to my
daughter if and when I believe the time is right. Any breach
of this condition will certainly cause an estrangement between
us, Ethelyn, and I am sure you do not wish to cause the severing
of the slim ties which still hold us together as a family.*

Without even a re-reading, Camilla sealed the letter and
sent it off. With considerable apprehension she waited for a
reply. But the days passed with no response, and at last, when
the day came for Pippa to leave, and there had been no word
from Wyckfield, Camilla realized that her sister-in-law had,
by her silence, indicated clearly that she wished to do nothing
to jeopardize Pippa's visit. In a way, the silence revealed also
that Camilla had achieved a victory in the clash of wills. But
she felt no sense of triumph. She watched her daughter board
the carriage with a heart fluttering with misgivings.

Before Miss Townley could follow her charge into the
coach, Camilla drew her aside. "You'll be sure not to permit
Lady Ethelyn to persuade you to extend the visit, won't you,
Ada?"

"I've told you a dozen times, Miss Camilla, that you needn't
trouble your head on that score. I won't stay in Dorset one
minute longer than I have to."

"Good. But there's something else." She turned her head
away so that Pippa, waving happily at her from the coach
window, wouldn't see her troubled frown. "My sister-in-law
may wish to engage you in conversation about... about my
possible remarriage—"

"Remarriage?" The governess's eyes lit up with delighted
speculation. "Miss *Camilla!* Are you—"

"No, I'm not, so you may wipe that expectant smile from
your face. But if Lady Ethelyn presses on you the virtues of

a certain clergyman—a Mr. Josiah Harbage by name—you are to give her no encouragement. Just tell her you're certain I would not be interested."

Miss Townley looked at her employer shrewdly and shrugged. "If that's what you wish me to say, that's what I'll say."

"Thank you. And there's...er...one other matter. She may ask you if you know anything about a...a Mr. Petersham."

"Petersham? Who's Mr. Petersham?"

"No one. That is, just say you haven't met him."

"Well, since I haven't, what else can I say?" the governess retorted.

"Exactly. Just remember to say you haven't met him, and change the subject."

"All this sounds very havey-cavey to me." Miss Townley squinted at Camilla suspiciously. "Are you up to somethin' smokey? Who *is* this Mr. Petersham?"

"No one. I'll tell you all about it...*him*...when you return. But for now you'd better go along. Sybil will be on tenterhooks by this time. Take good care of the girls, Ada. I'm counting on you."

Chapter Ten

It was the first time Camilla had been separated from her daughter, and she was overwhelmed with despondency. To shake herself out of the doldrums, she threw herself into the preparations for the dinner party. She knew it was ridiculous to make so great a to-do over the prospect of a tiny party, but it was the very first such occasion she would be arranging completely on her own. For the sake of her self-esteem, she wanted everything to be planned and executed with perfection.

She and the cook had already planned a most sumptuous menu. They were to start with a soup of creamed cucumbers, followed by English turbot in lobster sauce, rolled veal, a timbale of macaroni *Napolitaine,* some poultry filets *à l'Orleans,* little mutton *patés,* orange biscuits, cabbage flowers, Spanish celery, other assorted vegetables and a complete array of cakes, *soufflés,* jellies and creams.

A magnificent Persian carpet had recently been laid in the hitherto-unused formal dining room, and although the room was somewhat large for such a small assemblage, Camilla was determined to use it. She had Hicks remove all the center leaves of the table to make the seating arrangement more intimate, and she ordered large pots of flowers to fill every corner. On the afternoon of the event, she herself arranged three huge bowls of fresh blooms—one for the entryway, one to set before the dining-room windows and one for the center of the table.

Before she went upstairs to dress, she surveyed the scene with Hicks at her side. The dining room glowed from the efforts of a household of servants who'd scrubbed, aired, dusted and polished for two days. "Everything looks lovely, Hicks," she said with satisfaction, "and you are very impressive in your tails. Just make sure that Daniel and Thomas have done everything proper with their livery. And, Hicks, see that they don't overdo the hair powder. I have a nightmarish vision of Thomas clapping his hand to his head and loosing a cloud of white flour into the air! Warn him not to do anything the least bit out of the way, will you?"

By the time Betsy had dressed Camilla's hair and helped her into her favorite gown (a plum-colored creation of Genoa velvet with long sleeves and a positively wicked *décolletage*), Camilla was feeling festive, excited and optimistic. Everything had been arranged down to the last detail. Everything and everyone was prepared and ready. There was not a thing she could think of which could go wrong.

Her guests arrived promptly and were in the very best of spirits. Lady Sturtevant, sensing that this first dinner party was special to her friend, had seen to it that she and her two escorts were dressed with appropriate grandeur. They gathered, glittering with elegance, in Camilla's drawing room, where Sir James offered the ladies many effusive compliments on their outstandingly impressive looks. The wine, which was served by Hicks with flawless formality, was pronounced by Edgar (who considered himself a connoisseur in such matters) to be superior, and Sir James heartily seconded his brother-in-law's judgment. By the time dinner was announced, several glasses had been consumed and even the taciturn Edgar had unloosened enough to laugh at his wife's jokes and make one or two sallies of his own.

The first course passed with equal success. The food was much praised, and Sir James asked for his plate to be refilled so frequently that Camilla was convinced that his kind words were more than mere flattery. The two footmen, impeccable in their formal liveries, handled the serving without a slip, even Thomas behaving with such restraint that he was barely noticed. By the time the first course had been removed, Camilla knew that her party was a success. Edgar, surprising everyone by emerging from his usual reticence, took over the conversation, starting with a toast to his hostess. He lifted his wine glass and said, "To Camilla, who should teach my wife how to organize a dinner as memorable and free from disaster as this one."

Georgina laughed good-naturedly. "Never mind," she riposted. "When she has five children to get in her way, even Camilla will find it difficult to organize her dinners as well as she does now."

Camilla sat back and smiled contentedly. Everything was going just as she wished. There was nothing more to worry about.

Edgar, his tongue loosened by wine and good spirits, began to expound on the subject which occupied all his waking thoughts—politics. Prodded by the others (who eagerly grasped at this unwonted opportunity to learn about the situation in Parliament from an insider's point of view), he told them how discontent the house was with the leadership of Mr. Addington. "It looks more and more as if he will be stepping down before the year is out."

"Will he?" Georgina asked interestedly. "You don't think your Mr. Fox will succeed him, do you?"

"No, I'm afraid not. But I will not be sorry to see Pitt take over again. He's the best we have to lead us in time of war."

"Pitt?" Sir James asked, his mouth twisted into a cynical sneer. "If you ask me, he's too old and tired to be as effective as he once was."

"Perhaps," Sturtevant agreed, "but the country admires him. And he is perceived as being a strong leader."

"He *is* strong, when you compare him to Mr. Addington," Georgina said in support.

"Can't argue with that," Sir James laughed. "Have you heard the rhyme that's being bruited about?"

"You mean 'Pitt is to Addington as London is to Paddington,' don't you? We've been hearing that one for months."

"Are you saying, Edgar," Camilla asked shyly, never having had the opportunity before to discuss politics with men of power, "that you would *support* the return of Mr. Pitt? I thought you were a staunch supporter of Mr. Fox."

"I am, but these are unusual times. With Napoleon massing troops at Pas de Calais, we are being threatened on our own doorstep. We need a strong, *tried* hand at the helm. Already the talk of Pitt's possible return has caused an increase in the number of volunteers for the militia. I've heard rumors that the number may reach half a million."

"Half a million? Remarkable!" Sir James muttered, reaching for the port. "If only the Navy could inspire volunteers in such numbers."

"Perhaps they will," Edgar said optimistically. "We English are a surprising breed in time of crisis. Perhaps they will."

"Huh!" came a snort behind him.

Every head in the room turned toward the sound. It had obviously emanated from the throat of the footman standing just behind Lord Sturtevant, a decanter of wine in his hand. *"Thomas!"* Camilla exclaimed, shocked.

"Did you say something, fellow?" Sturtevant asked curiously.

"No, my lord," Thomas muttered and bent over to fill his glass.

"Yes, you did," Sir James accused, peering at him narrowly. "We all heard you."

Hicks stepped forward from his place at the sideboard. "I'm sure, sir, that Thomas was only . . . er . . . clearing his throat." He looked at Thomas threateningly. "Isn't that right, Thomas?"

Tom looked from Hicks to Lord Sturtevant, his face impassive. "I'm very sorry, your lordship," he murmured.

But Edgar's curiosity was piqued. "Never mind the apologies, fellow. What did you *mean* by that sound? I had the distinct impression that you were making a comment on my remark about volunteers for the Navy. Do you think I'm *mistaken?*"

"I'm sure that Thomas meant nothing at all," Camilla said, frowning at her footman with eyes flashing angrily.

"Of course he didn't," Sir James said flatly. "What does a footman know about such matters, anyway?"

"Don't jump to conclusions, James," Lady Sturtevant put in, grinning. "This fellow is a very unusual sort of footman."

Hicks came up behind his troublesome underling and gave him a shove in the back. "Take this tray of dishes to the warming room, you idiot," he hissed softly. "and *don't come back!*"

But Edgar wouldn't be put off. "Let the fellow speak," he insisted. "If he has an opinion, I'd like to hear it. Don't you believe that the Navy will get volunteers, fellow?"

"No, your lordship, I don't."

Sir James leaned forward. "What on earth do *you* know about it?"

"I know enough to remember the mutiny at Spithead, and how little has been done since to better a sailor's life," Tom retorted.

Hicks met Camilla's eye with a look of pained helplessness, a look that was returned in full measure.

"But improvements *have* been made since Spithead, haven't they?" Sturtevant asked, staring at the footman interestedly.

"Minuscule ones. Just ask yourself this, your lordship. With a man like Nelson as Admiral—a man who's a hero to every man and boy in the land—why is it still necessary to have press-gangs roaming the coastal towns for recruits?"

"Press-gangs!" Sir James snorted scornfully. "Nowadays there're no such things! They're just bogeymen, concocted from stories told at ale houses. We've the best Navy in all of Christendom, and every man of sense knows it."

"Bogeymen, eh? Let me tell you, sir, that—"

"Watch your tongue, Thomas," Hicks interrupted sharply. "Take this tray—!"

"Damnation," Thomas burst out, "I think these gentlemen ought to be *told* what goes on in the real world! Bogeymen, my *ass!*"

"*Thomas!*" Hicks, white-faced in fury and alarm, thrust the heavily laden tray into Tom's midsection. "Take this and *go!*"

While everyone watched in shocked silence, Tom took the tray to the door. But before he left, he looked back at Sturtevant and Sir James. "It would be better for the Navy and this country if you gentlemen stopped fooling yourselves. Go down to Southampton or Portsmouth and see for yourselves what goes on." With that he pushed the door open with his back, walked out and pulled the door closed behind him with his foot.

"Heavens, Camilla, where did you find that—" Sir James began.

But he was interrupted by a great crash of crockery. Out

in the corridor, Thomas must have dropped the tray.

Camilla shuddered. With a wince, she put a shaking hand to her forehead. Her lovely dinner, ruined! She looked up at her dinner guests in humiliation and caught Georgina's eye. Georgina was trying very hard not to laugh. Suddenly Camilla felt herself relax. "So much for my well-organized, disaster-free dinner," she said with a rueful smile.

Everyone hooted with laughter. "But we can still say it was memorable," Edgar said when the laughter had died. "You seem to have learned Georgie's knack, Camilla, of finding eccentric servants."

"Eccentric is the word for him," Sir James put in. "Belligerent bloke, isn't he? What do you make of his remarks, Edgar?"

Sturtevant looked thoughtful. "I don't know what I make of them. They had a ring of truth. Don't know but that I won't do a little investigating of the matter, just as he suggests."

"Well, we'd better not think about it now," his wife pointed out. "We are already late for the opera."

The laughter and bustle of their departure didn't distract Camilla from her fury at her footman. Even though Thomas had cleared away any sign of broken china from the corridor by the time they'd emerged from the dining room, and even though he reappeared with Daniel at the front door, carrying the ladies' cloaks and looking as calm as if nothing untoward had occurred, Camilla had made up her mind. When he helped her on with her cloak, she whispered through clenched teeth, "I hope you realize, Thomas, that you've used your last chance. As of this moment, you have your notice. You are *sacked*."

The next morning, Hicks entered the breakfast room with an expression on his face of considerable agitation. Finding Camilla already there, he hastened to pour her tea. "Sorry I'm late, Miss Camilla," he apologized, "but the three of them are packing to leave, and I can't talk reason to any of 'em."

"By the three of them, I take it you mean Betsy, Daniel and Thomas?"

"Yes, ma'am. I knew from the first there'd be trouble with 'em. From the first moment they asked for places on this staff."

"But surely Daniel and Betsy have been satisfactory. They can't be so foolish as to wish to leave at this time. Betsy's baby will be coming in a couple of months."

"I know it. And they know it. But they won't listen." He sighed as he uncovered a dish of York ham and offered it to her. "Perhaps it's just as well they go, Miss Camilla. They've given you nothing but trouble."

"Daniel has given no trouble, and Betsy is a jewel. Really, Hicks, we *can't* let Betsy go. I'll talk to them. Send them all in to me at once."

She pushed aside her plate and sipped her tea thoughtfully, trying to find a way out of this sticky dilemma. Her mind was made up about Thomas—he had to go. But she was equally determined that Betsy should stay. The poor young woman would need care for the next few months, and Camilla was determined to see that she got it.

The three servants appeared before her in short order, dressed in the clothes in which Camilla had first seen them. "Hicks tells me," she said without roundaboutation, "that the three of you are packing to leave today. I'd like to know why."

Thomas and Daniel, both looking sullen, refused to answer. Betsy, after glancing quickly from one to the other of them, faced her mistress. "Please don't be angry at us, ma'am, but we're . . . er . . . sworn t' stick together."

"Rubbish!" Tom muttered disgustedly under his breath.

"That's a very foolish sort of pledge, my dear," Camilla said to her maid, trying to ignore Thomas. "The likelihood of your finding places in the same establishment—and soon—is very slim."

"We'll manage, m' lady," Daniel said looking at Thomas with a stubborn set to his mouth, making Camilla suspect that the two men had been arguing the matter long and hard.

"I won't pursue the discussion for now. However, I do wish to remind you that, even if you're determined to stick together, you needn't leave at once. Thomas has the usual fortnight's notice."

"There, Tom, didn't I tell ye?" Betsy said with some satisfaction.

Tom made an impatient gesture with his hands. "I don't *want* her damned 'notice.' I won't remain on these premises another fortnight!"

"See here, Thomas," Camilla said angrily, getting to her feet, "I won't have you spewing out your vile curses in this house! It would be well to remember to guard your tongue when in the presence of ladies."

Thomas bit back a sharp retort and turned away. Betsy wheeled on him angrily. "Ye've no call t' talk to her ladyship that way, Tom, and you know it. We *need* that fornight's grace, and if she'd good enough t' give it to us, we'll take it. You turn around and thank her proper!"

Thomas's shoulders seemed to sag. He turned round as he was told. "Thank you, your ladyship," he said with glum reluctance.

Camilla nodded in disdainful acknowledgement of his surrender. "Do I take it, then, that the three of you will remain for the fortnight?"

"Yes, ma'am," Betsy said quickly, "we shall. You're bein' very kind, an' we're *all* grateful."

Camilla smiled at the young woman and put an arm around her shoulders. "Perhaps you'll change your minds before the fortnight is over, Betsy," she said comfortingly, walking with the maid to the door.

"I'd like t' say we will, ma'am," Betsy answered with a small sigh, "but I don't think so."

"Well, go along and don't worry about anything, my dear," Camilla said to her, throwing a look of disapproval at the two men who were following them out. "I won't permit these two brutes to force you to have your baby on the street. See her upstairs, Daniel. I want to speak to Thomas alone."

When Daniel and Betsy had closed the door behind them, Tom turned to face Camilla with a show of bravado. "If you think all this is my fault, you're mistaken, ma'am. I've argued myself blue in the face, begging Daniel to stay."

"I've no doubt you did. You needn't sound so defensively belligerent."

"Then why did you call me a brute?"

"I called *both* of you brutes. And it was only a . . . a figure of speech. Actually, I find Daniel's loyalty to you rather touching, even if I don't understand the reason. One would think you'd saved his life or some such thing."

His eyes dropped from her questioning gaze. "We . . . we've been through a great deal together, that's all."

"A great deal?" she echoed, puzzled. "At the home of that doctor in Derbyshire?"

Tom fidgeted in discomfort. "In many places," he answered evasively.

She studied him for a moment with wrinkled brows and then

shrugged. "Well, if you don't choose to enlighten me, I shan't press you. I hope you realize, Thomas, that Betsy is in a difficult situation because of you. It's not just the birthing, you know. She'll be weak for quite a while afterwards, and she will have an infant to nurse and care for. Even if you *do* find posts together (which I very much doubt), your new employer may not be very sympathetic to the personal problems of the staff—"

"You needn't tell me that you're kinder than most. I'm not a fool," he interrupted brusquely.

"I didn't intend to flatter myself, and you know it! Really, Thomas, you can be the most irritating—! I only meant to make you see how difficult it might be for Betsy if you and Daniel insist on tearing her away from here."

"Do you think I don't know? Why do you suppose I've been arguing with Daniel all morning?"

Camilla bit her lip. "If you're trying to make me feel guilty for discharging you, you won't succeed, you know."

Thomas swore under his breath. "I *knew* you'd think this was a ruse! I *told* Daniel—!"

"Whether it's a ruse or not, I warn you that I won't be trapped into changing my mind about you, even for Betsy's sake. You're an *impossible* footman, and you should have been sacked weeks ago."

"I know it, ma'am. I agree with you."

"You agree with me?"

"Completely."

She stared at him in annoyance and dropped down on a chair. Shaking her head in bewilderment, she made a little, irritated rasp of sound in her throat. "Dash it all, why must you *agree* with me? Your agreement doesn't make me feel a whit better about this situation."

"Would it help if I disagreed?" he asked with an ironic smile. "If you like, I'll make some stupid defense of my behavior so that you can get angry at me and sack me all over again."

She gave a reluctant laugh. "You *are* an original, I'll say that for you. Perhaps I should send you to Lady Sturtevant. She indicated a willingness to take you on."

"No, thank you, ma'am. If I'm as impossible a footman as you say I am, I should soon be in Lady Sturtevant's black books as well as in yours. I've done with domestic service."

"Then what *will* you do?"

"I don't know. Something will turn up."

"That sounds much too vague a program for a man who has the responsibility of another couple on his shoulders . . . and one of them an expectant mother."

"You needn't remind me. I'm all too well aware of that responsibility."

"Then you do understand that you must convince Daniel and Betsy to remain in my employ, at least for a while."

"That's why I agreed to this blasted additional fortnight," he said frankly. "With the extra time at my disposal, I may be able to convince Daniel to let me go away alone. If I can convince him that this is the best place for the baby—"

"Yes, that's the best argument. Very well, Thomas, we'll see what happens. But you are not to think, if your arts of persuasion are ineffective, that I'll change my mind and keep you on. At the end of the fortnight, out you go. I'm determined on it."

"Don't worry, my lady," Tom said with a rather bitter smile. "You can't be more eager for my departure than I am."

She shot him an irritated glare and motioned with her hand for him to go. He bowed and turned to the door. But before his hand touched the knob she stopped him with a word. "Why?" she asked in plaintive curiosity.

He turned back, his brows raised. "Did you say something, ma'am?"

"I asked why you are so eager to leave these premises. You admitted before that I was kinder than most. You've been well treated here, haven't you? And until your dreadful exhibition in front of my guests last night, I've put up with all your . . . eccentricities. Haven't I?"

He stared at her for a moment, his eyes unreadable. "Yes, you're very kind. Yes, I've been well treated. Yes, you've put up with me with remarkable patience," he said flatly. "And I hate it here."

For some inexplicable reason, she felt stricken. "But . . . *why?*"

"Don't you know?"

"I wouldn't ask if I did."

His lips turned up in a sardonic smile—the kind she'd seen on his face before. "Because, ma'am," he said quietly, "while I remain in this house I have to see before me, every waking hour of every day, that which I can never have."

Without waiting for her acknowledgement or dismissal, he turned and left the room. She didn't call him back to reprimand him for that breach of protocol. She was glad he'd left. If he'd remained, he would have seen how burning hot her cheeks had become.

Chapter Eleven

Lady Sturtevant had been quite right in predicting that her little Sybil would prove to be too much for Lady Ethelyn to handle. Ethelyn took a dislike to the child from the moment of their arrival, a reaction not much to be wondered at, for Sybil had three traits which were immediately manifest and which seemed to be specifically designed to drive Ethelyn berserk: one, she never walked down the stairs—she slid down the wide bannister of the main stairway as if it were her personal passageway; two, she peppered every sentence with such vile epithets as "Hang it all!" and "Egad!"; and, three, she ran, skipped or jumped about the house but never walked. And no one, not Miss Townley, nor Philippa nor Ethelyn herself seemed able to restrain her.

But what Ethelyn most disliked about the child was her influence on Philippa. It wasn't that Philippa had changed in any fundamental way—she was still perfectly ladylike, affable and polite. But she showered the most unaffected and warm-hearted admiration on her friend, seeing nothing reprehensible in any of Sybil's pranks. "Don't take on so, Aunt Ethelyn," she would say to her aunt in her soothing, mature way. "It's only high-spiritedness. I think Sybil is wonderfully energetic and imaginative. She means no harm at all."

As a result, Philippa was led into the most shocking misdeeds which would never otherwise have occurred. For example, when reading to Sybil a book about the Red Indians of America, Pippa agreed to Sybil's "imaginative" plan to paint their faces Indian-style with the pigments in Pippa's old box of watercolors. When they appeared in the drawing room to show the result to Aunt Ethelyn, the poor woman shrieked in fright. Another time, when the two girls went out riding, they outraced the groom, managed to escape from his supervision and rode off the property. They didn't return for four hours, during which time every servant in the household was enlisted to scour the countryside for their bodies, while Ethelyn took to her bed in hysterics despite Miss Townley's assurances that the girls were excellent horsewomen and would probably come to no harm. By the time the girls reappeared, perfectly safe and in time for dinner, Ethelyn was in need of the ministrations of a doctor.

But the straw which broke Ethelyn's spirit was the occasion of the curricle ride. The two girls stole into the stable, harnessed the curricle to a pair of chestnuts and tried to teach themselves to drive "a curricle and pair." Before anyone in the household even realized they'd gone out, they managed to drive the vehicle into a ditch, cracking the curricle beyond repair. (Fortunately, the chestnuts were a placid pair and didn't bolt.)

But the incident threw Ethelyn into trembling disorder. *Please send your carriage for the girls at once,* she wrote to Camilla, *for my nerves will not endure another day of their misconduct. I would send them home in my own coach if their behavior was the least bit reliable, but I cannot face shouldering the responsibility for their safety. Your Miss Townley, incidentally, does not seem any more capable of handling them than the rest of us, so I cannot count on her either. I trust your grooms and coachmen are more capable of dealing with such hoydenish behavior than mine have been.*

As a result, Camilla's coachman drew up at the Wyckfield Park gateway two days before the visit was scheduled to end, and Thomas, who had been selected to ride behind, climbed down to call for his charges. Camilla had given him the strictest of instructions. "Say as little as possible to Lady Ethelyn" she'd ordered, "for my sister-in-law is very short-tempered and is a high stickler in matters of decorum. If you should fall into verbal altercation with her, I shall be most provoked. So remember to say a simple 'Yes, your ladyship,' help Miss Townley to pack up the girls' things, and depart for home with as much dispatch as you can manage. I've chosen you to perform this vital errand for me merely because you seem to have a way with Sybil. But if you let me down by the *merest slip* of your unruly tongue, the *slightest* eccentricity or the *tiniest* dereliction of duty, I shall never forgive you nor shall I write a *single word* of commendation in your behalf. I hope you heed me, Thomas, for I was never more in earnest in my life."

With those words ringing in his ears, Tom presented himself at the door of the mansion at Wyckfield Park with considerable trepidation. After sternly warning himself not to talk back to Lady Ethelyn no matter what the provocation, he heard from her butler that the lady in question had taken herself to her bed and would not emerge until the girls had gone. With relief, he went up to the girls' room. They greeted him with the effusive delight of old friends, showed him their packed valises and declared themselves ready to start for home, a declaration heartily endorsed by Miss Townley, who had had quite enough of Lady Ethelyn's taunts and Sybil's unruliness.

Tom could scarcely believe his good luck. An errand that promised to be fraught with difficulty was turning out to be as easy as bowling down a hill. Cheerfully, he tucked the valises one under each arm, took the girls' hands and led them down to the waiting carriage, Miss Townley trailing along behind with her overstuffed bandbox. As they climbed aboard and tucked the lap-robe about them, Tom took their luggage to stow away under the coachman's box. There his good spirits were given their first blow. The coachman stood leaning his forehead against the corner of the carriage, his shoulders sagging pathetically. "Is something wrong, Russ?" Thomas asked.

The coachman looked up. He was white about the mouth, and his cheeks were pale. "I dunno, Tom. Feel sum'at strange in me stomach. Do ye think we could wait round 'ere 'till tomorra?"

Tom scratched his chin worriedly. "Her ladyship's expecting us back by tonight. She'll be frantic if we don't appear until tomorrow afternoon. Is it very bad?"

Russ shrugged. "Bad enough. It ain't unbearable, I s'pose."

"Then why don't we start out. If you begin to feel worse, just pull over, and I'll take the reins myself."

"Mr. 'Icks wouldn't like that. 'E says a cook cooks, an' a butler butles. 'E wouldn't want t' see the footman take the reins."

"Even in an emergency?"

"I dunno. Can you handle four horses?"

"I don't know. I've never tried."

"Then we better not chance it."

"So you're saying we'd better stay here for the night, eh?" Tom couldn't help feeling dismayed at the prospect of disappointing the girls, causing Lady Ethelyn further displeasure and stirring up nightmares of alarm in Camilla's breast, alarm that was certain to beset her if the journey had to be delayed for eighteen hours.

"What's the trouble?" Miss Townley asked, lowering her window and peering out.

Tom went over to consult with her. "Russ is feeling poorly, Miss Townley. We were wondering if we should chance pushing on or postpone our departure until tomorrow."

The girls, overhearing, groaned loudly.

"Are you in very bad case, Russell?" the governess asked.

"Not very. I've felt sick afore an' managed to 'old the 'orses."

"Then I say let's get started. If you become worse, we'll find an inn somewhere. That will be more amusing for the girls than remaining here."

Russ nodded and climbed up on his box, while Tom walked to the rear of the carriage and climbed up on his stand. He was filled with disturbing apprehensions. If the carriage had been a ship, he'd have felt more sure of himself. On a ship, he knew what to do in an emergency. A ship started out on the tide even if the weather threatened. If the storm broke, he'd know how to trim the sails. But horses were something else again.

For more than an hour the carriage rolled along smoothly. Tom, feeling the sharp wind in his face, closed his eyes and pretended he was at sea. The smell was quite different from the sea winds, but the bite was not unlike them. With eyes closed he could almost imagine he was standing at the taffrail, the deck swaying beneath his feet and the polished wood of the railing under his hand. He felt the familiar lash of pain that struck every time he reminded himself that he'd never stand on a deck again. Riding the back of a shaking coach was a poor substitute for sailing.

But suddenly the rocking under him seemed to change its quality. He opened his eyes in instinctive alarm. The carriage seemed to be swaying more than before. He blinked into the wind to see if he could make out Russ's high hat over the top of the carriage. He was just in time to see the hat sink down and out of sight. *"Russ!"* he shouted, his chest constricting.

There was no answer. The carriage gathered speed and then, to Tom's horror, he saw Russ fall from his seat and roll to the side of the road. "Oh, God!" he muttered as the carriage rushed past the prostrate body. Tom's first instinct was to jump off and help the stricken coachman, but immediately he realized that there were two little girls and their governess inside the carriage and four horses running unguided along the road. There was nothing to do but to climb over the top of the coach and try to grasp the reins himself.

The horses, feeling the sudden lack of restraint, began to race wildly, and the lurching of the coach was sickening. Within, the two girls began to scream in fright. Tom, his blood turning to ice, tried to pull himself up on the roof, but there was nothing to hold on to. The swaying of the coach was worse than the rocking of the deck of any ship he'd ridden in a storm. If he didn't move quickly, he'd surely be thrown to the ground.

He could never have said later how he managed it. In mind-numbing terror, he heaved himself up on the roof and, flat on his stomach, he inched himself forward. When he reached the front, he let himself fall head first on the coachman's seat. As soon as he righted himself, he looked for the reins, but they were flapping on the ground completely out of his reach. The wind roared in his ears, not quite drowning out the screams of the girls, hanging out of the carriage windows behind him.

He stared for a moment at the dangling reins and the blurred hooves of the four wildly galloping horses. Then, in a last-ditch act of desperation, he jumped for the yoke of the two horses closest to him. He hung from that for a moment, his legs dragging painfully on the ground, and then he heaved himself up so that he hung from the yoke by his midsection. The weight pained the horses, who reared up angrily, but Tom clung to his position. Holding himself in place with one hand, he reached out for the reins with the other. He grasped them after several attempts, quickly wound them tightly about one of his wrists to keep them secure, and pulled with all his might.

The rearing of the foremost pair pulled him right off his perch. He thought it was the end of him, but he managed to hook his free arm on the trace of one of the foremost horses as he fell. Even with his lower body dragging on the ground, he was able to keep hold of the reins which were still twisted about his wrist. For a moment he felt paralyzed—fearful that he would never be able to move—but some inner force kept his mind alert. He began to inch his arm along the trace until he felt the buckle of the horse's bellyband under his fingers. With that hold secure, he focused on taking the slack out of the reins which were still clutched in his other hand. By turning his arm in a kind of swimming motion, he twisted the reins round and round his wrist. He didn't feel any pain, so deep was his concentration on shortening the reins. Finally, when he'd tightened them sufficiently, he yanked on them as hard as he could, at the same time pulling down on the bellyband with his other arm. Miraculously, the horses responded. They slowed down sufficiently for him to draw himself erect and, by digging in his heels he was able at last to pull them to a stop.

With a shudder, he fell down on his knees in the dust, his legs seeming to give way beneath him. He sat there for a moment while he caught his breath, but the sound of sobbing from the carriage quickly shook him into action. He got unsteadily to his feet. With every muscle quivering, he unbound his wrist and ran to the carriage door. The moment he opened it, two weeping little girls threw themselves into his arms.

He could see, behind them, that their governess was slumped into a corner in a swoon but apparently unharmed. Pippa, her slim little body shaking, was clutching him tightly round the neck and sobbing into his shoulder, while Sybil, on his other side, was staring at him through red-rimmed eyes, her childish mouth agape and her lips trembling pathetically. He hugged the children to him with a convulsive groan of relief. Dropping down on the carriage step, he rocked them silently in his arms. It was a long time before any of them could speak.

By the time the carriage drew up at the door of the house in Upper Seymour Street, it was long after dark. Camilla flew down the steps, fire in her eyes, She'd spent three anxious hours pacing about the drawing room, the last one occupied with rehearsing the furious epithets she would hurl into Thomas's insolent face, for she had no doubt that whatever had happened was his fault. But the sight that greeted her eyes drove everything else from her mind.

First she noticed that there was no footman at the back of the coach. Next, Sybil's head appeared in the window, her bonnet askew and her hair alarmingly disheveled. Then she saw that it was Thomas on the coachman's seat instead of the coachman . . . a Thomas who'd been shockingly impaired. His livery was ripped and torn, his hat was gone, his nose mangled and bloody, and one of his eyes hideously blackened. "Oh, my God!" she cried out, "what's *happened?*"

Pippa opened the carriage door, jumped down and ran into her mother's embrace. "He saved our lives, Mama! You wouldn't have believed it could be done, but he really did it. He saved our lives!"

Sybil tumbled out close behind her. "It's true, Lady Wyckfield." she exclaimed excitedly. "Egad, I've never *seen* anything like it!"

Miss Townley tottered from the carriage and added her exclamations to theirs. Everyone was speaking at once. While Camilla tried to piece the story together from their incoherent ravings, Thomas slid down from the box and went round to the back. He ached in every bone and wanted only to stretch out on the bed in the narrow attic room that was his temporary home.

How he managed to climb the stairs he never knew. He let himself into his room, pulled off his ruined coat and threw it in a corner. He also tried to remove his shoes, but the effort proved too much for him. Gingerly, he laid himself down on the bed and shut his eyes. He thought fleetingly that he ought to wash himself and examine the extent of his wounds, but he didn't move. Of all the aches and pains he was aware of, he decided that his nose hurt him most. He wondered how badly mangled it was, and if he'd be disfigured for life, but he realized with surprise that he didn't much care. In truth, he felt wonderful. There was considerable satisfaction in having faced disaster head on and defeated it.

His mind roamed over the events of the day. Everything was quite clear except the struggle with the horses. That part was nothing but a blur. But the rest...the feel of the little girls' tears on his neck, the tension of the search for Russ in the hedges along the road, the relief when they'd brought him to the doctor in Aldershot (who'd said the coachman had had a heart seizure but would undoubtedly recover if he could remain in Aldershot in complete rest for a fortnight or so), the look on Camilla's face when her daughter had run into her arms...these were memories that would always give him a feeling of pride.

He was just drifting into sleep when he heard a tapping at his door. "Come in," he said, his tongue strangely thick.

The door opened, and Camilla, carrying a branched candlestick, came into the room, followed by Betsy who carried a basin and a small pile of clean cloths. While Camilla placed the candlestick on the room's one table, Betsy grinned at him from the foot of the bed. "We heard ye acted the hero again, ye cawker," she whispered fondly.

"Oh, good heavens, look at his poor *face*," Camilla moaned, staring down at him in horror. "Betsy, let's have the basin, quickly!"

Ignoring his thickly muttered objections, they bathed the blood and dirt from his face. There were several cuts and bruises, and the nose was undoubtedly broken, but Camilla doubted that there would be permanent disfigurement. They were just about to leave and send Daniel in to undress him when Betsy gasped, "Oh, my lady, just look at his *wrist!*"

Camilla sank down on the edge of the bed, lifted his arm to her lap and pushed back his shirtsleeve. The sight of the raw wounds made her wince. "Oh, *Thomas!*" she whispered, the tears filling her eyes.

"Don't make a fuss, ma'am," he said tiredly. "They'll heal."

"Betsy, run and fetch the herb ointment in my m-medicine drawer. And I think we shall need some more b-bandages."

Betsy scurried out. Camilla sat staring at the lacerated wrist in her lap, the tears rolling down her cheeks. Tom, feeling a drop splash into his palm, pulled himself up on one elbow and stared at her. "Are you *crying* over me?" he asked in amazement.

"Yes, I c-certainly am," she stammered with a little sniff.

"But there's no need. I'll mend soon enough."

"I kn-know."

"Then, why—"

She turned to him, her tears sparkling in the candlelight. The look in her eyes gave him a twist of pain so strong that it made his broken nose seem like a tickle. "I was s-so cruel to you . . . and you have g-given me the greatest gift," she said tearfully. "I am more beholden to you than to anyone in the world. I d-don't know what you did for D-Daniel, but if it was something like this, I now fully understand why he is so loyal to you."

He groaned in disgust and threw himself down on his pillow. "I don't want your gratitude, nor Daniel's either. Gratitude is a . . . a damned *puny* little emotion. That's not what keeps Daniel and me together. It's something much stronger, something not possible between you and me. So don't waste your tears, ma'am."

She got up, placed his arm gently at his side and gazed down at him. "If not gratitude, what is it you *want* me to feel, Thomas?" she asked softly.

He stared up at her, his eyes lingering on the wet cheeks, the curve of her throat, the glow of the hair that had fallen over her shoulder. But after a moment, he shook his head and smiled the ironic smile she'd seen so many times before. "No, I won't tell you now. In your gratitude, you might offer it to me, and it's something that goes ill with gratitude."

Slowly, with trance-like gentleness, she reached out a hand and touched his cheek. Tom, with every intention of brushing it away, put his hand on hers, but before he realized what he'd done, he'd lifted it to his mouth and pressed his lips into her palm. The skin of her palm was soft and incredibly sweet-smelling, and his heart began to pound. He heard her make a small intake of breath, and he knew that, whatever the cost— in physical pain now and in anguish later—he was going to take her in his arms.

But the door banged open, and Betsy bustled in, Daniel at her heels. Camilla, shaken back to her senses, snatched her hand away. With eyes lowered, she sat down beside him and applied the salve to his wrist. While she busied herself bandaging it, Daniel chortled with such pride over his friend's performance that Tom growled at him to stop making such a bother.

The wrists bandaged, Camilla and Betsy went to the door.

"You do realize, Thomas" Camilla said, pausing in the doorway, "that, under the circumstances, it will be quite impossible for me to sack you now."

Thomas lifted himself up on one elbow and fixed an enigmatic eye on her. "Will it, ma'am?"

"Of course." Her voice was unexpectedly choked and unsteady, and her eyes wavered from his discomfitting look. "You may remain in my employ for as long as you like."

There was a moment of awkward silence, during which Thomas peered at her outline silhouetted in the doorway. The candles at his bedside shone in his eyes, setting up a smokey barrier of light that obscured her face. He yearned to see her expression—to learn if a last, tiny remnant of that look he'd seen in her face a few moments ago still remained. But he could see only the halo that the light from the corridor made of her hair. *Damnation*, he thought, *it's the second time I've lost the opportunity to hold her in my arms.* He wondered if life would ever offer him another. The answer came to him in a wave of crushing despair; when, even if he remained in her employ forever, would there come another night like this?

Betsy, who'd been watching her mistress in immobile fascination, was the first to move. She made a motion of her hand to a puzzled, gaping Daniel to start taking off Tom's shoes. While Daniel bent to his work, Camilla raised her eyes and fixed them firmly on Thomas's face. "I shall bid you goodnight now, Thomas, because I . . . I don't know what else to say. But I hope you know that you will always have my gratitude . . . always . . . for what you did today . . . whether you wish for it or no. You may find it a puny emotion, but I am so . . . so filled with it that it doesn't seem at all puny to me."

She left the room, and Betsy followed, closing the door behind her. Tom fell back upon his pillow and stared up at the ceiling, letting Daniel remove his clothes and chatter away unheeded. *Gratitude!* he thought in disgust. She might be filled with it, but he didn't want it. Compared with what he wanted her to feel for him, gratitude was a crumb, a mote, a nothing!

She had offered it to him with a gentle, sweet generosity, and more than once. But the last time she'd offered it—there at the door, where he couldn't even see her face!—he recognized even without seeing her eyes that she'd bestowed it as a barrier—a wall she'd hastily erected to prevent any other emotion from finding its way inside her.

Well, he knew better than to butt against a wall. But as for her substitute of gratitude . . . let her keep it!

Chapter Twelve

In the warming room, Pippa sat up on the table swinging her legs and reading aloud from her very own collection of the plays of Mr. William Shakespeare, while Thomas performed his Wednesday afternoon chore of polishing the silver. He had read some Shakespeare in his youth and had always carried a dog-eared copy of *The Tempest* in his seabag, but he'd never seen a performance on the stage. The precocious child, perched on the table next to him, was reading aloud from *King John* with an enchanting dramatic verve, and Thomas's polishing cloth grew still very often as he paused to watch the girl with amazed and admiring enjoyment.

"Then King Philip says, *'How much unlooked for is this expedition,'*" Pippa declaimed in tones of convincing alarm. "And then the King of Austria answers,

> *By how much unexpected, by so much*
> *We must awake for defense,*
> *For courage mounteth with occasion.*"

She paused, looked up over her spectacles at the footman thoughtfully and asked, "What do you suppose he meant by that?"

"That courage mounts with the occasion? I suppose he means that one manages to act courageously when the situation demands it."

"Is that why *you* acted so bravely that day when we came home from Wyckfield? Because the situation demanded it?"

"Of course. Why else?"

"I don't know. It seems an inadequate explanation. *I* was in the same situation, and *my* courage didn't mount with the occasion. I was frightened to death."

"So was I, Miss Pippa, so was I! But you were much too little to do anything about the situation, and you knew it. I, on the other hand, am a rather big fellow—and I knew I was the only person on the scene who *could* do something. So I did it."

"Are you saying that *everyone* in such a situation would have acted as you did?"

"Most everyone. Isn't that what Mr. Shakespeare is saying as well?"

"It's what Mr. Shakespeare is saying that the Duke of Austria is saying. I don't believe that most everyone would have done it, and I don't think Mr. Shakespeare would think so either. After all, Miss Townley is a very good person, and *she* fainted dead away."

"That's not at all fair. Miss Townley was as helpless as you were," Thomas pointed out. He returned to his polishing with a troubled frown. "You mustn't make a hero of me, Miss Pippa. Heroes are for story-books, not for real life."

Pippa grinned. "You're heroic to be so modest about it, you know."

He shook his head. "No, I don't want to joke about this. I think its important that you understand. If you make an ordinary man into a hero, you'll expect him always to act heroically. But, since he's only ordinary, he'll be bound to let you down."

"You're not ordinary, Thomas. And you won't let me down." The little girl smiled at him with serene confidence and returned to her reading. But Thomas could no longer concentrate on her rendering of the drama. He was filled with misgivings. He didn't like being made a hero . . . not by Pippa nor by her mother. It made him deucedly uncomfortable. How would they feel if they knew the truth—that their hero was an escaped criminal with a charge of murder hanging over his head?

As the winter settled in with a dogged determination to keep the populace close to their firesides, the house in Upper Seymour Street became the quiet, comfortable haven that Camilla had envisioned. Callers stopped by when the weather permitted, and she and Pippa paid occasional visits to their new friends, but their social life was not as demanding as it had been during the holidays. As far as Camilla was concerned, this was just what she liked. Although the young Lord Earlywine still called more frequently than she wished, she'd learned that she could tell him flatly to go away, and the fellow would take himself off without offense. On the other hand, Sir James's attentions were just right for her purposes, for he was delighted to escort her to the theater and to parties without wishing for—or expecting—a real romance to develop between them. With Georgina as a friend and Sir James as an escort, Camilla's social life was as full as she wanted it to be.

There was only one fly in her ointment—the arrival twice weekly of letters from Wyckfield. There was not one which didn't mention the imaginary Mr. Petersham with disdain. Ethelyn wanted constant reports on the progress of the affair, obviously in the hope that matters would take a turn to cause Camilla to break off "this strange and suspect relationship." As a result, Camilla spent many hours at her desk, biting the tip of her pen as she concentrated her mind on the detailed creation of a perfect suitor.

She began to grow quite fond of her Mr. Petersham. She felt a bit like the author of a novel as she developed the details of his character and appearance. She made him very wise for his years, and very gentle in his dealings with others. She made him generous to a fault, telling Ethelyn that his friends frequently came to him to borrow money. *He even hands out soverigns to beggars on the street*, she wrote, *which makes me believe (although of course I have not asked him) that he is very well to pass*.

She began to see him in her mind and even to hear the quality of his voice. He was tall, of course, with thick sandy hair and a charming moustache. He had a youthful swing to his walk, a ready smile and a way of making her laugh at the most unexpected times. *The other day,* she related to Ethelyn, *I remarked that I hadn't heard what he'd said because I'd been lost in thought. "Were you?" he quipped. "I didn't know you were a stranger there."* Actually it was a jibe that she'd overheard Thomas throw at Pippa, but it served her purpose very well.

As the weeks passed and Mr. Petersham's character became more distinct, Camilla found herself almost enjoying the letter writing. There was something pleasing about creating a character, making him both unique and believable, and imagining how he would behave in various situations. She wrote to her sister-in-law about a dinner party and included a detailed account of what Mr. Petersham had eaten. (He would enjoy the roasts and the fowl, she decided, but he'd spurn the fish and the sweetmeats.) She created a little drama in which she was strolling with him down Bond Street which was crowded with people and carriages, and, right beside her, a pair of horses shied and broke into a gallop. *It was only by Mr. Petersham's quick thinking and adept manipulation in snatching me out of the way,* she wrote, *that I was saved from being hideously trampled to death.*

In response to that little tale, however, Ethelyn wrote frigidly that she remained unimpressed. *It is quite appropriate for you to feel grateful to Mr. Petersham, Camilla, but gratitude is scarcely a reason for betrothal. I have yet to read, in all the mass of detail you write about his character and manner, any proof of the rectitude of his morals, the depth of his religious convictions or the quality of his connections. Until these things are answered, I shall not feel easy in my mind about this association. Incidentally, Camilla, I hope that during that Bond Street stroll you and Mr. Petersham were not without chaperonage. Do not tell me again that you are of age. You are an unwed woman and should not be gallivanting about town with only a gentleman for company. I am assuming that a footman or some other servant was walking behind you, for otherwise you would have set tongues wagging. It can do you no service to be spoken of as fast. If ever that epithet attaches itself to your name, I shall not, even with my influence, be able to convince Mr. Harbage that you are suitable for him.*

Camilla seethed with rage. There seemed to be no end to her sister-in-law's determination to run her life. Angrily, she paced about the sitting room trying to find a way to end Ethelyn's irritating nagging. Suddenly a wicked smile lit her face. She ran over to her desk, trimmed a pen and impetuously dashed off a note to end these arguments over her suitor once and for all:

Dear Ethelyn,

Your last letter arrived yesterday and gave me much amusement, especially the realization that you still had hopes of making a match between your Mr. Harbage and myself. You will be surprised, I am sure, to learn that I am no longer available for Mr. Harbage or any other gentleman you may find suitable for me. Have you guessed, my dear? Yes, Mr. Petersham and I are wed! It was a small, simple ceremony befitting my status as widow and mother of a ten-year-old child, and it was followed by a dinner in my own dining room at which nothing unusual was served except champagne. You, my dear Ethelyn, are the very first to know. I hope you will be as happy for me as I am for myself.

It wasn't until she'd sent it off that Camilla began to feel misgivings. The letter had seemed, at first, like a little prank— a playful slap at Ethelyn's overweening presumption. But once the letter had been posted, she recognized that she'd indulged in an enormous, bald-faced, impulsive and shameful lie. It was so great a lie that she winced inside at the realization that she was capable of such deception. What if someone close to her, someone here in London, learned what she'd done? How could she face the world?

Worse than anything, what if *Pippa* learned of it? Pippa, to whom she'd never told a lie in all these years. How would Pippa regard a mother who'd erected a complete, elaborate structure of fabrications and deceits?

She would have to confess to Ethelyn, of course. That was the only solution. But a confession would have unbearable ramifications. Her head swam with sickening terror just thinking about them. First Ethelyn would write several vituperative, stinging letters about Camilla's sinfulness and depravity. Next would come the accusations that she'd fallen into corruption only since moving to London. Then would follow the insistence that they return to Wyckfield. And when Ethelyn had achieved *that,* Camilla had the horrifying premonition that she would find herself *married to Mr. Harbage* just to expiate her sin!

For the next few days, Camilla moved about the house in

a kind of trance. She was aware that Pippa and Miss Townley watched her with worried eyes, but she couldn't seem to rouse herself to make a decision on a course of action. The problem circled round and round her brain. On the one hand, the lie was too enormous to live with. On the other, Ethelyn's revenge was too unbearable to contemplate.

In her attack of guilt and fear, she didn't think about Ethelyn's more immediate reaction to the news of her supposed marriage. In her agony over what to do about the lie, it quite slipped her mind that, to Ethelyn, the news of her wedding at this time was still the *truth*. So when she came to the breakfast room one morning, only four days after the letter had been posted, she had no inkling that matters were about to be taken out of her hands.

She kissed Pippa on the cheek and said good morning to Miss Townley with forced good cheer. Pippa and Miss Townley exchanged worried glances. "Are you feeling well, Mama?" Pippa asked in concern.

"I'm fine, love. Why do you ask? Do I look hagged?"

"Not hagged," the girl said kindly. "Just a bit . . . tired."

"You look worse than hagged," Miss Townley contradicted bluntly. "I'd guess you haven't had a good night's sleep in a week. You can't make me believe, Miss Camilla, that there isn't somethin' amiss."

"Don't bully her, Miss Townley," Pippa said in staunch defense of her mother. "She'd tell us if there was something really wrong, wouldn't you, Mama?"

Camilla smiled at her daughter fondly and rumpled her hair. "I would if I felt it was your concern," she said, taking her place and reaching for the teapot.

"That's not right, Mama. Not right at all. If something was troubling *me,* you'd expect me to reveal it, even if it weren't your concern, wouldn't you?"

"But *everything* about you is my concern, dearest."

"And everything about you is mine," her daughter retorted promptly.

"The child is right," Miss Townley declared. "You've been wanderin' about this house like a frightened ghost for days now, and we think it's time you told us about it. But I won't bully you. Just want you to know we're more worried *not* knowin' than we'd be if we were told. That's all I'm goin' to say. Now drink your tea and read your letter in peace."

"Letter?" Camilla asked, the teacup beginning to shake in her hand.

"Right there beside you," Pippa said. "It's from Aunt Ethelyn. I recognize the hand."

Camilla slowly put down the cup. Aware that Miss Townley and Pippa were watching her, she concentrated on keeping up an appearance of calm. She picked up the letter, broke the seal and, with her lips pressed tightly together, she scanned the page.

Before Pippa's and the governess's horrified eyes, Camilla's face turned ash-white. "Mama! What *is* it?" Pippa cried.

"Good God!" Camilla gasped. "Ethelyn . . . she's *coming here!*"

Chapter Thirteen

Camilla's announcement seemed to her listeners to be completely inadequate to explain her evident dismay. "Is Aunt Ethelyn coming for a visit?" Pippa asked, puzzled. "I don't see . . . Is there something troubling about that?"

But her mother didn't answer. She just stared straight ahead of her with unseeing eyes. Miss Townley, with the familiarity of life-long closeness, reached over and pulled the letter from Camilla's nerveless hand. *"My dear Camilla,"* she read aloud, *"if you are expecting our good wishes, you will be disappointed. Oswald and I are shocked and offended that you saw fit to take such a step without first seeking our approval . . ."* She looked up at Camilla curiously. "What step?" she asked bluntly.

Camilla turned to her and made an attempt to answer. But her courage and her voice failed her, and she merely pressed her lips together and shook her head. With a helpless wave of her hand, she signaled her old governess to go on.

Miss Townley returned to her reading. *"Our first reaction after the shock of your announcement was anger. We almost decided to cut ourselves off from any connection with you at all. But after a night filled with prayer and meditation, I thought better of taking such a drastic step without seeking further enlightenment. After all, I do have Philippa to think about. Therefore, we have decided to meet your Mr. Petersham before we judge him . . ."*

"Who's Mr. Petersham?" Pippa asked.

Camilla cast her daughter a look of agonized shame and dropped her head in her hands.

"Petersham . . . Petersham . . ." Miss Townley mused. "You've mentioned that name to me. I remember! The day Pippa and I left for Wyckfield. Who *is* he, Miss Camilla? What sort of fix have you fallen into?"

"J-Just read the rest," Camilla mumbled from behind her hands.

". . . before we judge him. As much as I despise the prospect of setting foot within the environs of that loathsome city where you've chosen to reside, Oswald and I will pay a visit and see for ourselves what sort of husband you've chosen. Good God! *Husband?"*

Pippa gasped. "Mama? Has Aunt Ethelyn gone mad?"

"No, dearest," Camilla said, lifting her head and throwing her daughter a glance of abject shame, "I think *I* have."

"Have you *married* someone?" Miss Townley asked, aghast.

"No, of course not. That is . . . not exactly."

"Not exactly?" Miss Townley frowned at her in disgust. "What sort of answer is that? Either one is married or one isn't."

"I'm not married. Surely you must know that." Camilla's cheeks became suffused with color. "But I've let Ethelyn believe I am."

"Good heavens! *How?"*

"I just wrote and told her I'd done it."

"But, Mama, do you mean to say that you concocted a *lie?"* Pippa stared at her mother with something akin to awe.

Camilla's eyes filled with tears, and she nodded in humiliation. "Yes, I did. Oh, Pippa, I'm so *ashamed*—"

"What I'd like to know," Miss Townley demanded, "is *why?* I've known you too long, Miss Camilla, to believe that you'd do such a thing without provocation."

Camilla shook her head. "Thank you for saying that, Ada. It's kind of you to try to find justification for what I've done. And I *did* have provocation, but it doesn't excuse—"

"I ain't impressed with self-flagellation," Miss Townley growled. "Just tell us why you did it."

"Well, you see, Ethelyn had taken it into her head that it was time for me to remarry. She'd even found someone whom she considered suitable. Pippa, my love, I hope you're able, at your tender age, to understand and forgive me for what I've done and what I'm going to say. I was not very happy in my marriage to your father, you see, and—"

"Oh, I knew that. I've always known. Papa was not the sort with whom one could be . . . well, comfortable."

"Pippa!" Camilla blinked at her daughter in astonishment. "I didn't dream you could discern—"

"Children can discern a great deal more than parents imagine. Sybil and I were talking about it just the other day. But do go on with your explanation, Mama. I'm all agog to learn who this Mr. Petersham is."

"He isn't anyone. That is, he isn't anyone real."

"I'm becomin' very muddled, Miss Camilla," the governess sighed. "I wish you'd tell the story straight."

"I'm trying to. Oh, dear, where was I?"

"You were saying that you weren't very happy in your marriage," Pippa reminded her.

"Yes. And I am determined not to marry again. Ever. I want us to be able to remain just as we are now, all by ourselves, with no one to order us about or dominate our lives. And things were going along so well for us when Ethelyn started to thrust her Mr. Harbage before me—"

"Harbage?" Pippa's eyebrows rose. "Mr. *Josiah* Harbage?"

"Yes." Camilla was baffled. "How did you know?"

"He came to dinner while Sybil and I were at Wyckfield. I *met* him. He *couldn't* be the man Aunt Ethelyn wants you to wed."

"But he is."

Pippa whooped. "Mr. *Harbage?* He's as fat as Uncle Oswald and as sour as a lemon! All he ever talks about is vice and sin. He lectured us on all of the deadly ones except gluttony, which is the sin he forgets about because he indulges in it all the time. Aunt Ethelyn must think you're past your last prayers."

For the first time that morning, Camilla laughed. "But I *am* past my last prayers, you goose. What sort of man besides the Josiah Harbages of this world would want to wed a thirty-year-old matron with a saucy daughter?"

"I'll wager there are scores of eligibles who'd jump at the chance. After all, you *are* beautiful, and Sybil says that *that* is what counts most with gentlemen."

"Be that as it may," Miss Townley interjected crisply, "I've yet to learn the identity of the mysterious Mr. Petersham."

"It's no mystery, Ada. I just made him up."

"What?"

"Well, what else was I to do? I didn't want Mr. Harbage foisted upon me—for I didn't need Pippa's description of him to guess what he was like—and I couldn't seem to convince Ethelyn that I wished to avoid wedlock at all costs. So I created a suitor for myself as a sort of protection. And, since I had to refer to him in my letters, I gave him a name. Mr. Petersham."

"Oh, Mama, *Petersham?*" The child giggled disparagingly. "You could have given yourself away right there. Didn't you see the *sham* in it?"

"Of course I did. It was there on purpose."

"Well," Pippa conceded, "it was an inventive plan, I'll grant you that."

"Thank you," her mother said drily.

"Very artful. I had no idea, Mama, that you were so ingenious."

"Does that mean," Camilla asked, eyeing her daughter hopefully, "that you don't despise me?"

"Despise you? How silly! I only wish I could have *helped* you. I might have thought of a better name than Petersham."

"No doubt you would, you little egotist," her governess said, "but we still haven't heard the whole. Miss Camilla, what gave Lady Ethelyn the impression that you've *wed* this nonexistent Mr. Petersham?"

Camilla's eyes clouded over, and she got wearily to her feet. *"I* gave her that impression. I announced my wedding in my last letter. It was a foolish and impulsive lie, and I don't know what to do about it." She walked to the window and looked out at the small, winter-browned garden below. "In a fit of pique, I wrote her that I'd wed him, hoping to silence her on the subject of Mr. Harbage once and for all. The moment I posted the letter I realized how stupid I'd been. Now I shall

have to admit to her that I've been lying to her for months."
Her head, lowered in dejection, rested on the glass, and her
voice became choked with tears. "Heaven only knows *what*
she'll demand of me in atonement. Nothing short of wedlock
with the gluttonous Mr. Harbage, I suppose."

"Oh, Mama, no! You *wouldn't!*"

"Of course she wouldn't," Miss Townley snapped with as-
perity. "After all, Lady Ethelyn doesn't *own* her. I don't know
why your mother can't seem to be able to stand up to that
woman."

"You think me cowardly, don't you?" Camilla turned around
to face her accuser. "But it's not as simple as that. Pippa is a
Wyckfield, you know, and will be head of the family when
she comes of age. If I permit a rift in the family now, it will
be Pippa who'll have to mend it later."

"Rubbish. You're only looking for excuses. Pippa already
handles Lady Ethelyn better than you do."

"Nevertheless, it will not serve my daughter well to antag-
onize her only family. She'd not thank me for it in years to
come."

"But, Mama, you can't make a sacrifice of yourself just to
keep peace in the family, you know."

Camilla sighed. "I know. That's why I made up that ridiculous lie. But I've only succeeded in making matters worse.
Now it seems that my only alternatives are either a complete
rift or complete self-sacrifice."

Pippa leaned her chin on her hand thoughtfully. "There *is*
another way . . ."

"What other way?"

"We can find a Mr. Petersham for Aunt Ethelyn to meet."

Miss Townley and Camilla both turned to Pippa openmouthed. "What's that you say?" the governess asked in bewilderment.

"But Pippa, Mr. Petersham doesn't exist," her mother reminded her.

"I know he doesn't exist. But couldn't we find someone to
play his part while Aunt Ethelyn is visiting?"

"Play his part?" Camilla came back to the table, peering at
her daughter in fascination. "But that's . . . impossible . . ."

"I don't know, Miss Camilla. Per'aps the child has somethin' there. We *could* convince some gentleman to play the
part, couldn't we?"

"I don't see how. And besides, what good would it do?"

"He could stay here for the length of Lady Ethelyn's stay. We'd coach him to behave in as proper and decorous a manner as possible, so that Lady Ethelyn would approve of him. Then, as soon as he's won her over, she will go home in perfect contentment, and we shall go on as before."

Camilla studied the two upturned faces that gazed at her expectantly. They seemed to her to have gone mad, both at the same time. "This is utterly ridiculous. That both of you, who are always so sensible and wise, should have agreed on so wild a plan quite amazes me."

"It's not so wild, Mama. We have to concoct *something*, you know. You've seemed so happy these last months. I don't want to see you sad again."

"Nor do I," Miss Townley agreed. "If it will take a Mr. Petersham to keep Ethelyn from making you miserable, a Mr. Petersham you shall have."

"But how? Where? *Who?*"

"How about your young caller, Lord Earlywine?" Miss Townley suggested.

"Earlywine? He's only a boy of twenty-two! Ethelyn would never believe—! I told her *all about* Mr. Petersham. I described him in every detail—how he looks, what he's like, even what he *eats!"*

"Well, what *is* he like? Describe him to us."

"He's thirty-five years old, for one thing. He's tall and sandy-haired, for another. And he's generous, kind, humorous, open-hearted—"

"Quite a paragon," Miss Townley muttered drily. "You don't suppose Sir James might pass?"

"Sir *James?* Out of the question."

"Why? He's old enough, and his hair might pass for sandy—"

"He's *too* old. And much too stocky. And he's too hearty and boisterous to pass for my Mr. Petersham. Besides, I'd be much too embarrassed to ask such a thing of him."

Miss Townley drummed her fingers thoughtfully on the table. "Then I suppose the only thing to do would be to advertise for an actor—"

"An actor?" Camilla echoed in revulsion. "How can you suggest that we bring a stranger into the house? Really, Ada, you *must* see how impossible—"

A gasp from her daughter interrupted her. Pippa had been listening to the discussion with silent but rapt attention, her eyes growing wider and wider as an idea occurred to her. Now her whole face lit with excitement. "I know who'd be *perfect*," she announced importantly.

"Who?" Miss Townley leaned forward in fascination.

"We need someone tall, right?"

"Yes," the governess prodded.

"Lean?"

"Yes . . ."

"With sandy hair . . . and just a few years older than Mama?"

"Yes! You can't mean that you know someone who *fits*, do you?"

"Don't be so silly, Ada." Camilla was finding the discussion ludicrous. The entire scheme was too far-fetched to consider seriously. "Who can the child know who has those attributes, as well as being generous—"

"Generous, kind, humorous and open-hearted?" Pippa laughed triumphantly and jumped from her chair. She wheeled around to her mother and threw her arms about her waist in an effusive embrace. "He'd be *perfect*, Mama! Absolutely perfect!"

"Who, child, *who?*" her governess queried avidly.

"Thomas, of course!" The child whirled her mother about in dizzy delight. "Our *very own Thomas!*"

Chapter Fourteen

"Thomas?" Miss Townley knit her brows. "Thomas *who?*"

But Camilla knew, from the first mention of his name, whom Pippa meant. "She is referring, I believe, to our footman."

"Miss Pippa, you can't be serious. You can't expect your mother to embark on this plot with an ordinary *servant*."

Pippa drew up in offense. She couldn't see any validity in the objection. "I certainly do! Why shouldn't she? He has all the necessary qualities. Besides, Thomas *isn't* ordinary. He reads Shakespeare."

Miss Townley, on second thought, had to agree that he wasn't ordinary. "But... but it just isn't *done*," she muttered, trying to rationalize her objection.

Camilla had to laugh. "Making up a husband out of whole cloth isn't done either, for that matter."

"That's true enough," the governess conceded, trying to imagine Thomas as master of the house. "And the fellow certainly *looks* the part."

"And he speaks as well as Lord Earlywine," Pippa pointed out. "Better, if you ask me."

"And I wouldn't be surprised if he could charm Lady Ethelyn

right out of her shoes with that crooked smile of his," Miss Townley mused. "Betsy says that half the maids are openly in love with him, and the other half pretend they're not."

"You don't say," Camilla muttered in disgust. "I'm surprised we get any work done in this house at all, with that sort of thing going on."

"But you do agree, don't you," Pippa insisted, "that he's the perfect choice?"

"Seems a good possibility to me," Miss Townley concurred.

"You are both being utterly nonsensical. Even if Thomas *were* suitable, which I don't agree at all that he is, the plan is still unworkable.",

Miss Townley glowered at her. "I don't see why you say that."

"Look here. Suppose we do fool Ethelyn, and suppose she goes off convinced that I've made a satisfactory match, don't you see that it's only a temporary reprieve? Sooner or later she's bound to learn the truth, and then I'll be in worse case."

"Why would she be bound to learn it?" Pippa asked.

"Why indeed?" Miss Townley seconded. "All you need do is keep concocting stories about him."

"But what if Ethelyn asks to see him again?"

"You can make excuses," Miss Townley suggested. "Say he's gone abroad. Or he's engaged in important governmental activities."

"Or," Pippa added mischievously, "you can say he's 'passed to his reward,' just as Papa did."

"Pippa, what a shocking thing to say! Do you *see* what I've done, Ada? I've made a lying little devil out of my daughter!"

Pippa grinned. "Yes, isn't it appalling?"

"Pippa, this is no laughing matter! If Aunt Ethelyn had heard that last remark, she would have been quite justified in saying that I'm poisoning your immortal soul."

"Oh, stuff and nonsense!" Miss Townley declared. "No one can tell me that heaven wouldn't forgive a little girl for devisin' an innocent fabrication to protect her mother from the revenge of a domineerin' dragon."

"But I don't *wish* to be protected by my daughter. What sort of milksop do you take me for? I shall tell Ethelyn the truth and face whatever comes of it."

Pippa looked up at her mother with her calm, older-than-her-years directness. "And let Aunt Ethelyn bully you on the subject forever more?"

Camilla winced. "Do you think it will be as bad as that?"

"*I* think," Miss Townley declared, "that she'll be at you until you give in and wed someone she picks out for you."

"So do I," Pippa said.

Her mother glanced at the child and then at the governess, the frown-lines deepening on her brow. "If you both have combined forces to unsettle me, you are succeeding very well," she muttered, sinking upon a chair.

"Let's try the ruse, Mama," her daughter urged.

"If it works, you may win yourself a long period of peace," Miss Townley pointed out. "And if it fails, you won't be in worse case than you are now."

Pippa came up behind Camilla's chair and put an arm about her mother's sagging shoulders. "Don't be afraid, Mama. Thomas will make the scheme work, I know he will. But even if he doesn't, think how much fun we'll have had in the meantime."

"*Fun!*" Camilla gave a tearful little laugh and pulled her daughter into her lap. "You naughty puss! You've become so much like your friend Sybil that I almost can't tell you apart. When all this is over, you and I shall have to have a talk about your new attitudes. A *very long* talk!"

Pippa snuggled into her mother's embrace. "Does this mean you're going to *do* it?"

Camilla hesitated. "I don't know, Pippa. My Mr. Petersham is a very gentle sort..."

"So is Thomas."

"Thomas, *gentle?* Really, Pippa, I know he saved your life and all that, but you mustn't make a paragon of him."

"That's what Thomas tells me, too. But he's always very gentle with *me*, you know."

"And Lady Ethelyn won't know what a sharp tongue he can have when aroused. She's never seen him, after all," Miss Townley added.

"But what if he lets his spirit loosen his tongue in front of Ethelyn?" Camilla wondered.

"We'll train him not to. How much time do we have to prepare?"

"Not long. I believe Ethelyn said in the letter that they

plan to arrive as soon as the weather eases. Mid-March, I expect."

"Mid-March? That gives us almost a month." Miss Townley rose briskly. "I should think that will be plenty of time in which to prepare ourselves. Meanwhile, Miss Pippa, I think it's time you and I made for the schoolroom. We are already late for your history lesson."

Pippa slipped from her mother's lap and followed her governess to the door, while Camilla reached for the teapot to try to soothe her upset nerves with a fresh cup of tea. "Good heavens!" she gasped suddenly. "I forgot!"

"Forgot what?" Miss Townley asked, turning in alarm.

"That my Mr. Petersham has a moustache. I wonder how long it takes for a man to grow one. Do you think, Ada, that Thomas will be able to grow one in a month?"

As far as Miss Townley was concerned, the moustache was the least of the problems. A more immediate concern was getting her mistress to generate enough courage to ask Thomas to participate in the masquerade. Somehow, Camilla kept postponing the task. The whole subject was so embarrassing to her that she felt too uncomfortable to tell the footman the details. Every day she promised Miss Townley that she would do it "tomorrow."

Finally, Miss Townley took matters into her own hands. One frigid evening, when dinner was over and Pippa had gone up to bed, Miss Townley sought the footman out in the servants' dining room. "Her ladyship'd like to see you, Thomas," she said mendaciously. "She's in the sittin' room."

But Camilla was not expecting to see anyone. She had settled into a comfortable easy chair with a copy of Marie Edgeworth's novel, *Castle Rackrent,* which Georgina had given her. She'd taken off her shoes and was toasting her toes on the hearth, completely engrossed in the romantic tale with its unusual Irish setting, when the tap on her door distracted her. "Come in," she called, scarcely looking up.

"You wished to see me, ma'am," he asked.

She snatched her feet from the hearth. "I?"

"Yes, ma'am. Miss Townley said—"

"Oh, *did* she?" Camilla colored to her ears and tried to tuck her stockinged feet under her. "Then I suppose . . . yes, well, come in and . . . er . . . close the door, Thomas."

He did so with perfect, footmanlike precision and then stood erect at her elbow. She noticed with wry amusement that now, when it didn't matter, he was beginning to master the techniques of inaudible, invisible service. She cast him a sidelong glance, rubbed her forehead with nervous fingers, and sighed deeply. "I have something to ask of you, Thomas . . . a most enormous favor . . ."

"Yes, my lady?"

She hesitated. "Dash it all, I can't explain this to you while you're standing over me in that stiff, impersonal way. Do sit down."

"Sit down, ma'am? You can't mean it. Is this some sort of test of my sense of decorum? If there's anything I've learned since I've been in your service, it's that I must *not* sit down in the presence of my mistress."

"Yes, but I wish to ignore the rules this once. *Please* sit down."

"Very well, ma'am, but if Mr. Hicks should come in and see me, I hope you will explain to him that I'm doing it only in obedience to your orders."

"Good heavens, but you've become a stickler. Or else you're roasting me with decidedly malicious enjoyment. Are you going to sit down or not?"

"Where would you like me to sit, ma'am? On the floor at your feet?"

She glared at him. "Now I know you're roasting me. Sit down anywhere you like, and keep your barbs to yourself."

He sat down on the hearth before her and, with a kind of natural grace, stretched one long leg out before him. She couldn't help but notice how well it was shaped, for the tight breeches of his livery and the knit stockings revealed every curve and swell. She smiled to herself, remembering her conversation with the tradesman who'd sold her the servants' uniforms and liveries. He'd tried to sell her some special pads which, he explained, all the footmen in the great houses put in their stockings to make their calves appear well-developed. "Ye wouldn't want yer footmen to 'ave legs like sticks, would ye, me lady?" he'd asked. She'd responded that sticks would suit her well enough so long as the owner could walk on them. It was just as well she hadn't bought those pads. Thomas certainly had no need of them.

"Does this place suit you, ma'am?" Thomas asked from the hearth.

"Yes, that's fine." But it was not really fine, for his back was to the fire, and she had difficulty seeing his face. However, she didn't see how she could comfortably ask him to change his place after she'd given him free choice. "I asked to see you, Thomas, because I...I..." Her courage failed her. "How's your nose these days?" she asked, switching the subject abruptly.

"It's healed, ma'am. No pain any more. Just this funny little knob on the bridge."

"And your wrist? Is it badly scarred?"

"No, my lady, it's not. And since I assume you didn't request my presence just to ask about my health, I'll save you the trouble of making further polite inquiry by telling you that the rest of my anatomy is in equally satisfactory condition."

She glared at him. "I sometimes wonder, Thomas, if your doctor in Derbyshire really died. He isn't dead at all, is he? If I wrote to him, I suspect I'd learn that he drove you out without a recommendation, because of your saucy tongue. It's hard for me to believe that your brazen wit hadn't landed you in trouble long before I came into contact with it."

"No one ever said, ma'am, that my tongue didn't land me in hot water before my meeting with you. It's gotten me into difficulty more times than I care to remember."

"Then one would think a person of your sense should have learned, by this time, to curb it."

"Yes, one would think so, wouldn't one?" He grinned up at her unabashed. "The answer must be that I'm not as sensible as you think. But about that favor you wished to ask of me..."

"Favor? Oh...yes." She closed the book on her lap and fiddled nervously with its ribbon, a device which should have been used to mark her place. "This is a very awkward subject to have to discuss with you, Thomas, and I don't know quite how to begin. It...concerns my...er...marital state."

"Yes?"

She wished desperately that she could get a better look at his face. Were his eyes mocking her? "I am, as you know, a widow, and my late husband's sister has taken it into her head that I should remarry." She paused awkwardly, wondering just how to phrase her synopsis of the whole, unpleasant situation, especially the humiliating request she had to make of him.

"You're surely not asking if I concur with your sister-in-law's suggestion, are you?"

"No, of course not! What an arrogant idea!"

"Then you probably want to know which of the current candidates I would recommend, is that it?"

She gasped in outrage. "*What* current candidates?"

"Lord Earlywine and Sir James. If you ask me, neither one is worth a second look."

"I was *not* asking you! How dare you assume that I would consult you on such a matter!"

"Were you not? I beg your pardon, ma'am. Then what *did* you wish to consult me about?"

"I didn't wish to 'consult' you at all! I only wished to . . . to . . ."

"To ask me a favor. An *enormous* favor, I think you said."

She could sense, even if she couldn't quite see his expression, that he was enjoying—even savoring—her awkwardness. She was most disconcertingly aware how easily he could put her at a disadvantage whenever they conversed, yet she never knew where she'd gone wrong or what she'd done amiss. And now that she was beholden to him for saving her daughter's life, she couldn't even *dismiss* the fellow. The situation was truly impossible. And if she compounded her errors by asking him to masquerade as her husband, wouldn't matters be even *worse* when the masquerade was over? The answer was plainly affirmative . . . if she had a grain of sense she would *not* go through with this.

As if he were reading her mind, Thomas said quietly, "You needn't hesitate to ask me, you know, ma'am. There's very little I wouldn't do for you."

Those soft-spoken words completely overturned her resolve. "I . . . er . . . thank you, Thomas. That was kind." She shook her head in confusion. "I don't know how you always manage to be both arrogant and kind at once."

"If I'm arrogant, ma'am," he said in a voice that was suddenly serious, "it's only to remind the world from time to time that behind the livery there's a living human being."

"In your case, Thomas, the world is not likely to forget it." She paused, twisting the little ribbon tightly around her fingers. "But to return to the subject of the favor . . ."

"Yes, ma'am?"

"I did a rather foolish thing, you see. In order to put my sister-in-law off from her matchmaking, I . . . I told her a dreadful lie. And now she intends to visit here, and I am forced to . . . make that lie appear to be true by staging a . . . a rather elaborate masquerade. And for that I need your help."

"What sort of help?"

"I need you to . . . to play a major role in the masquerade."

"I'm afraid I don't quite follow, ma'am. What was that 'dreadful lie'?"

Camilla felt her cheeks grow hot. "It's most awkward to have to reveal it to you. What I told my sister-in-law was . . . was . . ."

"Since it's so difficult for you to speak of, perhaps I can guess. You told her you'd contracted a fatal disease, and you want me to play the part of a physician to convince her that you have less than a year to live."

A nervous little laugh escaped her. "That's very ingenious, Thomas, but—"

"No? Then let me try again. You wrote her that you'd discovered in your family a ne'er-do-well relation—a brother, perhaps—who had so sullied the family name that no gentleman of respectability would marry you. And I'm to play the black sheep."

"I can see that you can invent much better lies than I. I should have consulted you before I first wrote to Lady Ethelyn."

"Do you mean that I'm wrong again? Well, I've run out of ideas. I'm afraid you'll have to tell me the tale yourself."

She took a faltering breath. "You'll have to understand, Thomas, that it started as a lark. A little private joke that I never dreamed would come to this. I wrote my sister that . . . that . . ."

"That you'd already remarried."

She gaped at him in relief. "Yes, that's *it!* However did you—" Her eager smile abruptly died, however, as a sharp perception of the truth burst upon her. "You *knew!* You knew all along!"

He laughed, a long, deep-throated, taunting laugh. "Miss Pippa told me days ago."

She jumped up from her chair in a rage. "And you let me go on . . . stammering and stuttering like an idiotic schoolgirl!" She heaved her book at him, but he shied away in time. "Why, you . . . you . . . !"

"Bounder? Jackanapes? Make-bait? Muckworm? Dastard?" he supplied, laughing.

"All of them! Get out of my sight! I don't want to exchange another word with you!"

"Yes, ma'am." He got to his feet and backed to the door, the grin still wide on his face. "But don't you want to know if I'm willing to participate in your masquerade?"

"No, I don't." She turned her back on him. "I don't care whether you're willing or not. In fact, I don't care ever to speak to you again—or to my daughter either."

"Yes, ma'am. Then I'll just say goodnight."

She didn't turn until she heard him open the door. "Well, *will* you?" she asked, turning slowly, her head proudly erect.

"Play the role in your masquerade?" His broad grin had become a small half-smile, and his eyes held a warmth that made something in her chest clench. "I may have been deceitful in much of what I said tonight, my lady, but this one thing you may believe with absolute certainty: there's no role in the world I'd rather play than that of your husband."

Chapter Fifteen

Ethelyn's letter had specified that her visit would last no longer than three days, "that length of time being the outward extent of my ability to exist in the atmosphere of filth and decadence which London generates." Since the visit was to be so short (the only blessing in this troublesome situation), Camilla decided that it would be unnecessary to take anyone outside the household into her confidence. She might tell Georgie, of course, when they had a moment of private conversation, but the wisest course seemed to be to tell as few people as possible. If, during those three days, Hicks informed all callers that his mistress was not at home, none of Camilla's friends would encounter her in the company of her counterfeit husband, and thus she could avoid embarrassing explanations later.

As for the household staff, only Hicks, Miss Townley and Thomas were to know the whole truth. Hicks, as soon as he understood the circumstances, called the staff together and explained to them that Lady Wyckfield was going to play a joke on her sister-in-law by passing the footman off as her husband. "It will be only for a short time, and she's asked that you all try your very best not to give the game away. As soon as the joke is over, Thomas will return to his post, and everything will go on as before."

Hicks was also assigned the task of escorting Thomas to Bond Street to see that he was appropriately outfitted. He was measured for three waistcoats, two coats, trousers, breeches, linens, a complete ensemble for dinner wear, two pair of boots and a pair of evening shoes. The question of a riding costume— at which Thomas balked, claiming that he was too awkward a horseman to pass as a gentleman in that setting—was discussed among the memebers of the full committee (Camilla, Miss Townley, Pippa and Hicks), who concluded that activities out of doors would be discouraged for the three days of the Falcombes' visit; and if Oswald or Ethelyn insisted on venturing out, Thomas would make some excuse and avoid the outing.

Tom had agreed to the ruse with gleeful nonchalance, but he soon learned that he'd accepted an awesome responsibility. There was a great deal for him to learn in order to be successful at the role. First, Camilla charted an entire family tree for him to memorize. "My sister-in-law is bound to question you about your family, and you must be familiar with your ancestry in every particular," she explained, showing him the long line of descent which she had carefully worked out to avoid any possible connection with the Petershams of Lincolnshire, with whom Ethelyn had indicated a familiarity.

Then he was given a comprehensive course in deportment by Miss Townley. Every day, at a pre-assigned hour, she met with him and drilled him in manners, particularly in rituals of behavior at the table. She reviewed the use of the fork, she taught him how to carve a roast, how to make a toast and how to converse with comfort with the lady on his right. "That will be Lady Ethelyn herself, you know, my lad. The host's right is the place of honor. Lord Falcombe will sit at Miss Camilla's right, and she'll attend to *him*. But he's easy goin'. It's *you* who'll have the hard part."

Thomas groaned. All this was much more than he'd bargained for. His head was swimming with the tedious minutiae of his role, and he began to fear that he'd make some hideous error and spoil everything for his lady. At first the task had seemed to be a great lark—a way to engage in flirtatious badinage, as well as a chance to live for a time the enviable life of a member of the upper classes. But he began to see that the style of life was not so very enviable. It began to seem trivial and dull. He couldn't envy the gentlemanly classes if all they had to keep in their heads were inanities like the proper method of introducing an older lady to a younger one.

Nevertheless, he realized that if he made a *faux pas* or erred in any of these trifles, he would cause Camilla a great deal of trouble and distress. So he tried his best to put his disgust from his mind and concentrate on learning the foolish and superficial rules of gentlemanly conduct.

The day that his evening clothes were delivered from the tailor, Pippa suggested that they hold a trial dinner. The suggestion was seized upon eagerly by everyone. Hicks helped Thomas put on his new clothes and did some mysterious, tedious things with his hair. After more than an hour of preparations, Hicks, filled with pride, led Thomas down to the drawing room where the ladies had already gathered. "Your ladyship," he announced from the doorway with a grin, "may I present Mr. Petersham?"

Tom entered the room with studied nonchalance. "Good evening, my dear," he said, lifting Camilla's hand to his lips. "Good evening, ladies."

"Oh, Thomas, you look *splendid!*" Pippa cried.

He did indeed. Camilla and Miss Townley could only gape. This tall, lean, elegant creature looked every inch the gentleman. Hicks had curled and brushed his hair into the style of studied carelessness that was the height of fashion. His shirt-points were high and stiffly starched, his coat (cut straight across the waist in the latest, double-breasted mode) was buttoned only at the lowest button and revealed a magnificent waistcoat of striped satin in two shades of grey. His gleaming neckcloth, although tied very simply, made his skin look attractively dark. He appeared to be, from his stylish hair-comb to his patent leather shoes, a creature of taste, breeding and intelligence.

Camilla took note of the gleam of amusement in his eyes as they met hers. He was laughing at her again. Had he been able to read in her face her reaction to his altered appearance? Could he tell just by looking at her how impressed with him she was? She felt a tell-tale blush suffuse her cheeks, and she looked away, annoyed with herself for her inability to keep her feelings from showing. Nevertheless, she was proud of him. She became aware of a small thrill of pleasure glowing somewhere within her at the prospect of going through the pretense of marriage with him in the role of husband.

Miss Townley, meanwhile, was looking him over with sharp, critical eyes. "Needs a fob for his waistcoat pocket, I think. He looks too austere without a bit of jewelry, I'd say."

"Right," Hicks agreed, taking a folded sheet of paper and a stub of a pencil from a pocket and making a note. "Anything else?"

"I think he's perfect," Pippa said, running up and taking his hand. "Will you take me in to dinner, Thomas?"

"It'd be my pleasure, Miss Pippa, if the rules allow. Do they, Miss Townley?"

"You must call me Ada," the governess cautioned. "And call Pippa only by name, not with the 'Miss' in front of it."

"Yes, I know, but you don't want me to do it now, do you? I'm not playing my role yet, you know."

"You may as well become accustomed to it," Camilla said. "And you'd better begin to call me Camilla, too. If you slip and call me 'my lady,' we *shall* be in the soup."

"I won't slip, Camilla," he assured her, his eyes twinkling. "Not in that regard." He'd called her Camilla in his mind for so long, it was almost natural to do it aloud.

"I suppose I'd better call you . . ." She stopped and blinked at him with a momentary blankness. "Good gracious! I've never chosen a given name for Mr. Petersham."

"Then why not call me Thomas? It's as gentlemanly a name as any."

The "committee" voiced their agreement, and "Thomas Petersham" offered his arm to Pippa as they made their way into the small dining room. Pippa and Miss Townley took their accustomed places opposite each other, at the sides, while Camilla sat down at the foot. Thomas, eyeing the high-backed armchair at the head of the table, hesitated. "Go on," Hicks muttered *sotto voce*, digging Tom in the ribs with his elbow, "sit yourself down!"

Daniel, already in his place near the sideboard, waiting to assist in the serving, grinned at Tom as he passed. Tom answered with a wink and sauntered to his seat. But it was a strange sensation to sink down upon the massive chair. To Tom it was almost like a throne. He ran his hands over the carved wooden arms with a kind of proprietary pleasure before he settled back and looked down the length of the table at the faces staring at him expectantly. For a moment his mind went blank. Then he caught Miss Townley's eye. She gave him a little reminder by lowering her head, and he remembered that he was expected to say a grace. With unaccustomed shyness he recited a short one and looked up, wondering what he was supposed to do next.

Before he could begin to fidget, however, he found Hicks at his elbow, pouring a few drops of wine into his glass. "You needn't be so miserly, Mr. Hicks," he muttered. "I won't get drunk."

"I'm just plain Hicks to the master," was the hissed reply, "and you're supposed to taste the wine and give me the nod if you approve."

"Ah, yes, I forgot." He lifted the glass to his lips and sipped it with a pompous show of importance. "No, it won't do, my man," he said, playing the role to the hilt. "Take it away and open another."

Miss Townley whooped, but Hicks glared at him. "Just nod, you looby," he ordered, walking down the length of the table to pour the rejected wine for Miss Camilla. "Don't go putting on airs that don't suit you."

Camilla agreed. "He's right, you know, Thomas. You don't want to draw attention to yourself unnecessarily."

Thomas shrugged, but his lips twitched in amusement. "I can see that you're all determined to keep me from enjoying myself. Very well, ma'am, I'll only nod, even if the wine has turned to vinegar."

"There'll be no spoilt wine served in this house, of that you may be sure," Hicks said in high dudgeon.

"I think," Pippa pointed out mildly, "that if we all keep criticizing Thomas in this way, we won't be giving him the chance to act the master."

"That's quite true, Pippa, my love," Tom said brazenly. "You have more sense than the rest of us combined."

"That kind of talk will surely spoil the child, Mr. Petersham," Miss Townley said, settling into the pretense.

"I don't think so, Ada," he responded, watching Daniel

serve him his soup with a feeling of distinct discomfort. "She's well aware that she's a very clever little thing, yet it hasn't seemed to spoil—"

The door opened at that moment, and the parlormaid hurried in. She whispered something of apparent urgency into Mr. Hicks's ear.

"No, Gladys, you must be mistaken," the butler murmured. He turned to Camilla with a puzzled frown. "There's a carriage at the door, ma'am, with two occupants and a load of baggage. Gladys says it bears the Wyckfield crest. If I may be excused, I'll see what's going on."

Camilla nodded her assent, but her eyes widened with alarm. "It *couldn't* be!" she said to Miss Townley after Hicks and the parlormaid had left. "It's been less than a fortnight since her letter came, hasn't it?"

"Don't fall into a taking," Miss Townley advised. "All crests look alike to a girl like that."

"But who else would be arriving at our door with baggage?" Pippa asked.

Belatedly, the realization of what they suspected was occurring outside the front door burst on Tom. "Do you mean," he asked, starting from his chair, "that Lady Ethelyn and her husband may have *arrived?*"

"No, no," Camilla said hurriedly, waving away the thought with a nervous gesture of her hand, "it simply couldn't be. Her letter distinctly said that she would not come until spring."

"It said," Pippa corrected. "when the weather eases."

"But this is still *February!* No one in his right mind would expect the weather to ease in Feb—"

The sound of the door interrupted her. Hicks stood on the threshold, trying to hide the dismay that was apparent in his eyes and his chalk-like cheeks. "Lord Falcombe and Lady Ethelyn Falcombe," he announced in a voice of doom.

"My God!" Miss Townley groaned. "We're not *near* bein' ready!"

"Don't quail now," Pippa whispered confidently, getting up from her chair. "We shall brush through." With a bright smile, she ran to the door just in time to greet her relations who were bustling in. "Aunt Ethelyn! Uncle Oswald! What an exciting surprise!"

Chapter Sixteen

Ethelyn's large, black-clad frame filled the doorway. "Surprise?" she asked bending stiffly to allow her niece to kiss her cheek. "I wrote that I was coming."

"But you didn't say exactly when," Camilla said, crossing the room to exchange greetings. "But never mind. It is good to see you, even unexpectedly."

"Thank you, m' dear," Oswald said, entering the room and enveloping her in a bear-like embrace. "I've missed you, I don't mind admitting it. You must forgive us for falling in on you in the midst of your dinner." He looked at the table longingly. "We had hoped to arrive earlier—so that we'd be in plenty of time to change for dinner, you know—but the thaw has made the roads so deucedly muddy—"

"It's only by the Good Lord's grace that we managed to avoid an accident," Ethelyn elaborated with a shudder. "A dreadful trip, dreadful!"

"But you're here now," Camilla said comfortingly, "and we

don't care if you're dressed for dinner or not. We shall set two extra places at once. See to it, will you, Hicks?"

Ethelyn, having handed her black, plumed bonnet and heavy pelisse to the parlormaid, turned and looked about her. She fixed her eyes on Thomas at once. *"You,"* she said accusingly, "must be Mr. Petersham."

The room fell silent. Even Oswald, who was shrugging himself out of his greatcoat, stopped with his right arm still half buried in the coat's large sleeve to stare. Thomas crossed the room with a confident deliberation, a half-smile on his lips. "Yes, I'm Petersham, Lady Ethelyn," he said, raising her hand to his lips. "I've been anticipating this meeting for a long time, and with considerable interest."

"Have you indeed? You may be sure that your interest is not a bit greater than mine." She studied him with unsmiling directness. "You're younger than I expected. And where's your moustache?"

"Moustache?" He put a hand up to his face.

"Yes. I distinctly remember Camilla's writing to me that you had an impressive moustache."

Camilla and Miss Townley exchanged horrified glances. They'd completely forgotten the moustache! After the initial concern about the length of time necessary to grow one, the matter had completely slipped their minds!

"It's quite a coincidence that you should mention it," Thomas said, leading Ethelyn to the table. "I shaved it off just this week. Pippa didn't like it."

"No, I didn't," the child said with a giggle. "It tickled me when he kissed my cheek in the mornings."

"Should think it would," Oswald said, lowering himself into the chair at Camilla's right. "Plaguey nuisances, moustaches. Used to have one during my Admiralty days."

"Were you with the Admiralty?" Thomas asked, his eyes lighting with interest. "When was that?"

Oswald, flattered by the attention, embarked on a lengthy account of his earlier career. He was encouraged by the younger man's keen questions and obvious knowledge of ships and seamanship. Their conversation lasted through the second course and was only halted when Lady Ethelyn forcibly interrupted them to quiz Thomas about his family connections. But the gentlemen returned to the subject of the Navy after the ladies had left them to their ports, Oswald concluding the conversation by remarking that young Petersham should seriously consider embarking on such a career himself.

Camilla breathed a sigh of relief when Ethelyn declared herself too travel-weary to remain for long in the drawing room. As soon as they were joined by the gentlemen, she announced herself ready to retire. After Camilla had shown her sister-in-law and Oswald to their rooms and had tucked her incorrigibly optimistic daughter into bed ("I *told* you Thomas would be wonderful," Pippa had murmured as she'd snuggled into the pillows. "He can do anything!"), Camilla returned to the drawing room where Thomas, Hicks and Miss Townley waited, grouped round the fire. "Pippa thinks you were an enormous success," Camilla said when she'd shut the door behind her.

Thomas rubbed his chin warily. "Does that mean that you think otherwise?"

"I don't know what I think. We certainly haven't given ourselves away as yet, but I feel disturbingly apprehensive. We're not *at all* ready for this."

"I don't agree," Miss Townley declared, suddenly optimistic. "Everything went surprisingly well this evenin', despite the fact that we were taken completely unaware."

"But there are dozens of matters we haven't rehearsed . . . or even *discussed*, like choosing safe topics of conversation, or inventing a reason for Mr. Petersham to be living with us rather than we with him—"

"That's because he only had rooms in St. James," Miss Townley improvised promptly.

"Very well, but that still leaves matters like setting up a program of family prayers that Thomas should preside over—"

"Family prayers? But you don't hold family prayers," Thomas pointed out.

"I know, but Ethelyn will expect it of us."

"May I be permitted to make a suggestion, ma'am? I think it would be better to behave, not as Lady Ethelyn will expect, but as we would if I *were* your Mr. Petersham. Did you make him the sort of evangelical fanatic that Lady Ethelyn wished you to wed?"

"No, but—"

"Then you and Petersham wouldn't be holding household services, would you? It seems to me that we shall be more convincing if we act in a manner that would be natural to *us* rather than in an artificial way contrived to please your sister-in-law. Something as extraordinary as household prayers might even arouse her suspicions."

"But she's bound to disapprove of the lack of them."

"Let her. Our object is to make her believe you are well and truly wed, isn't it? You needn't win her approval to accomplish that."

"The fellow's right, Miss Camilla," Miss Townley said. "She's never approved of you anyway, and never will."

"But if she takes *Thomas* in dislike—"

"She won't," Miss Townley insisted. "I'm willin' to wager on it."

"Very well, Thomas, I'll take your advice. But that solves only one of our problems. I can't begin to enumerate all the others. There's your incompleted training, for one thing. For another, we haven't even *begun* to discuss how you and I are to behave toward each other—"

"Yes, and there's also the problem of where he's to sleep," Miss Townley added bluntly. "We can't have him sleepin' in the attic while Lady Ethelyn's here. She'll be bound to discover it."

"And there's something more," Hicks said worriedly. "His second coat hasn't yet arrived, nor his boots from Hoby's. He can't come down to breakfast tomorrow in his evening shoes."

"I can wear the shoes I've used with my livery. They'll do for a while. And the blue coat will do for tomorrow, won't it?"

"Yes, of course it will," Miss Townley said, nodding vigorously. "A little calm thinking is all we need to brush through."

"Right," the butler agreed, brightening. "I'll send Daniel out first thing in the morning to prod Hoby about the boots. Now what about his sleeping quarters?"

Camilla, pacing about the room thoughtfully, was so concerned about the possibility of forgetting some important detail (as she'd done about the moustache) that the butler's question failed to embarrass her. "With Ethelyn and Oswald occupying the two spare bedrooms, there isn't even a place for him upstairs."

"He ought to have a room adjoinin' yours," Miss Townley pointed out. "How about mine? I can have a bed set up in Miss Pippa's room."

It was an obvious and simple solution. "Of *course*," Camilla said with a relieved smile, pleased that a knotty problem had been so easily solved. But immediately after the words had left her tongue, a wave of mortification flooded over her. Miss Townley's room connected with hers through a door in her dressing room. Although it was inconceivable that Thomas would ever attempt to enter her bedroom that way (and besides, she could keep the door locked), the very thought of the *possibility* brought the color rushing up to her face. "That will do . . . er . . . nicely," she added lamely, turning her blushing face to the fire.

Miss Townley scurried off to arrange for a bed, and Hicks, declaring his intention to move all Thomas's things into his new quarters at once, followed the governess out. Camilla knew that it was up to her to deal with the largest remaining problem—how she and Thomas were to treat each other to give the appearance of a newlywed couple. She sank upon the sofa and looked up at him. "I don't suppose you've ever been married, have you, Thomas?"

"No. Why do you ask?"

She twisted her fingers together uneasily. "It would be helpful if *one* of us was familiar with the disposition and bearing of newlyweds . . ."

He studied her curiously. "But *you've* been married—"

"Yes, of course." Her eyes fell. "But it was a . . . a very long time ago."

So, he thought with a start, aware of a completely reprehensible feeling of satisfaction, *she wasn't happy in her marriage.* No wonder she didn't wish to be pushed into a second one. In wedlock, he suspected, even more than in other matters, once burned was twice shy. He looked down at her with a strong surge of sympathy. What suffering had her husband inflicted on her? he wondered. Sitting in the dim firelight, her eyes lowered shyly and her hands clenched in her lap like a frightened child's, she looked more vulnerable to the storms of life than the lowliest housemaid on the staff. This wasn't the first time he'd felt an urge to protect her from those storms, but tonight he felt it painfully. *He* could be a better husband to her than any nobleman he'd seen in her company (and evidently better than the one she'd had), but the conventions of society would never give him the chance to prove it. This game of pretense in which they were engaged was the closest approximation that life would ever offer him.

He sat down beside her, fighting the impulse to take one of her hands in his. "As to the disposition and bearing of newlyweds . . ." he began.

"Yes?" Her eyes flickered up to his face with a look of such hopefulness that it knotted his stomach.

"Their behavior shouldn't be very difficult to simulate. They'd behave like lovers, wouldn't they? Casting each other affectionate glances every now and again—"

"Yes," Camilla nodded, "and secret little smiles—"

"And slight touches of the hands as they pass each other on the stairs—"

She gave a flustered laugh. "Yes, that sort of thing. I suppose it will be quite awkward for us to have to engage in such goings-on—"

"Not for me," he grinned. "I shall not experience the least difficulty. And if it is difficult for you, an observer will only conclude that you are endowed with a most becoming modesty."

"Thank you for saying that," she murmured, getting to her feet and smiling down at him with greater warmth and relaxation than she'd been able to summon up since her sister-in-law had arrived. "You've been most helpful in this appalling muddle, Thomas—more than anyone could have had a right to expect. I am very grateful—"

He made a face at her as he rose. "Gratitude again! I wish to remind you, ma'am, that it's an offering which I don't prize."

"Very well, I'll try to leave it unsaid in the future. And now, I suppose, we may as well go up to bed. There isn't much else to be accomplished tonight."

They walked up the stairs in an uneasy silence. At the door to her room, they paused. "I suppose you know that the door to Miss Townley's room is the one just beyond," she whispered.

"Yes, I know."

"Goodnight, then, Thomas. I hope you sleep well."

But he didn't respond. He was staring at her with an unnerving intensity—a speculative look which, in the dim light of the corridor, she couldn't even begin to interpret. She blinked up at him questioningly, but before she could phrase an inquiry, she was pulled abruptly into his arms.

It had suddenly occurred to him that he'd almost kissed her twice before, yet each time he'd let the opportunity pass. Each time he'd hated himself for his vacillation. But now fate had provided him with an unprecedented third chance, and he was not going to miss it again. No vacillation nor hesitation this time. He tightened his arm about her waist, held her close and tilted her face up to his.

She stiffened in an involuntary, conditioned, immediate revulsion. "Desmond, *don't!*" she whispered, her eyes terrified.

He looked down at her, his eyes and voice gentle. "I'm not Desmond," he said and kissed her.

Slowly, firmly, with the mounting excitement caused by months of frustrated desire, he tightened his hold on her, his pulse racing. Not since the first time he'd thrilled to the effect of a wild wind on a schooner with fully expanded sails had he felt like this. Camilla, at first stiff and resistant in his arms, seemed slowly to melt in a sweet, heart-stopping submission, like a ship bending to the wind. *God, how I love her,* he thought exultantly.

At last he lifted his head, but he couldn't bring himself to let her go completely. She swayed in his arms, her eyes closed. After a moment the lids flickered open, her expression startled, as if she didn't know quite where she was. But almost immediately, she focused on his face and gasped. "Thomas! How *dare* you!"

He grinned and let her go. "Your Mr. Petersham is a fellow of rather warm affections," he said, his voice not quite steady. "You may as well get used to him."

He turned and proceeded down the hall with a step that was decidedly jaunty. She stared after him, openmouthed and breathless. When he reached his door, he looked back at her. "Goodnight," he sang out in a voice loud enough to be heard the entire length of the corridor. "Good-night, Camilla, my love."

He disappeared into the room, leaving Camilla in a whirl of confusion. Was he being insolent or merely playing his role? Or was there, in his vexatious, troubling, utterly disturbing behavior, some other motive entirely?

Chapter Seventeen

It was immediately evident to Betsy, waiting for her mistress in the dressing room, that Miss Camilla was in a state. The lady's lips were pressed together in agitation, her nerves seemed overwrought, and she answered all Betsy's inquiries about the success of the evening with abstracted monosyllables. "Is anything wrong, my lady?" Betsy asked, bending clumsily to help Camilla take off her shoes.

Camilla, with an effort, forced herself to attend. "No, of course not," she muttered, blinking herself into concentration. "What are you doing, bending down like that? Betsy, you mustn't do such things! Your time is too close—"

Betsy smiled and pulled herself erect. "It's nothin', ma'am. I feel perfectly well."

"Nevertheless, I don't wish you to over-exert yourself. Besides, you should be in bed at this hour. I told you not to wait up for me past ten—ever!"

"But ma'am, who'd be here t' undo yer buttons?"

"I can undo my own buttons, thank you. Go to bed at once, woman. I shall manage without you."

The maid went reluctantly to the door. "I laid out yer nightdress, ma'am, and—"

"Good *night,* Betsy," Camilla said pointedly.

"Well, if ye're sure there's nothin'—"

"I'm sure."

Betsy, opening the door, threw Camilla a last, worried look. "G'night, then, Miss Camilla. I hope ye sleep well." With a troubled shake of her head, she closed the door behind her.

Camilla stripped off her gown and slipped into her nightdress without being aware of what she was doing. The scene in the corridor had shattered the last of her self-possession, and she felt frightened and confused. She crept into bed and drew up the covers to her neck, but she found herself shivering all the same. Thomas had shaken her to the core.

The truth was that she'd never, in all her life, been kissed in such a way. The kiss had profoundly disturbed her. Her husband's kisses had been cold, astringent things, calculatedly indulged in and hastily dispensed with, like small hurdles he'd had to step over on his way to his goal. She had never been stirred by them. But Thomas's kiss had been fraught with emotion. She'd felt the tremors in his arms, the pounding of his heart, the stoppage of his breathing. The kiss had been no small thing to him. Despite his taunting insolence after he'd let her go, he'd been deeply moved. That understanding moved her deeply, too.

But what did it mean? That he loved her? Perhaps he did, but such a love could only bring him pain. She was sorry for him. But even more disturbing to contemplate was her *own* reaction to the embrace. She should have been horrified, as any lady would be, at such an unthinkable liberty taken by a servant. Yet she'd felt . . . what? Not horror at all. Oh, at first she'd been seized with a sort of habitual terror, not because her servant was taking liberties but because for a moment she was reminded of Desmond. But after that brief panic, she'd found her fear dissipating into the most astounding and blissful lassitude. Desmond had been threatening, but Thomas had made her feel, somehow, *safe.* She'd let herself relax against him, her blood tingling with the most delightful sensations. It had been a dizzying, rapturous awakening of feelings she hadn't known existed inside her. She'd felt positively regretful when he'd let her go.

She lay awake, staring into the glowing embers in the fire-place, trying to understand what had happened to her. She couldn't be in love with her footman—that was unthinkable! Besides, she'd surmised when she lived with Desmond that she was probably incapable of loving a man. Then how was she to explain to herself this strange stirring of the blood? She was either a too-easily-unbalanced fool or an amoral sensualist, she supposed, and neither one of these designations was particularly pleasant to contemplate.

But if she *were* capable of that sort of love—if she were ever to consider remarriage—she had the disturbing perception that Thomas, her footman, would be nearer an embodiment of her ideal of a lover than any of the gentlemen she was likely to meet. That perception was both thrilling and depressing—thrilling because she was, perhaps, capable of love after all; and depressing because, if true, she would be as subject to pain as he was likely to be. After all, what future could there be for them?

With all these upsetting questions still swirling about in her head, she entered the breakfast room the next morning tired, heavy-eyed and cross. Her mood was not abated by finding that everyone had come down before her; Ada had evidently finished earlier, but Pippa, Ethelyn, Oswald and Thomas were all smiling up at her from their places at the table. She gave them a feeble greeting, took her place and lowered her eyes to her plate. Like an ostrich, she hoped that by avoiding the eyes of the others in the room she would make herself invisible.

She was in no condition to face up to the nerve-wracking challenges which the day would surely bring. It had been a terrible night and had left her with a number of unanswered questions, dismaying possibilities and a headache. She tried to ignore the sound of the voices eddying around her by con-centrating on sipping her tea. But Thomas and Ethelyn seemed to be engaged in some sort of debate, and she surreptitiously lifted her eyes and looked over her cup to discover what was going on.

The faces were all quite cheerful. Ethelyn had apparently slept well, for she was smiling pleasantly at Thomas even though disagreeing with him. "But you must admit," she was saying, "that the draperies in this room, being made of that diaphanous material, are much too frivolous to be considered in good taste."

"I am no arbiter of taste, ma'am," Thomas responded, "but I find them most pleasing to the eye, besides permitting the light to filter in quite cheerfully. If you're saying that the choice of fabric is unconventional, I shall take your word for it, of course. But I'm not put off by unconventionality. Are you?"

"Well, I . . . I . . ." Ethelyn was at a sudden loss. She was, in reality, very uncomfortable with unconventionality, but she didn't like to admit it.

"I've heard Camilla's friends seek her advice very often on matters pertaining to the decoration of their establishments," Thomas said, pushing his advantage, "so I'm not alone in believing her taste to be admirable."

"What other opinion can I expect from a besotted newlywed?" Ethelyn said, smiling at him indulgently.

"Sybil says," Pippa volunteered, "that Lady Sturtevant and all her circle consider this house to be the most agreeably harmonious in decor of any in their set."

"You don't say," Ethelyn muttered, unconvinced. "Nonetheless, one must note that such draperies are woefully inadequate when drawn at night. How can they be expected to keep out draughts?"

"Since we never sit in here at night, that is a problem which doesn't much affect us," Thomas pointed out.

Camilla bent to her cup to keep her smile from showing. How delightful it was to have someone to fight her battles . . . someone at her side who could be counted on for support and protection! She felt her spirits rise and her tension ease. Ethelyn would have a difficult time winning an argument from her irrepressible footman.

It wasn't long before Ethelyn engaged him again in dispute, this time on a matter she considered much more serious than draperies. "Are you saying," she demanded in a voice choked with aversion, "that you don't hold family prayers *at all?*"

"No, we don't. I suppose you'll think us godless reprobates, ma'am, but—"

"I consider you to be a typical London *degenerate!*" she exclaimed. "Camilla, how *could* you—after all the warnings and instructions I gave you and the promises you made to me—

permit such neglect of your child's moral upbringing, to say nothing of your own—"

"I assure you, ma'am, that Pippa's moral upbringing has not been neglected," Thomas said firmly, "and that—"

"The child's name is *Philippa!*" Ethelyn cut in coldly.

"I *like* to be called Pippa," the girl said in loyal defense.

"Yes, Ethelyn," Camilla supported quickly. "It's only an affectionate nickname. Thomas uses 'Philippa' on formal occasions, just as he ought."

"But we are moving from the point, ma'am," Thomas said. "In regard to family prayers, it is our belief that—"

"*Our* belief!" Ethelyn scoffed. "I am thoroughly familiar with *Camilla's* beliefs, so you needn't waste your breath. Camilla is the sort, I am sorry to say, who bends to the strongest wind. It's quite clear to me that you've coerced her to accept your undoubtedly latitudinarian views against her own better instincts."

"Ethelyn, that's not *true!*" Camilla cried. "You have no idea *what* my instincts are in this regard. You've never let me express them."

"And as to coercion, Lady Ethelyn," Thomas said calmly, "you completely misunderstand how we live in this house. There is no coercion here. We long ago discussed among ourselves (for Pippa's views are as important to us as our own) our feelings about religious observances, and we were unanimously agreed that—"

"Are you trying to make me believe that both Camilla *and* Philippa willingly agreed to forego the very observances that had been so important a part of their former lives?"

"Not to forego them, ma'am. Only to change the outward form." He passed a plate of biscuits to Ethelyn with a smile. "Daily family prayers are very public displays, you know. We prefer to perform our obeisances in private."

"In *private?* What's privacy to do with it?"

"Well, if one thinks about it," Oswald interjected with unaccustomed bravery, "praying in private is more . . . more straightforward."

"More sincere," Pippa amended.

"Yes, that's true," Camilla said with unusual assertiveness. "In private devotions, one is less apt to be swayed by the practices and opinions of others."

"And less likely to mouth words by rote," Thomas said.

"Private prayers are less a matter of ritual and more a matter of honest faith."

"*Give me, kind heaven,*" Pippa recited a bit pompously, "*a private station,/ A mind serene for contemplation.*"

Ethelyn stared at the child, speechless. Philippa had even brought in poetry to join with the others at the table in giving support to a position which Ethelyn had, until this moment, found untenable. Now, however, she was quite at a loss as to how to argue the matter; one could hardly debate the value of attempting a private communion with one's God. She looked from one to the other of the faces surrounding her, shrugged and reached for the teapot. "Hummmph!" was all she said when she found her voice.

Thomas and Camilla exchanged looks of triumph, while Pippa squeezed her hero's hand under the table to show her pride in him. Thomas seemed never to let her down. She looked at her mother with an expression that said as clearly as words, *See? He's every bit as wonderful as I said he'd be.*

But Camilla, proud of his performance though she was, tempered her satisfaction with her awareness that she hadn't heard the last of the matter from Ethelyn. If she knew her sister-in-law at all, she was certain that Ethelyn would not let the subject of family prayers pass without further argumentation.

But the subject did not come up again. In fact, the day passed with surprisingly little strain. Ethelyn found nothing to complain about until teatime, when a small occurrence threatened to cause the break that Camilla had been fearfully anticipating all day.

Hicks, assisted by Daniel and the parlormaid, Gladys, had done the serving. The butler had not forgotten his former difficulties with the woman who was now a guest in the house, and he'd been particularly frozen-faced during the repast. After Pippa and Miss Townley had finished their tea and returned to the schoolroom, and the servants had taken their leave, Ethelyn remarked between bites of her sweet roll that she was surprised to see the butler still part of the household.

"Hicks?" Thomas asked in surprise. "Why should he not be?"

"The fellow is a dreadful incompetent, and rude in the bargain. Only Camilla's completely misguided loyalty explains his continued presence here," Ethelyn declared, brushing the crumbs from the impressive expanse of black bombazine that covered her bosom.

"But he's always seemed to me to be the most perfect of butlers," Thomas insisted.

"You are only a man. Men never take proper notice of the quality of their servants, except, of course, their valets."

"Hicks has doubled as valet for Thomas," Camilla said defensively, rising to her feet, "and he's never expressed the *slightest* dissatisfaction with him!"

"Pooh! That only proves that your husband is too easy to please. I'll have you know, Thomas, that your wife is notoriously incompetent in dealing with servants."

Camilla colored to her ears. "Really, Ethelyn!"

But Thomas, getting to his feet, couldn't help chuckling. "Is she indeed?" He crossed the room and put a comforting arm around Camilla's waist. "It has always seemed to me that she deals with her servants remarkably well," he said, looking down at her fondly.

Camilla's color heightened. To the onlookers they seemed the epitome of happy newlyweds. "That's because you're obviously bewitched," Ethelyn said placidly, helping herself to another bun.

Oswald chortled in agreement. "That much is quite plain. Smelling of April and May, the pair of you."

"But when the bloom wears off," Ethelyn predicted, "you'll discover for yourself what havoc a crew of incompetent servants can create."

Thomas looked down at the woman he held encircled in his arm. "I doubt that the bloom will ever wear off," he murmured. "Will it, my love?"

"Never," she answered, meeting his eyes with a wide-eyed glow in her own.

"So you see, ma'am," Thomas said to Ethelyn while bending to plant a kiss on Camilla's cheek, "the servants will never be a problem to us. We'll never bother to notice whether they're incompetent or not."

"That," Ethelyn responded acidly, "is nothing but foolishness. And I can't say I approve of such public snuggling and caressing, either."

"This isn't public," Oswald pointed out. "We're family."

"Nevertheless—"

"Nevertheless, Lady Ethelyn," Thomas said firmly, taking

Camilla's hand and leading her to the sofa, "this is our home, where we can behave as we like. We shall hold hands if we like, hold prayers where we like, hire servants whom we like. This is a happy house, you see, and we intend to keep it that way. We shall always be glad of your approval, of course, but we can't permit ourselves to seek that approval at the expense of our own happiness. You yourself would not wish us to act otherwise."

Camilla stared up at him, her throat contracted. Those were the very words she herself would have liked to say to Ethelyn but had never found the courage to utter. She lifted a hand to his arm and drew him down beside her. "Thank you, my dear," she said softly.

Ethelyn looked from one to the other. "Hummmph!" she said and took another bite of her bun.

Later, on her way up to dress for dinner, Camilla came upon her sister-in-law on the stairs. It was the first time since Ethelyn's arrival that they'd been alone in each other's company, and Camilla held her breath and waited for what she was certain would be the inevitable diatribe against the manners and morals of the husband she'd dared to select without her sister-in-law's permission. But Ethelyn only said, "Your Thomas is a man of strong opinions."

"Yes, I . . . I suppose he is," Camilla murmured, bracing herself for the attack.

"I don't hold with all his views, of course, but he's a great deal more sensible than I'd expected him to be."

Camilla, though inwardly breathing a sigh of relief, was nonetheless offended. "What *did* you expect, my dear?" She asked with a wry smile. "That I would wed an imbecile?"

Ethelyn paid no heed to the sarcasm. "Perhaps not an imbecile, but I *did* expect a weakling. I didn't think your spiritlessness would attract any other sort."

"Thank you very much indeed!" Camilla said curtly. "Now that you see that you were mistaken, do you find it possible to admit that I am, perhaps, not as spiritless as you thought?"

"Now don't climb up on your high ropes. I meant no offense. I've always told you that you were too amenable—"

"I might have appeared so . . . but only because I didn't wish forever to be arguing with you."

"Be that as it may," Ethelyn said, strolling down the corridor beside the younger woman in complacent self-assurance, "I will admit that no one can say your husband is a milksop."

Camilla gave a dry little laugh. "No, one certainly can't. 'Milksop' is the *least* fitting of words to describe my hus—er...Thomas."

"All things considered," Ethelyn mused, patting Camilla's hand approvingly, "it seems to me that you haven't done badly for yourself. Not badly at all."

With a satisfactory verdict thus pronounced, Lady Ethelyn saw little reason to prolong her visit. She informed Camilla the next morning that she and Oswald would remain for one more night only. "No matter how pleasant the company, my dear," she said, "London is still London. It is, and always will be, a blemish on the English isles. Now that I've seen for myself that your situation is tenable as far as your marriage is concerned, I feel no need to remain. We shall leave tomorrow after breakfast."

Camilla could scarcely believe her ears. A wave of relief swept over her so strong that she felt almost giddy. What a triumph! They had *done* it; the ruse had succeeded. Thomas's wonderful performance had transformed her deceitful tale into a most believable performance. And now she would be free—free of Ethelyn's interference, free of her past, free to live her life as she wished. She wanted to dance around the room in joy.

In the heady delight of the relief of her tension, she determined to make this last evening of her sister-in-law's stay as festive and enjoyable as possible. With Hicks and the cook, she devised a menu fit for royalty. Then, while Ethelyn took an afternoon nap and Oswald went out to stroll through the streets near Whitehall where he'd once spent so much of his time, the staff went to work to ready the large dining room for its second use.

The entire household was in a flurry. Daniel and the house-maids dusted the chandeliers, polished the plate, waxed the floor, aired the room and set the table. The kitchen staff bustled about in a frenzy, for her ladyship had decided on serving not only partridge filets *à la Pompadour*, a veal ragout with onions, a roast of beef, a fish stew *Bordeaux*, three kinds of bread and six side dishes, but, to please Lord Falcombe's sweet tooth, a lemon gelatine mold, a "Turkish Mosque" cream, and some tiny apple-filled pastries which took great effort to concoct.

Pippa was quite put out when she learned that she would not be permitted to attend the dinner party. "It will be Thomas's last dinner as your husband," she pouted, "and I had my heart set on observing him."

"I'm sorry, love," her mother explained gently. "but it is not appropriate for girls your age to attend such affairs. And besides, we shall take our places at the table at an hour much too late for you. I promise to observe everything very carefully and to tell you the whole tomorrow in great detail."

With that Pippa had to be content. But she instructed Miss Townley, who'd been invited to attend, to be equally observant. "I want to know *everything* that Thomas says and does," she requested, "so, please, Miss Townley, watch and listen as carefully as you can."

Miss Townley, who was busily letting out the waist of a gown which Miss Camilla had given her, merely grunted. "Ye'll turn into a regular busybody if you don't watch yourself," she said brusquely, biting off a thread. "Better get your nose back into that book and work on your French declensions."

By early evening, all was in readiness. But Camilla's careful plans were slightly disrupted when Oswald returned from his outing with the news that he'd met an old friend, Lord Jeffries, while walking near Whitehall. Lord Jeffries, who was still with the Admiralty, had been delighted to see him, and they'd spent more than an hour chatting about old times. Oswald had so enjoyed the encounter that he'd impulsively invited Jeffries and his lady to join them for dinner. "I hope, Camilla, my love," he apologized, puffing over his exertions to remove himself from his greatcoat, "that I haven't incovenienced you."

"No, of course not, Oswald. I shall simply have Hicks set two more places. It will be very pleasant to expand our party. Let's see . . . with you, Ethelyn, Ada, Thomas and me . . . that means we shall be seven all together. I'd better tell Cook at once."

But there were to be eight. When Lord Jeffries and his wife tapped at the door a little before nine that evening, they were accompanied by a naval officer in full dress uniform. "I hope your mistress won't mind my having brought an extra guest," Lord Jeffries said, handing his chapeaubras to Hicks.

Hicks, in turn, passed the chapeaubras to Daniel, who was standing just behind him, stiff and uncomfortable in his formal livery. The footman put out his hand to take the hat when he saw the face of the "extra guest." The chapeaubras fell from his suddenly nerveless fingers. It was all he could do to keep from gasping.

"I'm sure my mistress will be delighted," Hicks said with a polite smile, bending down smoothly and retrieving the fallen headpiece. He thrust it into Daniel's hand with a warning glare and, his face restored to composure, turned to assist Lady Jeffries with her cloak.

The "extra guest" handed his hat to Daniel and turned away, but Daniel had gotten a close-enough look to be certain he wasn't mistaken. The gentleman was sickeningly familiar. He was tall, thin, with iron grey hair and a neatly trimmed beard. The only thing unfamiliar about his face was a livid scar which ran from the bridge of his nose diagonally across his forehead to the left corner of his hairline. But Daniel knew quite well how the scar had come there . . . and he felt his blood run cold. *Oh, God,* he thought wildly, *how can I warn Tom?*

Hicks had removed Lady Jeffries' cloak, and he tossed it to Daniel as he led the guests toward the drawing room where the family waited. Daniel, in a helpless panic, followed them down the hall, hoping desperately for some sort of inspiration which would suggest a way out. But none came.

Hicks threw open the doors of the drawing room. "Lady Jeffries, Lord Jeffries, and Captain Everard Brock," he announced as the guests filed in.

While Oswald jumped to his feet (with all the alacrity that his huge bulk permitted) and began to make the introductions, Daniel peered over the butler's shoulder into the room. He spotted Tom almost at once and knew immediately that his friend had recognized the unexpected guest. Tom was poised, immobile, halfway between sitting and standing, his hand extended, a smile frozen on his face. Oswald was leading Captain Brock, of His Majesty's Ship *Undaunted,* across the room to meet him, but before the meeting took place, Tom's eyes met Daniel's. And, in that one timeless moment, each could read in the other's face the starkly terrifying certainty of impending doom.

Chapter Eighteen

"Captain Brock, may I present our host, Thomas Petersham? Thomas, the captain commands the *Undaunted*, which, you may know, distinguished itself at Camperdown."

Tom pulled himself erect and smiled. "Who doesn't know of the victory at Camperdown? This is indeed an honor, Captain Brock."

The men shook hands. Captain Brock squinted at Tom closely. "We haven't met before, have we? I have a feeling that—"

"I surely would have remembered meeting the captain of the *Undaunted*," Thomas said smoothly. "But come and meet my wife, Captain. She won't forgive me if I keep you too long to myself."

As the rest of the introductions were made, Hicks and Daniel passed among the guests offering glasses of sherry. Tom, reaching for a glass from Daniel's tray, moved aside with him as inconspicuously as he could. "We're cooked fer sure," Daniel whispered through unmoving lips. "Let's make a run fer it."

"No, I can't do that to her ladyship. I'm going to play the game through to the finish. There's a chance we'll brush through. He hasn't been able to place where he's seen me."

"It's a dreadful chance t' take."

"I know." Tom looked round at the captain, sitting at his ease and chatting comfortably with Oswald. "You keep yourself out of sight if you can. No use both of us getting caught in this trap."

He moved back to the group and took a stance behind Camilla's chair. The conversation seemed to concentrate itself on the Navy, with Captain Brock at the center of attention. Even the ladies questioned him about his voyages and battles. Tom listened but didn't dare to contribute to the conversation. The less he drew attention to himself, the better. He only hoped that the conversation would veer in another direction; all this talk of ships and the Navy was decidedly dangerous.

Camilla, who was beginning to know him better than he dreamed, noticed his unusual silence. Just before dinner was announced, she managed to draw him aside. "Is anything amiss?" she asked nervously. "You've been very reserved."

"This is the first time I've heard you complain on *that* score," he said with a quick grin. But something in his eyes— a look of wary tension—troubled her, and she couldn't return his smile.

The dining-room doors were thrown open at that moment, signaling the fact that dinner was ready to be served. "You haven't really answered me, Thomas," she whispered hastily. "Is there—"

"No, nothing. Don't trouble yourself about me," he assured her. "You'd better go along. Lord Jeffries is waiting to take your arm."

The dinner, served with inconspicuous efficiency by Hicks, Daniel and two parlormaids, was impressively lavish. To Thomas's relief, the food inspired a turn in the conversation. Lord Jeffries made a fuss over the fish stew, his wife sang the praises of the ragout and Oswald uttered effusive praise about everything. Lady Jeffries, a soft-spoken, fluttery woman with watery eyes and a way of hunching up her shoulders as if she were sitting in a perpetual draught, referred repeatedly to Camilla's remarkable ability to arrange so elaborate a dinner on such short notice. "And with an unexpected guest at the table as well!" she chirped in birdlike admiration. "You are much to be complimented."

"Yes, you do seem to have learned to set an admirable table, Camilla," Ethelyn admitted grudgingly. "I didn't dream you could manage so well."

While the guests continued to praise each dish set before them, a housemaid tiptoed in and spoke to Daniel. After a moment's exchange with Hicks, the footman followed the maid from the room. Tom, Camilla and Miss Townley all noted the occurrence and exchanged looks, but since Hicks did not appear to be perturbed by the defection, they did nothing about it.

The subject of food could not be expected to hold the attention of the diners indefinitely, and before Tom was quite aware of how it had happened, Oswald had turned the conversation back to the subject of the Navy. He spoke with patriotic optimism of the coming naval confrontations with Napoleon's fleet. "With men such as you in the Admiralty, Jeffries, with men like Nelson commanding the fleet, and with the like of Brock here captaining the ships of the line, we have nothing to fear," he declared expansively, lifting his glass.

"That's all very well," Jeffries said after swallowing his wine, "but the French have some ships of excellent design, very swift in the water—"

"Remarkably swift," Brock agreed. "I've seen them in action. They make many of ours seem like clumsy hulks."

"But we far outnumber them, don't we?" Oswald insisted. "And our men are better seamen. There's no fighter in the world like the British tar."

Tom felt himself stiffen, and his heart began to race. The closer they came to the subject of the recruitment of sailors, the more likely that Captain Brock's memory would be jogged. "Do you go to the theater a great deal, Lady Jeffries?" he asked abruptly, in a desperate attempt to turn the subject.

Lord Jeffries, about to embark on the subject of British seamen, blinked at his host in surprise. Falcombe had told him that afternoon that this Mr. Petersham had expressed some brilliant and original ideas about naval practices, and he'd looked forward to discussing those ideas with him. Yet the fellow had uttered hardly a word all evening and was now embarking on a completely irrelevant matter. What was wrong with the chap?

Lady Jeffries, accustomed to being overshadowed by her

influential, opinionated husband, was taken aback by her host's unexpected interest. "Me?" she asked in her fluttery voice. "Why, no. I'm afraid not. My husband, you know, has little interest in drama and such fripperies."

"That's too bad," Tom murmured, seeing his heavy-handed maneuver about to fail. "I've become interested, of late, in seeing a performance of . . . of . . . *King John,* and I wondered . . ."

Everyone seemed to be staring at him. *"King John?"* Lady Jeffries inquired in confusion.

"Yes. Shakespeare, you know. I wondered if you'd ever seen it," he finished lamely.

"Oh, I see." She gave a helpless little giggle. "No, I'm afraid I'm totally unfamiliar with *King John.*"

"Silly play," Ethelyn said authoritatively, attacking the tender slice of beef on her plate with relish. "Full of illegitimacy and murder and pretenders-to-the-throne. I don't know why you wish to see it."

"Can't call it silly," Miss Townley objected, rushing to Thomas's defense. "After all, Shakespeare—"

"Don't know why you ladies always like to discuss plays and things when we can be speaking of really interesting matters like the naval war," Oswald said bluntly. "Didn't mean to cut you off, though, Miss Townley. If you want to prose on about Shakespeare, go right ahead."

"No, not at all, Lord Falcombe," Miss Townley said. "Don't mind droppin' the subject of Shakespeare for the Navy, if that suits you better."

"I must admit it does," Oswald said. "Couldn't ever understand why everyone's so fascinated with dead Kings. I'd much rather talk about the here and now. Like what Jeffries here had to say about our British sailors. What were you saying, Jeffries?"

"I was about to say that our ships are grossly undermanned. The most serious problem is, was, and will probably always remain, recruitment."

"Yes, I agree," Oswald said eagerly. "That's why I'd like you to hear Petersham's ideas on the subject. Had me quite caught up when we discussed the subject yesterday. Tell him your analysis of the problem, Thomas."

Tom would have liked to wring Oswald's neck. "It wasn't much of an analysis," he said with a dismissive wave of his hand. "And I'd much rather talk about . . . about your stables, Oswald. How does one go about developing a reputable herd like the one at Wyckfield?"

Oswald's mouth dropped open. "Nothing particularly reputable about our stock at Wyckfield. Can't imagine what gave you such an idea. See here, old fellow, why are you suddenly becoming so modest about telling us your theory of naval re—"

He was interrupted by the sound of a female voice in the hallway outside the dining room. *"Hicks? Camilla?"*

"Good gracious, what was that?" Ethelyn asked, her head coming up with a start.

"Camilla, are you home? Where *is* everyone?" The voice was closer and clearer now.

"Oh, good God!" Camilla gasped, jumping from her chair. *"Georgie! I completely forgot!"*

The door of the dining room opened, and Lady Sturtevant, absorbed in the complicated process of removing the enormous, feathered hat she'd chosen to wear, strolled into the room. She glanced up as Camilla hurried up to her. "Ah, there you are, you beast. I've been waiting for you an *age*. Did you forget we were to go to—*Oh!*" She stared at the diners in amazement. "You have guests!"

"Yes, I—"

Georgina's eyebrows shot up. That she should have broken in unannounced upon a dinner party was humiliating in the extreme. "I'm terribly sorry. I had no *idea* that—! I seem to have intruded." She backed awkwardly to the door. "I thought we were going to the opera. I must have mistaken the date—"

"No, Georgie, it was *I* who mistook the date," Camilla said, putting a trembling hand on her friend's arm.

"Very rude sort of behavior, I must say," Ethelyn muttered.

Camilla cast an agitated glance over her shoulder at her sister-in-law and turned back to her friend. "Yes, it was. Please forgive me, Georgie. I've been at sixes and sevens for the past two days. Lady Ethelyn and Lord Falcombe arrived, you see, quite unexpectedly—"

Georgina, offended at having been forgotten and excluded from these festivities by the person she'd considered her very closest friend, was about to withdraw her arm from Camilla's clasp and stalk out of the room in high dudgeon when she became aware of the tension in her friend's face. Something was very much amiss here. The names she'd just heard clicked into recognition. "Your *sister-in-law?*" she asked in an undervoice, realizing that Camilla was in some sort of difficulty.

Camilla nodded. Georgina, her irritation forgotten, gave her friend a speaking look of compassion.

"Well, *really,* Camilla, don't just stand there like a gawk. Ask your friend to join us," Ethelyn ordered in disgust.

Camilla reddened. There was nothing for it but to do as Ethelyn said. She would have to introduce Georgie to everyone at the table. But, if the pretense of the last two days was to continue, Georgie would have to behave as if she were well acquainted with "Mr. Petersham." How could she warn her friend to assist her in the deception? If only she'd found time to confide in her friend beforehand! Well, it was too late now. Her house of lies was about to come tumbling down about her head. "Yes, Georgie," she said, swallowing courageously, "you must join us. Come and let me make you known to everyone."

"Well, I shouldn't. I should be on my way to the opera. But I'll stay for a little while."

"Good," Camilla said, but her heart sank. She took her friend's arm and led her to the table. "Lady Sturtevant, may I present Lady Jeffries, Lady Ethelyn Falcombe, Lord Jeffries, Lord Falcombe, Captain Brock and Miss Townley, whom you've met many times. And . . . and . . ." She gave her friend's arm a warning pinch. "And of course, you know my h-husband—"

This was too much for Georgina. In spite of the pinch, her mouth dropped open. "Your *husband?* But that's *Thomas!*"

"Yes, of course," Camilla said, pinching her with greater desperation. "Thomas. Who else? Bring Lady Sturtevant a chair, will you, Hicks? And, Gladys, take Lady Sturtevant's hat and pelisse."

"Why do you look so startled, Lady Sturtevant?" Ethelyn inquired. "One would think you didn't expect to see Thomas at his own table."

"She didn't," Thomas said, smiling at Georgina broadly. "I was to have gone to . . . to the country yesterday, to see about some matters on my . . . estates."

"Did you postpone your journey on our account? That was very good of you, old fellow," Oswald said cheerfully.

"I still don't see why Lady Sturtevant should look as if she's seen a ghost merely because Thomas postponed his trip for a day or two," Lady Ethelyn said, staring at Georgina suspiciously.

"Our Georgie doesn't react well to surprises, do you, my dear?" Thomas said, looking at her with an affectionate grin.

"Evidently not," Georgina muttered, trying to recover her equilibrium. If Camilla was playing some sort of havey-cavey game with her footman, it was not *her* place to give them away.

"Do sit down, my dear," Thomas urged her. "We gentlemen have been on our feet all this time, waiting for you to take your place."

Georgina speechlessly sank down on her chair. Camilla, waiting behind her, pressed her friend's shoulder thankfully. "I'll explain everything later," she whispered and turned to go back to her own place.

But just as she and the still-standing gentlemen were about to reseat themselves, the door burst open again. Daniel stood in the doorway, his face white. "My lady," he cried, "it's the baby! I think it's *comin'!*"

"Daniel!" Hicks barked, appalled.

"Is everyone in this house *demented?*" Ethelyn demanded.

"The *baby?*" Camilla, almost tottering, ran across the room to him. "But, Daniel, it's too early, isn't it? Are you sure you're not mistaken?"

"I don't think so, ma'am. She's got these seizin' pains, y' know, what make her shriek . . . every couple o' minutes, seems like."

"That sounds very much like birth-throes to me," Georgina said knowingly.

"Does it? Then someone ought to run for the midwife at once." Camilla put a shaking hand to her forehead. "Daniel—?"

"Yes, ma'am," he muttered dazedly. "The midwife . . ."

"Quite an interesting household you've brought us to, Falcombe," Lord Jeffries remarked, reaching for the wine.

"It's a veritable madhouse!" Ethelyn said icily.

"Who is it who's . . . er . . . expecting, if I may inquire?" Lady Jeffries asked timidly of Lady Sturtevant.

"Camilla's abigail, I believe. The footman's wife."

"Unheard of, disturbing a dinner party in this vulgar way!" Ethelyn muttered irritably.

"Now, now, my dear," Oswald temporized, "these things will happen when they will."

"Not much Miss Camilla could've done to prevent it," Miss Townley defended.

At the door, Daniel stood leaning dazedly against the frame. "The midwife," he was muttering. "Where . . . ?"

"Oh, dear," Camilla said, studying him worriedly, "I don't think *he* can be relied upon to fetch the midwife."

Georgina rose from her chair. "Let me do what I can until *someone* fetches her. After five hatchings of my own, I ought to be capable of offering some assistance."

"*Would* you,' Georgie? I'd be eternally grateful."

"Shall *I* go for the midwife, Miss Camilla?" Hicks offered quietly.

Camilla threw a guilty look at her guests. "No, Hicks, I think we need you here."

Thomas, seeing an opportunity to escape from the nerve-wracking presence of Captain Brock (whom Daniel, in the shock of impending fatherhood, had apparently forgotten), jumped to his feet. "I'll go, my love. I can be spared more readily than our butler. Just give me the direction."

"Oh, yes, Thomas, that *is* the best solution," Camilla said in relief. "If you'll just settle Daniel into the sitting room before you go, Georgie and I can go up to Betsy, and all the others will be able to finish their dinners in peace."

Tom made his way across the room with alacrity, while Ethelyn shook her head in vehement disapproval. "In peace?" she said in tones of utter disparagement. "This is the least peaceful, the most disorganized dinner party I've ever attended in my life!"

Miss Townley frowned at her and got to her feet. "Miss Camilla, shall I—"

"No, Ada. Please stay here and play hostess in my stead."

"Come on, old man," Tom said to Daniel softly, putting a supporting arm about him, "let's get you down on the sitting-room sofa."

"You and I had better be prepared," Georgina warned her friend. "If Betsy's 'seizures' were afflicting her every few minutes, it may be too late for the midwife."

"Oh, *L-Lord!*" Daniel stared at her in horror and swayed unsteadily. "Tom, I . . . think I'm goin' t' *faint* . . ."

Tom grabbed him with both arms. "Hold on, Daniel. It'll

turn out all right." And bracing him up firmly, he tried desperately to hurry him out of the room.

"Hold on there!" came a sharp, cold command. "Don't either of you move another step!"

Everyone froze in his place. There was no mistaking the authoritative ring in that voice. It came from Captain Brock, who was leaning on the table with one hand and pointing at Tom with the other. Everyone in the room stared at him: Camilla and Georgina near the doorway, Hicks and the maids at their places near the server, the other diners surrounding the captain at the table, and Daniel and Tom framed in the doorway.

Oswald was the first to move. "Hang it, Captain, you've nearly made me jump out of my skin! What's the to-do *now?*"

"You, fellow—yes, *you,* the butler! Close the door! And Jeffries, you and Falcombe here, *seize that man!*"

"*Seize* him? Do you mean Thomas?" Oswald sputtered. "Have you lost your *wits?* That man is, roughly speaking, my *brother-in-law!*"

"I don't care if he's, roughly speaking, your *bastard son!* That's the murdering deserter who *cracked my skull!*"

Chapter Nineteen

Ethelyn shrieked, Lady Jeffries gasped and Daniel, shocked into alertness by Captain Brock's accusation, groaned. There followed a veritable explosion of sound: exclamations, questions, expressions of disbelief, gasps and outcries. Ignoring the hubbub, Tom turned to face the agonized question in Camilla's eyes. In painful silence, they stared at each other until he could no longer bear it. His eyes flickered down in abject shame. He didn't see her cheeks whiten or her hand fly up to her mouth to press back the cry that came unbidden from her throat.

Lord Jeffries, who had also remained silent during the first chaotic reaction, now joined the others in throwing questions at the captain and Tom. But the noise made sensible communication impossible, and he threw up his hands in disgust.

"Will you all be quiet!" Tom ordered at last. "I'll answer all your questions and accusations in good time. But first I must remind you that there's a woman upstairs in labor. Go to her, Camilla. And you, too, Lady Sturtevant. We, none of us, would forgive ourselves if she suffered from neglect while we engaged in this pointless altercation."

"The altercation will not be pointless, I assure you," Captain Brock said threateningly.

"Nevertheless," Lord Jeffries said, "Mr. Petersham is quite right in advising the ladies to go at once."

Georgina hurried from the room, but Daniel stopped Camilla on the threshold. "Take care of 'em fer me, my lady, if . . . if I should be gone by the time the baby comes."

"Gone? Why should you be—" Her eyes widened in sudden understanding. Daniel, too was involved in this frightening turn of events. Was he—and Thomas, too—about to be *carted off in irons?*

Only by the sheerest effort of will—made possible by imagining her Betsy writhing in agony upstairs—was she able to keep hold of herself. She turned about to face her guests, all of whom were on their feet, staring at her with expressions which revealed shock, curiosity or concern. "Lord Jeffries," she said in a voice surprisingly firm and steady, "I appeal to you, as a member of the Admiralty and as the only gentleman here who can deal with this matter with some impartiality, to promise me that you will permit no one of this household to be removed from here until I return. What happens to persons living in my house is of vital concern to me, and it is simple justice that I be consulted before decisions relating to their futures are made. But I can only cope with one crisis at a time. This man's wife is about to have a baby. Therefore, until that baby is born, I insist that nothing—or no one—in this household be disturbed or uprooted. Will you see to it, my lord?"

"I would like very much to oblige you, my dear, but—" He turned a questioning eye to Captain Brock.

The Captain shrugged. "If both these miscreants give their words not to make any attempt to escape, I'm willing to wait."

Tom and Daniel nodded their agreement.

"Very well, ma'am," Lord Jeffries said, "we'll take no action until the child is born."

Without another word, Camilla left the room.

"Now I think it's time we were given some sort of explanation," Ethelyn demanded as soon as the door had closed behind Camilla.

"The explanation is quite simple," Captain Brock said coldly. "These men were common sailors on my ship, brought before me for some infraction. They turned on their guards, knocked my mate senseless, swung a lantern against my head and jumped overboard. As brazen and revolting a pair of deserters as you're likely to find."

"That's nothin' but a pack o' lies," Daniel burst out.

"Is it, Petersham?" Jeffries asked.

"From start to finish."

"Are you trying to tell us," Brock sneered, "that you didn't give me this mark on my forehead?"

"Aye, I did. I won't deny that. But the circumstances leading up to it were not in any detail as you've related them, and you know it."

"All right, then, Petersham, let's hear *your* tale," Jeffries said, his voice tinged with suspicion.

"You won't like the truth any more than he does," Tom muttered, turning away, "so what's the good of telling it?"

"Why would I not? Your wife herself attested to my impartiality."

"No one of the Admiralty could be impartial, for my tale indicts you all."

"Does it indeed?" Jeffries said drily. "That's the sort of nonsense every criminal spouts, you know. It's never his fault—oh, no!—but only the fault of the system. Naval injustice, that's the cause. How sick I am of hearing *that*."

Thomas smiled grimly. "So you see, there's no point in my telling you the story, is there?"

"I suppose not," Jeffries said with a sigh. He peered at Thomas for a moment, wondering how an intelligent, audacious, personable young fellow like this had gotten himself into such a fix. "Well, if you don't wish to discuss the matter, we all may as well return to the table and finish our dinners, not that I myself have much appetite. Is there anything left that's edible—what's your name, fellow? Hicks?"

"Yes, my lord," Hicks said, clenching his fists to shake himself from the throes of a lethargy caused by his fear of impending tragedy, not only involving his nephew and Thomas but Miss Camilla as well. But he was head of the staff—he would carry on. "We've kept the beef warm . . . and the partridge filets. And we've still to serve the Turkish creams and the apple tartlets that Lord Falcombe likes so much."

Oswald shook his head glumly. He'd taken a strange fancy to Camilla's new husband, and this turn of events profoundly depressed him. His temporary return to the world of naval affairs had stimulated his spirit and roused him from his customary lethargy. Instead of wishing to run away from this situation, he wanted very much to be able to *do* something, but a course of action had not yet occurred to him. "No, no," he said with a sigh, "I don't want anything. Seem to have lost my appetite, too."

"The thought of returning to the table must be abhorent to all of us," Ethelyn said, her mouth turning down in an expression of acute revulsion. "What I wish, Lord Jeffries, is to get to the bottom of this affair—one which, I might add, only serves to support my conviction that this city is a place of godlessness and corruption."

"I don't see how we're to get to the bottom of it, Lady Ethelyn, if Mr. Petersham refuses to discuss the matter."

"But the little I've heard makes no sense. How can a Petersham of the Sussex Petershams—it was Sussex, wasn't it, Thomas?—have been employed aboard Captain Brock's vessel as a common sailor?"

"Yes, I've been wondering about that myself," Jeffries said. "How did that happen, Petersham?"

Hicks and Miss Townley exchanged glances of alarm. Any revelations about the Petershams of Sussex were bound to bring the truth of Camilla's duplicity to light. Miss Townley bravely intervened. "If you are all determined not to return to the table," she said loudly, "may I suggest that we'll all be more comfortable seated in the drawing room? Hicks can bring in some tea, and the sweets and creams, and we shall all do nicely." *There!* she thought. *That will postpone these revelations for a while.*

For more than two hours, Camilla and Georgina were too busily occupied with assisting the birth to exchange a single word about the mysterious goings-on downstairs. A little before midnight Betsy gave birth to a beautiful little girl, healthy and perfect. Georgina sent a housemaid to fetch Daniel. It was fully fifteen minutes, however, before he came. (Evidently there had been some reluctance expressed by Captain Brock about letting the fellow out of his sight.) But his face, when he gazed at his wife in the candlelight holding the swaddled infant in her arms, showed nothing but a joyful awe. Both Camilla and Georgina were moved to tears. They led him to a chair beside the bed and tiptoed from the room.

"And now," Georgina demanded, throwing off a blood-besmirched apron and assisting Camilla to do the same, "will you please tell me what in the world is going *on* down there?"

"I wish I knew," Camilla answered, the exaltation of assisting with the birth fading from her face. "All I can tell you is that Thomas is evidently not what he professed to be."

"That much I surmised already. He's a sailor, not a footman. But, Camilla, have you *married* him?"

"Married him?" For a moment, Camilla blinked at her friend's confusion. "Oh, *that*. This new trouble has driven that from my mind."

"You must have a very sponge-like mind to forget something like marriage to your footman!"

"I didn't marry him, you goose. It was only a pretense, to convince Ethelyn that her matchmaking scheme was quite hopeless. Strange, it seemed so important, just a little while ago, for my stupid hoax to succeed. Now I don't care a jot! All I can think of is . . . what I heard Captain Brock say. 'Murdering deserter.' My Thomas is a m-murdering deserter."

"'*My* Thomas'? Camilla! You're not in *love* with the fellow, are you?"

Camilla's eyes flew to her friend's face. "Would you think it . . . very dreadful . . . if I were?"

"Not dreadful. But . . . a bit tragic, under the circumstances." She peered at her friend closely. "You don't, do you? Love him, that is?"

"Oh, Georgie, I don't know! All I can say is that he's been more of a husband to me in the last two days than Desmond was in eleven years."

Georgina enveloped her in a tearful embrace. "Oh, my poor Camilla!" she murmured with deepest sympathy. "My poor, poor dear! Whatever shall we do now?"

They entered the drawing room to find the entire party waiting in glum silence. Hicks and Captain Brock were the only two on their feet, Hicks standing in his place beside the tea service and the captain leaning on the mantel of the fireplace and glowering into the flames. On the sofa, Miss Townley was determinedly occupying herself with some embroidery, while

Lady Jeffries was huddled in the corner, fast asleep. Ethelyn, sitting stiffly erect in one of the pair of wing chairs, was reading a book of sermons. In the other chair, Lord Jeffries lolled back against the cushion, his legs stretched out before him and his eyes half-closed in contemplation. Oswald had perched his expansive girth uncomfortably upon an ottoman and was staring with a worried frown at Thomas, who stood motionless in the window embrasure looking out into the blackness of the night.

On the entrance of the two ladies, everyone but Thomas and the sleeping Lady Jeffries looked up. "The baby—?" Miss Townley asked.

Camilla gave her a smile. "A lovely girl. All is well there. No, don't get up, gentlemen. Let us not stand on points at this late hour." She took a chair beside the tea table, while Georgina sat down beside Miss Townley. "I'm quite ready now, Captain Brock, to hear what you have to say."

"There's nothing much to say, ma'am. The authorities have been searching for that fellow for months. He is a deserter from my ship, and I intend to take him back with me to the *Undaunted*. After a shipboard court-martial, I shall administer whatever punishment I deem suitable."

Both Lord Jeffries and Oswald voiced immediate objections, but it was Tom whose words rang loudest through the room. "Damnation, I'll not go! Try me in a civil court or not at all! I'm no cursed bluejacket trapped in the King's service. I'm a free Englishman and demand to be tried as such!"

"What nonsense is this?" Lord Jeffries asked. "If you're a seaman of the Navy, I'll see to it that you're tried fairly in an Admiralty court—you have my word."

"I am *not* a seaman of the Navy. I was the mate of the merchant ship *Triton* when they tried to impress me to serve on Captain Brock's vessel."

"Come now, Thomas," Oswald said, trying sympathetically to caution the young man to guard his tongue, "you can't expect us to believe that an experienced officer of Brock's stature would try to impress the mate of a merchant vessel."

"No, I can't expect you to believe it, but it's true nevertheless. The fact is that the press-gang didn't know I was the mate. They thought I was just another poor devil of a seaman like Daniel. But when I was dragged aboard the *Undaunted*, I showed the captain my papers. He knew full well who I was!"

"Is this true, Brock?" Jeffries asked, scowling.

"The man's lying," Brock said coldly. "Let him show you the papers, if they exist at all."

Tom laughed bitterly. "He knows they don't exist. He burned them."

"I can't *believe* he'd do such a thing," Jeffries said, troubled.

"You'd be well advised to believe it," Tom said earnestly, "unless you want to face more mutinies like Spithead and Nore. What have you done, you at the Admiralty, in the six years since but shut your eyes and drag your feet! Whatever victories the Navy's won have come about because a few commanders like Collingwood and Nelson know how to inspire men, and because the ordinary British sailor has a pride in his service and a love of country stronger than his self-interest. But don't push your luck too far. Don't shut your eyes to the abuses— and they are notorious to those of us who sail—of such men as Brock, for there is a limit even to your best sailors' patience."

Oswald stared at the younger man with wide eyes. "Good God, Jeffries," he said after a long silence, "are matters as rotten as this? What's the matter with you fellows at Whitehall? This impressment business is bad enough, but do our captains have to resort to destroying a merchantman's identity to fill their rosters?"

"You are assuming, Falcombe," Captain Brock said with icy sarcasm, "that your 'brother-in-law, roughly speaking' is telling the truth. I say I never saw any papers. Will you believe him or me?"

"I'll be blunt, Brock," Jeffries said. "I'm inclined to believe *him*. In your initial account, you said he was one of your sailors, brought before you for an infraction. You told us nothing of impressment. Sounds to me as if you were not giving an honest account from the first."

Brock made a dismissive, nonchalant wave of his hand. "You can't expect me to remember the minor details of one interview with an ordinary seaman. The only reason I remembered the fellow at all was that he struck me with the lantern."

"That may be, but Petersham seems to recall everything very well. I see no reason to doubt him."

"No? Well, I'll give you one: his name. I can't recall it right now, but I'd wager it wasn't Petersham. It was something like Collinge . . . or Collford . . ."

"Collinson," Tom supplied.

"Collinson?" Ethelyn gasped. "Do you mean to say that

you're not a Petersham of Sussex at all?"

Tom threw Camilla a look of despair. "No, Lady Ethelyn, I'm not."

"I might have known!" Ethelyn fixed a disdainful eye on her sister-in-law. "It's just like you, Camilla, to be taken in. I warned you, but you took no heed. Now you find yourself married to a common criminal with, I'm certain, no family connections and no future. Serves you quite right, too!"

"See here, ma'am—!" Tom rounded on her angrily.

"No, Thomas, let me," Camilla said with calm astringency, rising and placing herself squarely before Ethelyn's chair. "Ethelyn, I've tried for years to maintain cordial relations with you, but tonight you've pushed me too far! I've been a coward long enough. Never again will I permit you to disparage me, insult me and manage me. The truth, my dear, is that I've know all along what Thomas's true name is. The name Petersham is *my* invention, not his. Thomas's only crime in this affair was to be kind enough to act the role of my husband for the length of your stay in his house."

"Do you mean," Ethelyn squeaked, aghast, "that you're *not married?*"

"Wha—? Who's no' married?" queried Lady Jeffries, waking with a start.

"No one. It's nothing, dear," Jeffries said, patting her hand. "Go back to sleep."

"Yes, Ethelyn," Camilla said, "that's what I mean. I'm not married at all."

Ethelyn fell back against the cushions, one hand clasped to her breast and the other to her forehead. "Oh, my heavens! This is worse than *anything!* The deceit! The *depravity!* You should be down on your *knees* asking the Good Lord's forgiveness for such sinfulness."

"Lady Ethelyn," Tom said furiously, "I can't remain silent when I hear such nonsense. There was no sinfulness and no depravity! Your sister-in-law's character is above reproach, and I won't stand here and listen to you villify her!"

"Hear, hear!" Lady Sturtevant cheered.

"I don't need lectures on morality from a common deserter," Ethelyn responded, drawing herself up in austere dignity. "You would be the *last* person to whom I'd listen when it comes to evaluating my sister-in-law's character."

"Ethelyn, be still!" her husband barked. So unaccustomed

was he to use that tone of voice that not only Camilla, Miss Townley and Hicks looked up in astonishment but he himself seemed surprised.

"What was that?" Ethelyn asked him in disbelief.

"I said be still!" He rose from the ottoman with lumbering majesty. "What right have you to evaluate Camilla's character? Besides, we've been acquainted with her long enough to know, without Thomas having to tell us, what sort of person she is. It begins to be apparent to anyone with half an eye that much of this is *your own fault!* If you weren't so deucedly tyrannical, Camilla wouldn't have had to resort to subterfuge, we'd never have come to London at all, and Thomas wouldn't have found himself at a dinner table facing Captain Brock. You've done enough damage for one night. Either sit here in silence or go up to your room. I'd like to try to see what I can do to *assist* this fellow, and it will be difficult enough without having the proceedings interrupted by your diatribes."

"Oh, Oswald!" Camilla cried tearfully, throwing her arms about his neck. "I never *dreamed* you could be so . . . so courageous."

"There, there, my dear," he said, patting her shoulder awkwardly. "No need to indulge in waterworks. I wasn't always a henpecked old pudding, you know."

"This is all very touching," Brock said drily, "but the hour grows late. Either let me take this make-bait back to the ship or throw him in irons into Fleet prison."

"Don't see why we should do either," Oswald said, leading Camilla back to her chair. "It seems to me a matter that can be settled amicably right here. The way I see it, Thomas was caught in an impressment trap, and when you found you'd caught the wrong fish, you decided not to let him go. Burned his papers. A very embarrassing peccadillo for you to have to explain, if it should come out. True, he scarred your forehead— an equally embarrassing peccadillo for *him* to have to explain. If he forgets *his* grievance, can't you forget yours?"

"Oh, hear, hear!" Lady Sturtevant cried, applauding.

Everyone in the room gazed at him admiringly. No one had imagined that the huge, clumsy Lord Falcombe could conceive so cleverly diplomatic a scheme. Even Lord Jeffries was impressed. And Camilla let herself breathe deeply again in relief.

But Captain Brock came forward, his lips curved in an icy smile. "No, my lord," he said, crossing the room toward

Thomas, "matters of this sort rarely can be settled so neatly. In the first place, I have never admitted that I'd burned any papers. In the second place, I do not consider this scar to be the result of a mere peccadillo. And lastly . . ." He put his hand on Thomas's shoulder and closed his fingers on it like a vise. ". . . lastly, you are quite forgetting about your man's most heinous crime of all."

"Oh?" Oswald asked, one eyebrow climbing up. "And what was that?"

"Murder, my lord. Nothing less than murder."

Chapter Twenty

Pippa wandered about the house next morning, too ill-at-ease to settle down. She'd visited Betsy and seen the new baby, but Daniel was strangely subdued, as if something worrisome was on his mind and not permitting him to enjoy the birth of his first child with the proper enthusiasm. Aunt Ethelyn was locked in her room and had responded to her niece's knock with a curt command that she was to be left alone. Hicks, looking pale and heavy-eyed, had told her that her Uncle Oswald had left the house early this morning on a mysterious errand. Miss Townley and her mother had not yet made an appearance. And Thomas was nowhere to be found.

Pippa was far from being a fool; it was clear to her that something dreadful had happened at her mother's dinner party. Aunt Ethelyn had probably discovered the ruse, but Pippa could not believe that the mere unmasking of Thomas could so depress everyone in the house. It had been nothing but a little game. Even Aunt Ethelyn could be made to see the humor of it.

Should she try again to talk to her aunt? Perhaps she could brighten up the situation.

But before she could put the thought into action, her mother emerged from her bedroom. One look at Camilla's red-rimmed eyes and wan cheeks and Pippa knew that matters were in a more serious state than she'd imagined. Without a word, she slipped her hand into her mother's and walked with her down to the breakfast room. She waited until her mother had drunk half a cup of tea before she spoke. "You promised me last night that you would tell me all. So Mama, please—?"

Her mother put down the cup with a shaking hand. "Oh, Pippa, don't ask me!"

"I *must*. I know something terrible's happened. Do you want me to go about imagining all sorts of horrible falsehoods? Wouldn't it be better if I knew the truth?"

Camilla propped her elbows on the table and lowered her head to her hands. "Pippa, love, not now. I just can't."

"Then just tell me where Thomas is. He'll explain things to me. He always gives lovely, direct answers to my questions."

"But that's the problem, dearest. Thomas is . . . not here any more."

"Not here? What do you mean? Where is he?"

"Well, you see, he's not really a footman at all."

"I surmised as much. He's a sailor, isn't he?"

Camilla looked up in surprise. "How did you know? Did he tell you?"

"No, but he always told sea stories so well. Full of details that a landlubber wouldn't know."

"Landlubber?"

"Yes. That's what he calls people who work on land. Has he gone back to sea, then? He wouldn't do that without saying goodbye to me, would he?"

"No, of course not. He's . . . oh, dear, I don't know how to tell you. He's been . . . taken into custody."

Pippa peered at her mother with stricken eyes. "Mama! You don't mean *prison!*"

Camilla tried to answer, but, afraid that she would burst into tears, put a hand to her mouth and merely nodded her answer.

Pippa drew in a breath. "But . . . *why?* What's he done?"

"I'm not completely sure," Camilla answered, choked. "The worst of it seems to be that . . . that, in a struggle with some men who were trying to kidnap him to serve on a naval vessel, he hit one of them so hard that . . . he d-died."

"Oh, Mama, *no!* What will they do to him?"

Again all Camilla could do was shake her head.

Pippa's eyes widened in horror. "Mama! They won't . . . they wouldn't . . . *hang* him!"

Camilla held out her arms to her daughter, and Pippa flew into them. They clung together for several minutes, too terrified even to weep. "Don't shiver so, love," Camilla said at last. "Your Uncle Oswald has gone to see what he can do to help. Perhaps he can find a way . . ."

Oswald returned late that afternoon and found Camilla sitting with Pippa near the fire in the sitting room. They both turned to him with faces of such eager hopefulness that he almost wanted to retreat. "My news is not all bad," he said in preparation, "but if you're hoping to see your Thomas come walking in that door, you'll be disappointed."

"Tell us what you've learned, Oswald. We can deal with disappointment, if we must, can't we, love?"

"You don't want Pippa here, do you?"

"Yes, she's all right. She loves Thomas very much, you see."

"Well, then," he said, seating himself on the edge of a chair and pulling a sheaf of notes from his coat, "let's see what I've accomplished thus far. First, there's some good news in Daniel's case. He's safely out of it. His papers were signed with an X, and when I showed the committee his real signature, they decided to rule that he had not legally been enlisted. Under the circumstances, no one seemed impelled to make an issue of his case, not even Brock. It's Thomas he wants."

"That *is* good news, Oswald. Betsy will be overjoyed."

"I wish I could say the same about Thomas's case. I discovered that the *Triton* is out to sea, which is a bit of bad luck because we won't be able to question the captain about Thomas's credentials until the ship returns. But most everyone I've spoken to on the Admiralty board seems inclined to believe that Thomas is telling the truth. Lord Jeffries is furious at this evidence of the continued activity of press-gangs—the Admiralty doesn't admit to sanctioning them, you know—and Lord Sturtevant is so angry about the incident that he threatens to bring the matter to the attention of Parliament if the Admiralty doesn't treat Thomas fairly. (He's quite impressed with Thomas, it seems, from some remarks he'd made at a dinner here. And Lady Sturtevant gave him a very dramatic account of everything that happened here last night.) I think Brock will find his friends at the Admiralty very cool to him as a result of all this. And if it turns out that Thomas has been telling the truth about being a mate on the *Triton*—"

"Don't worry, he has been," Pippa said confidently.

"If he has, then Brock will find himself in very hot water. But, of course, the murder is the sticking point for Thomas. Don't know what we can do about clearing him of that."

"But if he was defending himself, it isn't really murder, is it?" Camilla inquired, biting her lip.

"I don't know. Self-defense may not be applicable in this case." He looked down at his notes. "I've learned the name of the officer in charge of the press-gang, but no one seems to know the name of the deceased. Thought I'd ride down to Southampton and see if I can locate the officer. The prosecution will have to do it—they don't have a case without a victim—and I don't want them to have more information than we have. Don't know what good it will do, but there's no harm in learning all we can."

"When do you want to go?" Camilla asked.

"Right away. Why?"

"Because I'm going with you."

"I, too," said Pippa.

"No, dearest, you will stay right here. I'll give you a more difficult task to accomplish than chasing about with us in Southampton. Stay here and see if you can make matters right with your Aunt Ethelyn."

Moresby, the officer who'd led the press-gang, was not hard to find. But he seemed strangely reluctant to reveal the name of the murdered man. It was only after Oswald bribed him with a handful of sovereigns that the fellow managed to remember it was a Casper Jost who'd died that day.

"Where'd you bury him?" Oswald asked.

"I didn't bury him. It isn't my job," Moresby said.

"Who did, then?"

"How would I know that? Ask his widow."

"Where can we find her?" Oswald asked impatiently.

"Can't say. Jost was no friend of mine."

But with the help of an additional bribe, the officer remembered that Jost had mentioned having a place in Netley, a short distance south on the Portsmouth road.

On the way to Netley, Oswald castigated himself roundly. "Don't know why I dragged you on this goose chase. No point in it anyway. There's no good can come of it that I can see."

"Perhaps not," Camilla said, "but I'd like to talk to the widow anyway. It might ease her grief if I tell her that it was only an accident—that Thomas hadn't meant to kill her husband. And we can give her some money, too. Not that money could ever make up for . . . for . . ."

"I know," Oswald said, squeezing her hand.

The proprietor of the Netley Linendrapery pointed out the Jost domicile. It was the third from the corner of a long row of tiny, frame houses with identical front steps and little iron grillwork surrounding identical little front gardens. When the carriage drew up to the house, Camilla put a restraining hand on Oswald's arm. "Let me go alone," she begged. "I shall do better with the widow that way."

Oswald shrugged. She jumped out of the carriage and ran up to the front door. An ill-kempt, stoutish woman with a number of hairs on her chin answered the door. "Are you Mrs. Jost?" Camilla asked.

"That's 'oo I be. Whut ye want?"

"I . . . I've come to ask you some questions . . . about your late husband."

The woman squinted at her suspiciously. "Whut'd ye mean, me late husband? On'y got but one, an' he's sittin' back there in the kitchen, swillin' ale."

It was a jubilant Camilla who returned to Upper Seymour Street that night, and a jubilant Pippa she tucked into bed. "I *knew* my Thomas couldn't have killed anybody," the child grinned, hugging her mother tightly. "Will he be coming home tomorrow?"

Camilla eased her daughter on to the pillow and drew up the coverlet. "I don't know what will happen next, dearest. But I suspect Thomas will not be coming back here to live. He isn't a footman after all, you know, and we can't expect him to spend his life working at something for which he is unsuited."

"Yes, I understand that, but aren't you going to marry him?"

"*Marry* him? What gave you such an idea as that?"

"You did. When you invented a husband for yourself, you made him just like Thomas, didn't you?"

"No, I didn't. He wasn't like Thomas at all."

"Yes, he was. Tall, lean, sandy-haired, generous, kind and humorous. That's how you described Mr. Petersham, and that's just how Thomas is!"

Camilla flushed. "But, those are very general terms. They could equally apply to any number of people."

"I'll wager you can't name *one.*"

"Really, Pippa, you are becoming much too cheeky. You must take my word for it that Thomas and I would not suit."

"I can't agree. When you pretended to be wed, it seemed to me that you suited each other very well."

"It was only pretense." She smoothed the hair from her daughter's brow tenderly. "I know you wish to have Thomas near you for always, dearest, but you mustn't let your desires run off with your reason. I can't be expected to marry everyone for whom you take a fancy, you know."

Pippa hitched to her side, turning her face away from her mother and pulling the coverlet up to her neck. "I thought you fancied him also," she said, her voice melancholy and suddenly very childlike.

"Well, I'm sorry to have to disappoint you, love. But isn't it enough that the man Thomas injured is fully recovered and that Thomas will soon be a free man? And that we can go on living contentedly here in London, near our friends the Sturtevants, just as before? Isn't that *enough* to be happy about?"

"I'm happy about Thomas being a free man, of course. About the rest, I shall have to think before I answer. For things will *not* be as they were before, with Thomas gone. Goodnight, Mama."

Camilla closed her daughter's door quietly behind her and walked thoughtfully down the hall, wondering why she'd been reluctant to reveal to the child how close her own desires were to Pippa's. But before she could find an answer, she thought she heard her name being called in a quavery voice. "Ethelyn?" she asked hesitantly, pausing before her sister-in-law's door. "Did you call?"

"Yes. Can you come in for a moment?"

She opened the door with considerable trepidation and looked in. Ethelyn was sitting up in bed, a prayer book in her lap. Camilla came in and stood at the foot of the bed, studying her sister-in-law curiously. Ethelyn was wearing only her night-dress. Somehow she looked much less formidable in the white muslin gown with its soft lace at the neck and with her greying hair loosened from its knot and falling round her shoulders with unaccustomed softness. It occurred to Camilla that she'd never seen Ethelyn except in the darkest of colors and the most formal of costumes. In this bedtime informality, her usually awesome sister-in-law looked almost frail. "Is there anything I can do for you, Ethelyn?"

"I wish to speak to you," Ethelyn said, her eyes lowered. "Will you sit down, please? Here at the side . . . that is, if you wish . . ."

"Yes, of course." Camilla took the chair indicated and waited for what she expected would be a long lecture on the blessings of redemption.

"I have had a number of long talks with Pippa since you left for Southampton," she said quietly, after a moment of silence. "Did the child tell you?"

"Pippa?" How had her ingenious daughter managed to convince her aunt to call her that? "No, she didn't tell me."

"She is quite remarkable, you know. She believes we . . . you and I . . . don't have an adequate understanding of one another."

"Oh?"

"She is probably right. It gave me pause, especially after what you had said . . . and Oswald, too. I've been thinking a great deal . . . and praying. And I've come to the conclusion, Camilla, that I have been . . . grossly at fault."

"Ethelyn, I didn't mean—"

"No, don't soften just because you see me shaken. I d-drove you to fabricate a large falsehood—"

"A very large falsehood."

"Yes, and I didn't want to admit that I knew . . . I *knew* . . . that lying is not characteristic of you. I knew it even when I accused you . . ."

"Please, Ethelyn, you don't have to—"

"But I *do*. You and Pippa and Oswald . . . you're all the family I *h-have!*" Astoundingly, she put her hands up to her face and burst into tears.

"Ethelyn!" Camilla gasped.

"I don't want to l-lose you!" the older woman wept.

"Oh, my dear," Camilla murmured, moving to the bed next to Ethelyn and putting an arm around her shoulders, "have no fear of that. I think Pippa was right. If we take the trouble to learn more about each other, instead of always judging each other, we shall do better."

"Then you . . . forgive me?"

"You don't need to ask."

"I shall not, ever again, give you orders, Camilla. I promise."

Camilla laughed. "Then *I* promise, if ever I *do* find a suitor I wish to wed, to bring him round for your approval."

Ethelyn looked up in surprise. "What do you mean?" she asked, wiping the wetness from her cheeks with the back of her hand. "Aren't you going to wed Thomas?"

"Thomas?"

"Yes. Oswald told me it looks as though he'll be completely exonerated. I assumed, therefore—"

"Tell me, Ethelyn," Camilla said, watching her sister-in-law from the corner of her eye, "if I *did*, would you approve?"

"Well, I approved of him before, didn't I?"

"Yes, but you thought he was a Petersham. Of the Sussex Petershams."

"What difference does that make? A man is more than a pedigree."

Camilla, trying not to laugh, got up and looked down at her sister-in-law with hands on hips. "Did you know the fellow was my *footman?*"

Ethelyn's eyebrows rose. "What has *that* to say to anything? We are all equal in the eyes of God, you know. Really, Camilla, I hope your months in this mad, corrupt environment have not made a snob of you." She opened her prayer book and began searching for her place. "Thomas would be much more suitable for you than anyone I could think of, including Mr. Harbage. Goodnight, my dear."

Chapter Twenty-one

The *Triton* was rumored to be returning to port by the end of the month. As soon as it arrived, and Thomas's status could be verified by its captain, a final dispensation of his case would be made. In the meantime, Ethelyn and Oswald decided to return to Wyckfield. Ethelyn explained that she missed the sweet country air, and Oswald, whose increased activity had caused him to burn off a half-a-stone of fat, declared that if he stayed in town much longer he'd waste away. They therefore bid Camilla and Pippa a fond farewell, extracted a sincere promise from Camilla that she and Pippa would pay a visit to the country soon, and were embraced with a great deal more affection than they'd received on their arrival.

Camilla and Pippa, after a week of silence on the subject of Thomas's welfare, decided to pay a visit to Fleet prison. But a guard informed them that Thomas Collinson was no longer incarcerated behind those walls; he'd been released in the custody of Lord Jeffries. Camilla was hurt and angry that he'd sent her no word of his change of address, and she returned home feeling strangely empty. After all that had passed between them, was he now going to forget her existence?

There was nothing to do but wait and see. Despite Pippa's urging, her pride did not permit her to write to Lord Jeffries for information. If Thomas had wished them to know his where-abouts, he surely could have found a way to inform them of it.

Life returned to its previous pattern, but with a subtle difference. Camilla was aware of a certain joylessness, and it seemed to her that even Pippa had lost some of her serene good spirits. But a few weeks later, early in April, Oswald appeared without warning at the door of the breakfast room. "Put on your wraps, my dears. I'm going to take you both for a long ride."

"Oswald! What are you doing back in town? Is Ethelyn with you?"

"No questions now. We don't have time. Hurry, hurry, for you are about to have the most exciting surprise."

"You're not taking us off to Wyckfield, are you?" Camilla asked as he ushered them into his carriage. "I told you not to expect us until May or June."

"No, not Wyckfield. I'm taking you to Southampton."

"Southampton!" Pippa squealed in delight. "It's *Thomas!* You're taking us to Thomas!"

"That's right, you little magpie. You guessed it."

"Oswald! What's happened. How did you find him? And why have we not heard anything?"

"I didn't have to find him. I've been in touch with him all along. He didn't want to see you until everything had been cleared up. So that he could look you in the eye, he said."

"Has everything been cleared up, then?"

"Without a black mark remaining. The captain of the *Triton* not only vouched for him but said that he'd been unable to replace him with anyone of equal caliber. And Jeffries has taken the fellow under his wing. Trots him out to talk to every-one interested in naval matters. And the last surprise is that he's found him a berth on a John Company ship."

"John Company?" Pippa asked. "That's the East India Com-pany, isn't it? Thomas told me they're the finest merchant ships afloat."

"So they are. As mate of the *Athena*, he'll have master's

papers before he knows it. Jeffries hopes that, by that time, he'll have gotten over his prejudice against the Navy and will join up to captain a ship of the line. He has a very promising future, this lad of yours."

"Oh, fiddle-faddle, Oswald. He's no 'lad of mine,'" Camilla said with a toss of the head. But her heart was leaping about in her chest quite uncontrollably, and she had to turn her head to peer out of the window so that Oswald wouldn't see her cheeks.

The carriage rolled right on to the pier, and before it had come to a complete stop, Pippa jumped down. She stared in awe at the huge, three-masted ship *Athena*, anchored at the end of the pier and, spying Thomas waiting at the top of the gangplank, resplendent in a blue uniform with a cocked hat on his head, went flying aboard. She leaped right up into his arms. "Oh, Thomas, Thomas, I've missed you so!" she whispered into his neck.

"And I've missed you, Miss Pippa," he said hoarsely, squeezing her tightly.

His greeting to Camilla was much more subdued. Except for a certain tremulousness of the voice, his how-de-dos were very polite and formal. After shaking Oswald's hand warmly, he took them on a full tour of the ship, pointing out everything from the hold to the crow's nest and from the prow to the taffrail. He pointed out the Indian teak beams and the copper fastenings; he told them about the tonnage, the battery mounts, and the types of sail; he explained about the disposition of the crew of one-hundred-and-thirty-three men as well as a couple of dozen passengers. To Oswald and Pippa, it was all fascinating.

While he talked, Camilla studied him from under lowered lids. His blue uniform was trimmed with black velvet lapels and cuffs, and was embroidered with gold braid, not unlike officers of the Navy. It gave him a look of distinction that filled her with pride. And she was impressed by the diffident way in which the passing sailors greeted him. And the animation of his face while he spoke, and the way his hand lovingly caressed a rail or pole, completely revealed his feelings. He belonged here.

He took them to tea in the captain's quarters, where the bronzed, heavily jowled captain greeted them kindly and chatted with them for the better part of an hour. Before they'd realized it, the sun had begun to set. "Looks like it's time to disembark, as the sailors like to say," Oswald announced.

"Before you go, Lord Falcombe—" Thomas began.

"Lord Falcombe, is it? You called me Oswald easily enough when you were nothing more than a footman. Surely you can do so now."

"Oswald, then. Do you think you'd like to show Pippa the sailors' mess? And the galley?"

"Oh, *yes*, Uncle Oswald, I'd like that," Pippa said, her excitement boundless.

Oswald threw the young man a narrow-eyed look and laughed. "Come along then, Pippa. But I warn you that all this scurrying about is wearing me out."

As soon as they were out of sight, Thomas took Camilla's arm and led her across the deck to the port-side railing where they could look out to the sea and watch the setting sun. Her heart began acting strangely again. What, she wondered, was he preparing to say to her?

"Oswald told me what you did for me, Miss Camilla, and I—"

"I did nothing, Thomas. Nothing at all."

"Nothing? You changed my condition of life from murderer to hero. From my point of view, that's a very great deal."

"Hero?"

He grinned. "Yes, so it seems. You should have seen me holding forth, spouting my views to all sorts of Important Personages—Admirals, MPs, even the Duke of York. Lord Jeffries couldn't seem to stop parading me before anyone and everyone with an interest in British seamanship. I'm thankful that this place was found for me before I'd become completely transformed from sailor to speaker."

"It's wonderful, Thomas. I . . . we're very proud of you."

"But it's all because of you. Oswald says he'd never have bothered about finding Jost if you hadn't persisted. I've been waiting all these weeks to tell you how . . . how grateful I am."

"*Grateful?*" She stared up at him, her heart sinking. "But you're the one who told me—a very long time ago, it seems—that gratitude is a very pallid emotion."

"I said it was a *damned puny* little emotion, and so it seemed when it was directed *at* me. But now, you see, it's turned the other way. Now I feel what you were feeling . . . and I find it quite overwhelming."

And now I feel what you were feeling, she thought, *and I hate it!* Gratitude! How very unsatisfactory it was when one wanted to inspire another type of emotion entirely. *Oh, Thomas,* she wanted to cry, *is this all you wish to tell me? Is this why you sent Pippa and Oswald away? Have we nothing else to say to each other?*

But she said nothing aloud, and they stood watching the sinking sun until Pippa and Oswald returned. Thomas escorted them to the gangplank, still sunk in silence. Oswald asked when the ship was to sail and how long the voyage was to be. Thomas answered, somewhat glumly, that they were to leave in a week for a three-month sail to the Indies. They shook hands vigorously, and Oswald wished him good fortune. Pippa kissed him goodbye and made him promise to visit them as soon as he returned. And, at the last, he kissed Camilla's hand. It seemed to her that he held it a bit longer than he should have, but perhaps the impression had been only the inaccurate measure of her aching heart, seeking some small sign of hope.

They went down the gangplank, Camilla in a bewildering fog of despair. All the way back to London she was unaware of her surroundings and what Pippa and Oswald were saying. She must have responded coherently, for they showed no signs of being disturbed by her behavior, but she was not aware of having spoken to them at all.

The fog in her brain persisted for two days. Then a question that Pippa put to her at the breakfast table brought her up sharply. "Are you *sure* you haven't taken a fancy to him?" the child asked.

"What?" Camilla asked, startled.

"I'm speaking of Thomas. Are you sure you haven't taken a fancy to him?"

Camilla frowned. "You asked something of this sort before. I thought I'd answered you. Why do you bring it up again?"

"Because you've been acting very strangely since we visited the *Athena.* I know this subject is not one on which I have any knowledge, but it does seem to me that you're in a state of confusion similar to lovers in books. They are always disturbed, distracted and distressed."

"Pippa, you can sometimes be a very irritating child." She propped her chin in her hands and looked at her daughter lugubriously. "But you're right, of course. I *am* in a state of confusion."

Pippa nodded knowingly. "I thought so. So is Thomas."

"Thomas? What do you mean?"

"He seemed similarly distracted when we saw him."

"Nonsense. I never noticed anything of the sort."

"Well, I did. So did Uncle Oswald. He said he thought Thomas was sick."

"Neither of you need worry," Camilla mumbled. "If he felt anything at all, it was *gratitude*."

Pippa shook her head dubiously. "I don't think gratitude can make one sick, do you? He loves you, Mama, I'm sure of it."

"You, my love, are letting your wishes get the best of your judgment." She got up from her chair and began to wander absently round the room. "And even if he does, it makes little difference. He's off to sea on a three-month voyage."

"Not yet. They don't sail until Thursday."

She stopped in her tracks. "Pippa, you goose, what are you suggesting? That I rush back to Southampton and *throw* myself at him?"

Pippa considered the matter in all seriousness. "No," she said after due reflection, "that wouldn't be proper. But..." She looked up at her mother with a wicked glimmer. "...there's something you *can* do."

"Really?" Camilla asked with her eyebrows raised superciliously. "And what is that?"

"You could pack up some things and book passage on the ship. They take passengers, you know. Thomas said so."

"Book *passage?*" The idea was so unexpected that she could only gape at her daughter in awe. But then she shook her head impatiently. "I know what's in your mind, you little vixen. You'd like nothing better than to sail off to the Indies on Thomas's ship."

"I'd love it above anything, of course, Mama, but *this* time I think I'd better remain behind. You may take me on the *next* voyage, after your honeymoon is over."

"*Honeymoon!* Honestly, Pippa, I can't imagine where you pick up these ideas."

"Everyone knows about honeymoons, Mama, even Sybil. By the way, I think I'd like to stay with her while you're gone. Do you think Lady Sturtevant would permit it?"

"Yes, of course she would. Oh, good God, what am I

saying? I really *must* be disturbed, distracted and distressed."
She dropped down on her chair, giving a little shiver of excitement. "Oh, Pippa, love, do you really think I *should?* It seems the most impulsive, irresponsible, *wild* sort of plan."

Pippa grinned at her. "Yes, doesn't it? It's just the sort of thing Sybil might have thought of. I do believe I'm picking up some of her qualities at last. Isn't that *prodigious?*"

"Prodigious," Camilla agreed drily, making a face at her.

"Does that mean that you'll *do* it?" Pippa's face lit up with hope.

For a long moment her mother didn't answer but stared speculatively into space. Then, with a little shake of her head, she roused herself and jumped up. "Very well, I'll do it. I'll *go!* So don't just sit there, my girl. This is *your* idea, you know, and if it's to succeed, you haven't time to sit dawdling over breakfast. Come along. We have a thousand things to do!"

She seized her daughter's hand and, laughing, pulled her to the door. But as they crossed the threshold, Camilla stopped short. "I've just had the most mortifying thought. What if, after the ship has put to sea, I discover that Thomas doesn't want me after all?"

"He wants you. I'm sure of it."

"But what if you're mistaken? I know you're very gifted, but you *can* make mistakes, you know."

"Then, Mama," Pippa answered with her remarkable aplomb, "at least you'll see the Indies."

There followed a flurry of packing and preparation that was unprecedented in Camilla's experience. Miss Townley was convinced she'd lost her mind. Georgina, on the other hand, was enthusiastic. "It's just the sort of madcap adventure every woman ought to have. And don't worry about Pippa at all. After three months in my disorderly household, I'll return your admirably well-bred daughter to you healthy, unharmed and transformed into a wildcat."

Camilla felt as if she were living on the edge of hysteria. Her moods swung wildly between exhilaration and depression. In moments of optimism she packed her portmanteau with eager haste, only to pull everything out of it in fearful despondency a few moments later. She packed and unpacked three times in the next two days. But through it all, she knew she would go.

For the first time she would gamble dangerously with life. The prospect made her blood dance in her veins. Never before had she felt so truly alive.

On the afternoon before her departure, while repacking the portmanteau for the fourth time, she realized that her favorite Norwich shawl was missing. Either Miss Townley or Betsy must have taken it to have it pressed. "Ada? Betsy?" she shouted like a hoyden. "Whose taken my shawl?"

There was no answer. Where were they? Unless the activities of the various members of the household could be better organized, she would never get off on time the next day. And if she departed late, she might arrive in Southampton and find that the ship had sailed without her!

Feeling more than ordinarily hysterical, she ran out of her room to the top of the stairs. "Hicks?" she called. "Can you come up here, please? I need some assistance."

Again there was no answer. "Where *is* everybody?" she snapped impatiently. "Will someone come upstairs to me?"

"Yes, ma'am," came a muffled voice from the nether region.

She sighed in relief. "Thank you, Daniel. And bring up the small hat box which I left on the table in the sitting room, will you?"

She dashed back to her bedroom and began to pull her hats and bonnets from her wardrobe. She tossed them, one after the other, on her bed. It was difficult to decide which headpieces would be most suitable for shipboard wear. After all, she'd never sailed to the Indies—or anywhere else—in her life and had no idea what the weather conditions would be. Small bonnets that could be firmly tied to the head would probably be best, she surmised.

There was a tap at the door. "Come in, Daniel," she said, not looking round. "Just put the box on my dressing table, and then come and see if you can close the portmanteau."

"Yes, ma'am."

The sound of the voice made her breath freeze in her chest. She wheeled around. *"T-Thomas!"*

He was standing in the doorway, dressed in his footman's everyday livery and holding her hatbox before him as if it were a present on a silver tray... the very model of footmanly decorum. "Yes, ma'am?" he asked politely.

"Wh-What are you *doing* here?"

"You called, I believe."

"Stop that!" she almost stamped her foot in impatience. "I don't want to joke. What are you doing here?"

"I'm employed here, am I not, ma'am? I don't believe I've been discharged. In fact, if I recall, you said I had a position here for as long as I wished."

"You are *not* employed here! You're the first mate of the *Athena,* and you are sailing tomorrow. Now what is this all about?"

"I *was* the first mate of the *Athena.* I've run off. I found that I couldn't sail with her."

"But that's nonsense! You love every plank and sail of that ship. You belong there."

"No, not after *you'd* been there." He tossed the hatbox on a chair and came up to her. "I kept seeing you on the deck . . . and remembering what a coward I'd been that afternoon. I began to realize that there was no joy in it for me any more. You weren't there, you see."

"I don't understand . . ."

"It became clear to me that I'd find life more bearable if I were close to you— even as your footman— than if I were far away as a seaman," he said softly, smiling down at her.

Her knees seemed to give way. "Oh, Thomas!" she breathed, sinking down upon the bed, ignoring the fact that at least two of her bonnets were being crushed beneath her.

"May I not come back on the staff, ma'am? I shall be the most invisible, inaudible footman that ever was."

She gave a tearful laugh. "A likely tale! You can't be invisible and inaudible to me any more. I should always be watching you from the corner of my eye to see if you were going to pull me into your arms and kiss me, as you did so brazenly before."

He grinned. "I can see where that might present some difficulties. Then if I won't do as a footman, do you think you could try me as a husband? You've already given me a kind of trial. I didn't do badly, did I?"

"No, you didn't." She looked down at the hands clenched in her lap. "I . . . liked you as a husband very much indeed."

"Oh, Camilla!" He swept a few of the bonnets aside, sat down beside her and took her in his arms. "I do love you so," he murmured and kissed her hungrily.

"But, Thomas," she asked when she could speak again, "you cannot have been serious when you said that you'd run away from the *Athena*. You do want to sail on her, don't you?"

"I've taken a day's leave." A small, worried frown creased his forehead. "But I won't sail on her if you have objections to being a sailor's wife. Hang it, Camilla, let's not talk about it now. Ever since I let you leave the ship the other day, without telling you . . . I've been like a man possessed. I must kiss you again . . . just to convince myself that I really have you in my arms at last."

After a while, she put her hands to his chest and held him off. "We are really behaving in a shockingly disreputable way," she said, blushing. "This is my *bedroom!*"

"So it is." He lifted his head and looked about him happily. "Do you know, my love, that you are sitting on your hats?"

"Am I?"

"In fact, the room seems in an inordinate state of disorder. I think you *need* another footman, ma'am. From the look of things, you need all the assistance you can afford."

"I do *not* need another footman. I am going on a voyage, and a footman would be decidedly in the way. This confusion is only because I've been packing."

"Packing? For a voyage?" A light seemed to flare up at the back of his eyes. "A voyage where?"

"To the Indies, of course. Where else?"

He grasped her shoulders with eager intensity and pulled her to him. "Oh, God! Don't joke, woman! Were you *really* coming to me?"

"Yes, isn't it shameful? I couldn't bear to be without you either." She lifted a hand to his cheek. "Don't look at me in that adoring way, my love, or I shall cry. Do you think you might just . . . kiss me instead?"

Pippa and her friend Sybil, strolling down the corridor together, passed the open door and peered inside. "Egad!" Sybil exclaimed. "Who's that?"

Pippa beamed. "That's *Thomas!* I *knew* he fancied her."

"Your mother is sitting on her bonnets."

"Yes, I see. It's love sickness, I believe. It makes one a bit confused."

"Does it? Then I hope I never catch it."

"Love sickness? They say it's very enjoyable when you're older."

"It looks very dull to me. They haven't moved at all since we've been watching," Sybil observed in disgust.

"Well, I expect that kissing is more entertaining to *do* than to watch. Would you like to do something else?"

"Yes. Let's go back to your room and sit on your bonnets."

"All right. It will probably make them easier to pack." And the girls turned away from the still-embracing couple and strolled back down the hall.

Heart-stirring Regency Romances by

Elizabeth Mansfield

__ THE COUNTERFEIT HUSBAND	05336-9/$2.25
__ DUEL OF HEARTS	04677-X/$2.25
__ THE FIFTH KISS	04739-3/$2.25
__ THE FROST FAIR	05362-8/$2.25
__ MY LORD MURDERER	05029-7/$2.25
__ THE PHANTOM LOVER	05078-5/$2.25
__ A REGENCY CHARADE	04835-7/$2.25
__ A REGENCY MATCH	04514-5/$2.25
__ THE RELUCTANT FLIRT	05088-2/$2.25
__ A VERY DUTIFUL DAUGHTER	05226-5/$2.25